Hunts and Home Fires

Surviving Fifty Years of Alaska
And Other Interesting Things

Dennis Lattery

For Butch
Dennis Lattery

PO Box 221974 Anchorage, Alaska 99522-1974
books@publicationconsultants.com — www.publicationconsultants.com

ISBN 978-1-59433-089-6
Library of Congress Catalog Card Number: 2008937142

Copyright 2008 Dennis L. Lattery
—First Edition—

All rights reserved, including the right of reproduction in any form, or by any mechanical or electronic means including photocopying or recording, or by any information storage or retrieval system, in whole or in part in any form, and in any case not without the written permission of the author and publisher.

Manufactured in the United States of America.

Dedication

To MY Lifelong, patient, partner, my wife Sharon, for all her support while I did this.

Table of Contents

About H*unts and Home Fires* 7
Growing up in Alaska...9
Rose Cochran's Nasturtiums..14
Life As An Alaska Entrepreneur 18
My First Rifle 24
An Apology to Miss Rodland 27
Recreational Gold Hunting 31
The Dunking of E. Waneta Coring..34
Alaska Statehood, A Big Night! 37
Working for Nick 38
The Local Jacket 44
Hunting Mine Mountain 46
Don't Eat the Putshki!...51
UofA Engineers Day 53
Trouble Bruin..55
My First Client..61
Land Otter Man..68
Twins for the Pot...70
The Kids at Skwentna..75
Sheep Fever 78
A Day Worth Spending...84
The Weather Spirit of Birch Creek..87
Little Tok Grizzly 93
Dyea Beach 96
The Other House 97
The Goats of Victor Creek..100

Who Speaks for the Salmon?	107
Mom's Broke Leg	111
The Three-Legged Deer	114
On Keeping a Diary	117
Alaska Range Moose	119
Murder Lake, Fact or Fiction?	127
Alaska Bowhunting Details	129
The Woodstove	135
Needed, Support from America	136
Three Culprits in Bear Country	142
How Fairbanks Came to Be	147
A Hunting Partner	149
West Kodiak Passage	153
Lamentations of a Camp Cook	161
"Oh My God, I'm Dead!"	164
The Fly Fishing Malady	170
Powerful Confused, but Never Lost	173
Have We Been Here Before?	178
Bear-Baiting Myths	179
Sourdough Don't Fly	183
Remembering Fred Bear	186
A Memorial for The Futz	189
A Good Mulligan	192
The Rock and the Hard Place	197
Picking the Ideal Client	199
South Fork Reflections	203
When Optics Are Your Best Friend	205
On Following Your Nose	208
In the Midst of Bears	211
Calling All Moose	218
"Packing" in Alaska	224
Mystery of the Kenai	228
Living in Earthquake Country	233
Fire on the Tsiu	238
Octopus—Care and Cleaning	244
Test Your Dead Reckoning	248
Dipping Copper River Salmon	251
Bibliography	255

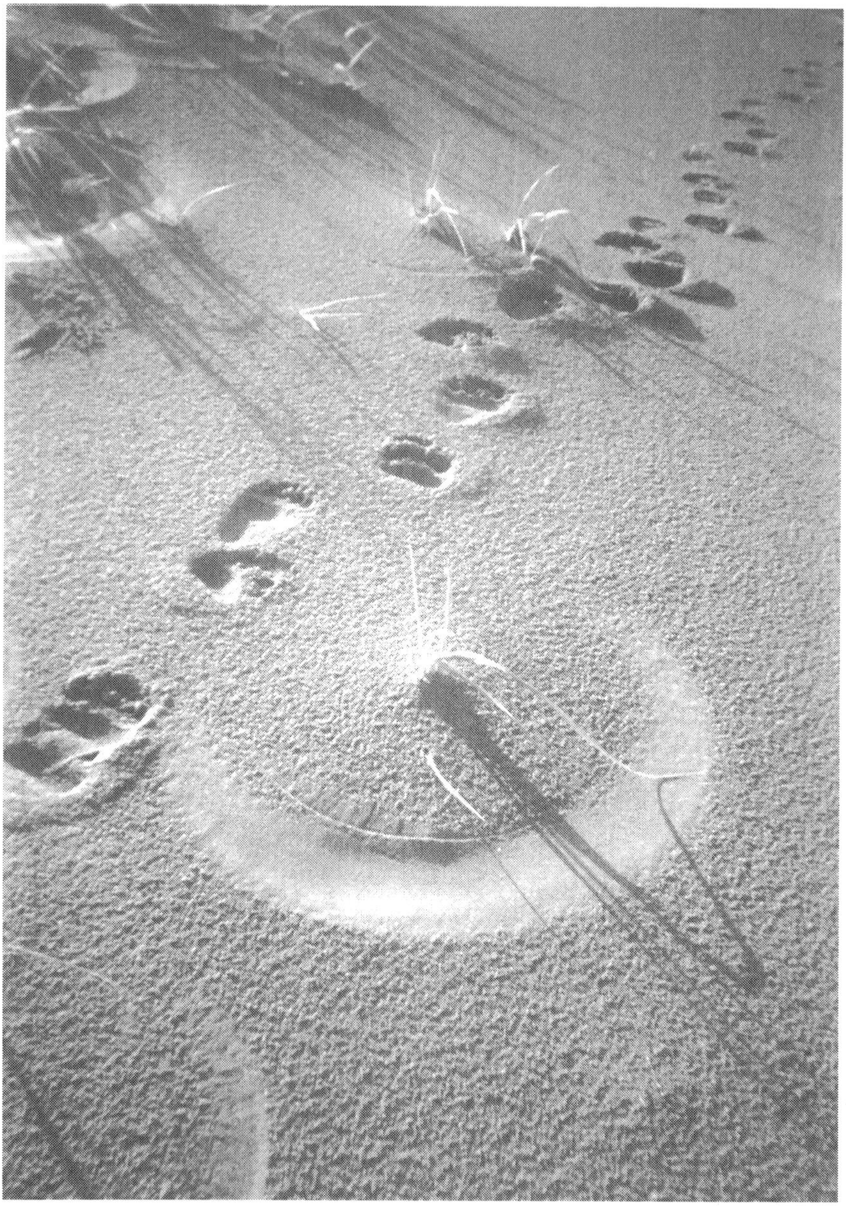

Introduction

About Hunts and Home Fires

WHO KNEW, YEARS AGO, THAT SOMEDAY I WOULD develop enough interest in writing to put together a pile of words high enough to pose as a book? Certainly not I, and definitely not any of my frustrated English teachers from those painful days of education in the Alaska public school system.

The hardest part of producing this narrative was writing this section and, in particular, offering a plausible explanation of exactly what this work of art is all about.

It is not an autobiography. A complete story of my life would hardly be worth reading, and certainly not worth writing.

It's not fiction, at least not most of it, as I have tried to be straight with the facts in all cases, maybe omitting a thing or two here and there to protect the innocent.

Essays about my youth (*Growing up in Alaska; My First Rifle; Working for Nick; Rose Cochran's Nasturtiums*) speak for themselves.

It is not a historic work, although I have thrown into the mix a few items of Alaskana which I hope a reader might find interesting, just to spice up the narrative (*How Fairbanks Came to be; Living in Earthquake Country*).

Most of what is written here comes from me, representing pages from my life, many times I am sure, along the slant of my personal opinion (*Needed, Support from America; Bear-Baiting Myths*).

Where I felt I have trod heavily on a subject (*Land Otter Man*), or I have related much on what I understand to be fact (*How Fairbanks*

Came to Be), I have included some published sources in a short bibliography, in support of what I have said as well as for those curious enough to want to explore a subject a little further.

I have tried to inject some humor (*Sheep Fever; Have We Been Here Before?; The Fly-Fishing Malady*), a few educational things (*A Good Mulligan; Alaska Bowhunting Details; The Three Culprits In Bear Country*), and a few things on the serious and practical side (*Powerful Confused but Never Lost; Calling All Moose; A Good Mulligan*). There are a few essays (*Who Speaks for the Salmon; South Fork Reflections*), and even a snippet of poetry (*Dyea Beach*)!

The backbone of the book is hunting stories, a number of which have been published in state and national magazines. The stories previously published have been so noted, including where and when. Using this format, I am stealing a page from my favorite Alaska outdoor writer, Russell Annabel. Most of his five books are composed of published stories of his Alaska hunting adventures, written principally for *Field and Stream* magazine during a period extending from the 1950s through the 1970s.

You will note that most of my published stories are related to bowhunting, a sports affliction I picked up on the east coast of America while down that way in the service. I hardly used a rifle between 1969 and 1985—but times change. These days I don't hesitate to shoulder my little Marlin .45.70 and head out into the hills behind my Kodiak area cabin chasing Sitka blacktails.

Amid the stories, anecdotes, and fodder, the underlying theme here is, I guess, gratitude for the fact that I have been fortunate enough to survive over fifty years of living in Alaska. Not a small accomplishment for a person who has had the pleasure of rubbing his nose in this modern-day wilderness as often as he tried to. I have always maintained that Alaska will kill you in a heartbeat if you give her half a chance. It would take only one foolish, careless, or even innocent mistake.

Big thanks here to my daughter Denise Trutanic for her writing skills and ongoing technical computer support and to a dear friend, writer, and retired English teacher, Sandra Larsen, for her proofing skills.

I hope there is something of interest in the following pages for everyone.

Chapter 1
Growing up in Alaska

I HAVE LIVED IN, FIRST, THE TERRITORY OF ALASKA, then the state of Alaska, for more than fifty-five years now. Although very young when we moved here from Canada, I still remember clearly that warm, sunny morning in the spring of 1949 when we steamed up Gastineau Channel aboard the Canadian steamship *Princess Louise* and landed at the dock in Juneau. That morning we were truly "fresh off the boat."

My father died in a river drowning in 1947 and Mom, my sister, Lorna, and I had a tough go at earning a living since Dad had been taken from us. These were not good years in any of our lives.

Mother's mom, Grandma Ada, lived in Juneau and worked as a cook in the old federal jail, a somber, gray fortress on top of a hill overlooking the city and Gastineau Channel. The ominous rumor among kids on the street was that they hanged people up there. At that time they probably did! The old jail was torn

Sister Lorna and me on the beach in Juneau, circa 1950.

down many decades later to make way for a new state office building, which now *truly* looks like a blockhouse fortress on top of that hill! Grandma's advice to us back in Canada had been to come to Alaska. There was plenty of work, she advised. "Come up here and get a fresh start." I guess that's what we set out to do.

Mom found work and eventually married again, a wedding which marked the beginning of four years of cosmic connubial disaster. *Especially* these years are not a tenderly remembered part of my younger life!

I always kept myself in pocket money working at something or other (more about work later), but the main job my sister, Lorna, and I had at that time was getting through elementary school.

We lived mostly on Willoughby Avenue, a segment of the main arterial extending through Juneau, in a pretty rough neighborhood. Getting up the hill to the Fourth Street School, without walking a long way around, necessitated passing through a section of Willoughby known as the Village where mostly Native people lived. Over time, not being the smartest fellow, I cultivated the disdain of a number of Native kids my age to a point where I often found them laying for me. Many days I either had to fight my way to school or fight my way home again, and on some days both. There were times I found myself badly outnumbered and had to run for it. Contending with this gauntlet I soon learned I could outrun any of my tormentors if necessary. Over time this environment served to develop both my young legs and lungs to a considerable extent. I don't recall anyone ever being able to catch me in a flat-out, fair race to the sanctuary of my front door.

In late 1953, our dysfunctional family moved to Ketchikan, where our "head of household" found work in construction of the new Ward Cove pulp mill. In 1954, Mom and I fled north on an Alaska Coastal Airlines flight to Juneau. We didn't just leave that part of our lives, and a miserable marriage, behind—we fled from it. Sister Lorna had already quite understandably bailed out and returned to live back in Canada for a time.

In the spring of 1955, Mom took a job as a cook working for the White Pass & Yukon Railroad in Skagway, a beautifully scenic but very windy little city located at the head of Lynn Canal at the northern end of southeast Alaska's Inside Passage.

The name Skagway is reported to have evolved from the Native name *Skagua*, meaning "home of the north wind," or the Tlingit Indian term *sch-kawai*, meaning, "end of the salt water." Although here is no accepted authority to determine which is correct, "Home of the north wind" is, very appropriately, the locally accepted translation.

In this little place we found peace, made a home, and truly started over. Mother met and married Alf Kalvick, a lovely little second-generation Norwegian carpenter, a displaced North Dakota Lutheran, and one of the finest men I have ever known.

It was during these tender years growing up in Skagway that I developed and sharpened my hunting, fishing, trapping, and a general love for being out of doors, that was to be such an important part of my later life. During high school I kept busy fishing the canal, trapping the beaches, and chasing up the surrounding mountains after coastal Rocky Mountain goats.

I made it through Skagway High School mostly because I played basketball. Quite literally, at the time I didn't really care if school kept or not. I don't believe I would have made it without the spirit and personal glory of playing ball during those school years which held my interest firm enough to keep me going. I went to school to play basketball, not to get an education. If today you try to convince me of the importance of high school sports in the lives of our young people, you can save your breath. You'll be preaching to the choir.

Soon after graduation, my high school sweetheart, Sharon Hermens, consented to be my wife and we were married in July 1960. I had a good taste of the hard, cold task of earning a living during the winter of 1960 and didn't like what I saw. This set us looking hard at our future and we were soon plotting and working toward attending college at the University of Alaska in Fairbanks.

College was a rude awakening for the kid who had never cared if school kept or not. I had to develop some study habits I had never acquired in high school—and very quickly! I played basketball for the University of Alaska, Fairbanks (UofA) for four years, trying, I guess, to relive some of the spice of the four years of high school sports I had loved so much. Unlike in high school, nobody cared if I got the grades or not. If you didn't pass you didn't play. I know my grade point average in college suffered for the time spent with basketball, and later regretted that. I would have traded all four years of my college basketball career for just one more year of playing for Skagway High School!

We worked hard at the "getting through college" plan, sitting out only one semester in 1965 when our daughter, Denise, was born.

Each fall, out of Fairbanks, I chased after moose and caribou, which provided the bulk of our winter's meat supply.

I graduated from the university in the spring of 1967.

We had to make a family decision at the end of my sophomore year.

Should I enter the Reserve Officer Training Corps (ROTC) to pursue becoming an officer and serve a two-year tour in the army? The Vietnam war was in full swing at that time and chances were bleak of serving a two-year obligation anywhere but in Vietnam. I had some strong personal feelings about serving my country, unlike many other "men" during that time who fled to Canada to avoid the draft, leaving other draftees to run the risk of serving in their place. But that's another story. Anyway, we hoped for the best, or at least a chance for the kids from Skagway to do some traveling, and I signed up for the advanced ROTC program.

After infantry officer basic training at Fort Benning, Georgia, followed by aerial photo schooling at the Army intelligence school at Fort Holabird in Baltimore, Maryland, I spent the remainder of my service time as an aerial photo interpreter cranking rolls of film for the Defense Intelligence Agency (DIA) in Washington DC. I interpreted many rolls of aerial film from Vietnam but never got there.

My family was with me the whole while. We never regretted volunteering for the military. It gave us a chance to travel to the Deep South, a paid tour of the entire east coast, and the experience of living a ping-pong ball's throw from our nation's capital was thrown in as part of the deal.

During this period, hunting pheasants in Pennsylvania and chasing whitetails in Maryland were bonuses which served to keep my hunting instincts in tune. I also developed a love for bowhunting. A one-week gun season in Maryland at the time, versus a two-month bow season, was a no-brainer. I took to bowhunting—an affliction I still have.

In 1969 my military obligation was satisfied. Several options were available to us. We (this was a family deal!) could be promoted to captain if we re-upped for another year, we could take a civilian photo interpreter's job with the DIA and stay in Washington DC, or muster out and head for home. Alaska called. No contest. We were soon headed north.

After a short time at home in Skagway, I was offered a job in Anchorage working for the state highway department. This was the beginning of a long career in state government as a professional real estate appraiser. Work sent me traveling all over Alaska, a job I enjoyed so much I sometimes couldn't believe they were actually paying me for doing it. This would span the next twenty-eight years, the last twenty-one of which I served as Chief Review Appraiser for the State Department of Natural Resources. (DNR)

I took an early retirement at age fifty-eight in 1997 and hardly even looked back, leaving the real estate appraiser profession behind me.

I had been working for other big-game guides as an assistant guide, using up most of my annual leave from the DNR for that purpose, since the late 1980s. I met all the requirements, so I tested for and received my registered big-game guide license in 1997.

This was the beginning of a whole new career. I had been putting together hunts for companions most of my adult life and figured it was about time for a little pay for what I had already been doing for free for so long.

Perhaps most surprising during this later period in life was the emergence of an interest in writing, an interest which had surfaced only in snippets during the past. In the 1990s I gradually began having articles published in national magazines. It looked like at least a few people liked what I wrote. My interest in writing grew with each publication; and, although I never believed I had enough words in me to play at a book, here I am.

Chapter 2
Rose Cochran's Nasturtiums

ANYONE GROWING UP ON SOUTH WILLOUGHBY AVENUE in Juneau, Alaska, in the early 1950s, is sure to remember Rose Cochran's Lunchroom. It was a drab little yellow one-story building fronting on the north side of the street just a few doors west of Stevenson's Market. It had a period false front, an old awning over the entry, and a huge flowerbox under a big front window facing out across Willoughby.

At that time, Rose was a lady who must have been in her late sixties. She always appeared neat, wearing light-colored dresses, and usually an apron covering her front from neck to hemline. Her hair was short, mostly grey, and curly. She always wore white shoes resembling the kind I recall school nurses of that time wearing, and when she sat, legs crossed, talking, she had the habit of running her index finger through the top inside edge of her left shoe like she was either rubbing or scratching the upper edge of her foot arch. Not the best of unwitting habits for someone in the food service.

Inside the establishment, on the left, was a counter with no more than six stools and there were about three or four small tables with checkered tablecloths against a wall along the right side. Each little table allowed for two people, comfortably. This provided ample serving room down the aisle between the counter stools and tables—as long as there wasn't a third person seated at a table in the aisle. If a third person sat at the table, Rose had to squeeze around the outside customer to wait on anyone further along toward the front door. There

Chapter 2— Rose Cochran's Nasturtiums

was a doorless opening into a small kitchen at the inside end of the lunch counter. This was a no-frills lunchroom and the usual fare was a hamburger with fries or soup and a sandwich. In the morning, folks in the neighborhood could usually tell the soup of the day by the cooking smells coming from Rose's kitchen. I rarely ate there, save for a burger or two, or maybe an order of her long, fat-cut French fries, but it sticks in my mind that she always served a good cup of coffee.

Rumor had it that Rose was the mother of an up-and-coming stage actor at that time. His name was Steve Cochran, a man who was soon to become quite a Hollywood star, famous for playing tough-guy crime roles and westerns. Years later, Steve reportedly bought his mother a home outside and moved her out of Alaska; if this is true or not, such an eventual success story for her was to be years after the time frame of this little tale.

The great impact Rose Cochran had on my life was not due to her food or to her movie star son—it was due to the nasturtiums growing in the window box in front of her establishment.

Most every gardener with any experience knows that nasturtiums are an edible flower and most kids who grow up around the plant know that a small taste of honey-sweet nectar can be had by biting off the back tip of that flower's blossom and sucking out the tiny bit of delicious fluid to be found there. I knew this and had the good fortune, or *misfortune* as it would turn out, to live in a house almost directly across the street from Rose's blasted garden box.

I was a young lad of about nine or ten years at the time. Over the course of early summer I watched the flowers grow into bloom. I was sorely tempted by the thought of a nectar treat but hesitant to prey on the plants for fear of being caught in the act. The porch which housed the window box was quite open and exposed to the view of the prying eyes of many potential witnesses.

This went on for weeks until finally, late one quiet evening, long after the lunchroom was closed, I was out later than I should have been and temptation got the best of me. I had neither a sensible plan of attack nor the cover of darkness needed for a safe raid. The famous midnight sun had me exposed to near full daylight. I should have gone home to bed but instead, overconfidence took me. Willoughby Avenue was deserted, save for an occasional passing car. I stole down the street a distance and then crossed over to the sidewalk on the lunchroom side.

This was to be a bold frontal attack. I would walk slowly down the sidewalk to the entry, quickly check for observers, slip up to the flowerbox and harvest the number of bright orange, red, and yellow blossoms I felt it would be prudent to get away with—hopeful of getting away without being caught. From the start a foolish plan!

My intention was to take only a small bit of plunder. But as I plucked the blossoms I became consumed with greed. The more I had in my hands, the more I wanted. If ten were good then twenty were twice as good, so I kept on picking. I didn't take them all, but I nearly did.

If there were prying eyes I didn't see them. My bold plan appeared to work without a hitch and soon I was enjoying the fruits of my petty larceny hidden in some clandestine salmonberry patch down the street. Then I slipped home and into my bed with no one the wiser.

Next morning I arose as usual and went about the daily business of a nine-year-old. At the time, Mom was a housewife and not employed. Sometime after noon my baby seagull stomach drove me home for something to eat. As soon as I opened the door, and saw Mom looking at me through the narrow slits where her eyes normally resided, I knew I was in trouble.

I was exposed! By whom I never knew, but someone had spotted me doing the dirty deed and had told Mom that morning and she was laying for me at home. There was nothing I could do but face my comeuppance and take whatever I got without a peep; and, as it turned out, this was to be a good one!

Ma was fighting mad and set about whaling on me for the thoughtless transgression. I was large enough at the time to have resisted the clobbering, had I a mind to, but I didn't. I just curled up in a corner and took it. My size probably had a frustrating effect on Mom who knew that hitting me harder produced nothing but greater wear and tear on her and little, if any, of the desired effect on me. This punishment imbalance was soon to turn around, however. At the time she was wearing a pair of wooden shoes, heavy clogs with wood soles. Unable to produce the desired damage with her small hands she took to kicking me, curled up on the floor, in the buttocks and thighs. Apparently, after a good number of swift kicks, she was satisfied I had finally paid the appropriate price and the parental lesson ended. I don't know where she went, but she left the house, and me sitting on the floor rubbing the sore spots.

That was the one and only thrashing I can remember my mother ever giving me. In later years we would make light of the tanning, a more or less private joke between mother and son. She told me many times, in jest, when she thought I was out of line regarding some minor issue, that I had best be careful or she would "get out the wooden shoes!" When she said this I always took the spirit of the statement as a hint of regret and apology as much as an intended joke. I never failed to reassure her, "Never mind, Ma, I had it coming."

Chapter 3
Life As An Alaska Entrepreneur

DURING MY YOUTH HERE IN ALASKA I DON'T RECALL ever having an allowance. Although there were probably times when I begged money from my parents, it must have been so far back that I don't remember doing so. But, in fairness to the folks, neither do I recall ever being refused money, nor being lectured that if I wanted something I would have to go out and work for it. I just never asked.

There was always a roof over my head, which seldom leaked, plenty of food, and adequate clothing, but if I wanted or needed something else, I worked to earn the money to buy it. Some opportunity always seemed to present itself which allowed for making pocket money. I was always quick to recognize such opportunities and take advantage.

One of my jobs in early grade school was peddling the *Juneau Empire* on the streets of Juneau. Each daily issue was published early in the afternoon. The paper at that time, including the press and the circulation office, was located on Main Street, a few blocks up the hill and quite near the downtown area. Those of us who were street hawkers, as opposed to paper route delivery boys, picked up our papers at the circulation office and then ran like hell for the main drag through the center of downtown, South Franklin Street, to hit the bars. Bars were the absolute best places to peddle papers. Nobody ever stopped a minor from coming into a drinking establishment if he was delivering the news. During this narrow daily window of opportunity, speed was obviously important, and if you were smart in the race down South Franklin, you passed up the smaller hole-in-the-wall watering estab-

Chapter 3— Life As An Alaska Entrepreneur

lishments for the larger ones. The first paperboy through the door usually sold an issue to at least every other person in the place—and you most often got some sort of tip. Every one of us working the streets then knew that a customer with a couple of drinks in him tended to be generous. When the race was over and it looked like the downtown paper market was thoroughly saturated, you took the remaining papers back to the circulation office, handed over the money (less the tips!), and were paid a percentage on the spot for the number you had sold. Not a lot of money was made, but it was surely lucrative enough for an hours work for a grade school kid.

I tried a paper route for a year but there was not enough profit in that end of the newspaper business to suit me.

During the early fifties another of my capitalist adventures was shining shoes. Ink Ingledue operated Ink's Barbershop in the uptown area on South Franklin Street. This was one of the busiest foot traffic locations in Juneau at that time for either a barbershop or a shoeshine stand.

While passing one day I noticed that the three-seat shoeshine stand in the front of the shop was idle and approached Mr. Ingledue to inquire if he needed someone to operate that end of his business. He took me in on a trial basis and I was soon shining shoes every afternoon after school and all day on Saturdays. Several of my best customers were bellmen at the Baranof and Gastineau Hotels who would drop off several pairs of shoes a week to be shined up like mirrors. I was absolutely unabashed about drumming up business for my shoeshine concession. When things were slow, I was out in front on the street like a New Orleans street vendor crying out the word that shines were available inside.

I worked for Ink for less than a year. Later I tried my hand at a shine stand in front of the original Red Dog Saloon, also on South Franklin, but soon gave that up also. Between both experiences, at the very least I learned how to put a fine shine on a pair of shoes.

Few people who have lived in Alaska a good number of years fail to remain untouched by the commercial fishing industry in some way or other. My first experience with the business, at a very tender age, was on the Juneau waterfront.

One day, while watching halibut boats unloading their catch at the Juneau Cold Storage dock, I spied several older Native ladies standing on the dock beside an unloading table. Two Cold Storage em-

Hunts and Home Fires

ployees were up on the table, 3 feet or more above the level of the dock, and, with the aid of cargo hooks and very sharp machete-like knives, were cutting heads off halibut being unloaded with cargo nets from the holds of fishing boats. The decapitated fish were then slid off the table into huge wheeled carts inside an open door in the building. The severed heads, I noticed, were courteously being slid over to the side of the table where the ladies were waiting. They would pick the heads off the table, skillfully cut out the halibut cheeks, and then slide the cheekless heads under the table, down through a trapdoor in the dock and into the channel. When they had all the cheeks (the very best eating part of a halibut!) they wanted, the ladies left. The employees continued cutting off heads and dumping them, cheeks and all, down through the trapdoor into the drink. Here, I thought, was an opportunity for profit.

I soon set myself up in business. All that was required was a sharp knife and a couple of liver cans, square, galvanized, five gallon cans, with large lids, used for storing and transporting fish livers. The Cold Storage employees were as cooperative with me, at first, as they had been with the Native ladies. The bigger the fish the bigger the cheeks and it was an easy proposition to cut a 5-gallon can full in an afternoon. I made a small fortune that summer selling halibut cheeks through the back doors of small local restaurants.

Most good things soon come to an end, it seems. More and more people, seeing me and a few others cutting cheeks, began to horn in on the deal, the result was a crowd of too many people around the unloading table reaching for halibut heads. The employees swinging razor-sharp machetes became concerned about lopping off a hand, so we all were abruptly forbidden to salvage any more cheeks on company property. But the heads continued to be dropped down into the bay through the trapdoor. It looked like the company had killed my golden goose—or had they?

In one last, desperate effort to save my niche in the Alaska fish business, I conceived a bold plan to keep things going. I secured a small skiff from a friend and, waiting until halibut unloading was in full swing, worked the little boat through the pilings under the Cold Storage building to a point under the trap door. I soon saw the error in the plan. It was like being under a meteor shower. While I did recover a few heads, the distance from the dock down to where the skiff floated was far too great and the larger heads nearly drove themselves through the bottom of the boat. In addition, huge chunks of ice, which often accompanied the fish up onto the unloading table from the hold of the unloading boat, were also discarded down through the trap door. Any number of these could have easily killed me and, unknown to anyone up on the dock, I was forced to row for my life.

It was not until the family moved to Ketchikan that my career as a young entrepreneur really flowered. While there I once again entered the newspaper business, expanded into magazines, found new opportunity in the metals market, and prospered once again in the fishing business.

In Ketchikan we lived about 2 miles or so north of town up the North Tongass Highway. I could walk to town most of the way on the beach and while doing so, pick up enough scrap copper, brass, pot metal or lead to make the walk worthwhile. Near the end of the beach walk was a conveniently located junk shop which bought scrap metal. I rarely took the scenic beach route without picking up a couple dollars for scrap metal I had collected along the way.

Profit from the news end of my business affairs came from two sources. Both required some up-front money—which usually came from my metals market earnings.

First was the sale of *Seattle Post-Intelligencer*, affectionately referred to by readers and those of us in the newspaper business, as the Seattle P.I. Whenever an Alaska Steamship tour boat was in town I bought every available Seattle P.I. in the dock neighborhood, effectively cornering the market. I then went aboard the docked Alaska Steamship boat and proceeded to sell my copies for fifty cents per issue above what I had paid for them. The crews working aboard these boats were based out of Seattle, hungry for local news, and gladly paid the inflated price.

On other days when Canadian Princess tour ships were in town, I substituted the *Alaska Sportsman* magazine for the Seattle P.I. and sold magazines to the tourists above the cover price. The Totem Press office, which printed the *Alaska Sportsman*, was located only a few blocks from the boat dock. They sold the magazine over the counter at the cover price just a few minutes' walk from the end of the ship's gangplank. The tourists didn't know this and I certainly never volunteered to tell them.

In Ketchikan, like in Juneau, I was not allowed access to halibut heads to cut cheeks. But, by going directly to the boat owner, I was still able to turn a profit on the waterfront.

My first choice was bumming the boat owner out of his catch of incidental, or "by-catch" fish, other than halibut. These kinds of fish were always hauled up out on the fishing grounds by accident. Various species of rockfish, particularly yellow-eyed rockfish—often erroneously referred to in Alaska as red snapper—were my favorite target. As the halibut were being unloaded, these by-catch fish were thrown up on deck out of the hold, to be taken care of later in some manner. The fish processors didn't want these fish and most often neither did the boat skipper. Usually, if I asked, the skipper would tell me I could have them, and that was that. These I filleted and quickly sold through the restaurant back doors.

If the skipper balked at just giving the fish to me, the next tactic was to offer to wash his pam boards in exchange for them.

This is a job every fisherman hates. Pam boards are boards in the hold of the boat which compartmentalize the hold area into sections. As fish are caught, they are iced down in these compartments in the hold. The front of each compartment in the hold is a removable wall of these pam boards. Their function is to hold the fish and ice in each compartment. The boards slide up and down in grooves like sluice gates and can be added, or removed, as necessary, when either icing down fish or during the process of unloading. As the boat unloads, these boards are slid out and thrown up on deck. They are covered in fish slime and someone has to wash them. They need to be scrubbed clean before being put back down in the hold. This requires lots of running water and a good brush scrubbing for each board. Not a really fun job. I was always careful to note that the fish I was going to get would be well worth the work. If the fish looked not to be worth it, I never made the pam board offer.

When times were tough, and there was no by-catch worth working for, there were instances when I offered to wash pam boards for pay. It was seldom that I was refused this dirty job when I asked. I never negotiated for wages in advance for the job, choosing to leave my pay entirely at the discretion of the skipper who hired me. I think this strategy played well on the skipper's sense of guilt over what might be a fair price for scrubbing those slimy boards, because I don't ever recall not being generously compensated.

As a side note, Ketchikan in 1953 and 1954 was a rough little town. A local boom was in progress with the building of the Ward Cove pulp mill, and a major road construction project was underway on the

Tongass Highway through much of the downtown waterfront area. Prostitution was in full swing and brothels along Ketchikan's notorious Creek Street red light district, not far south of the center of town, were thriving. Scantily clad women could be seen advertising their wares as they hung out of every other doorway along the Creek Street boardwalk. Crime was on the increase and members of the local police force frequently made headlines in the city paper amid charges of being on the take. Those were fast-moving times.

Later, growing up wild in Skagway, I worked as a bull-cook (cook's helper, table waiter, and dishwasher) for the railroad, and held a wharf watchman's job working on Sundays and holidays all through high school (I bought my own car while in high school and paid for all maintenance and gas). I worked on the railroad section or bridge and building crews during the summers and always did odd jobs between jobs.

Dad Kalvick was a carpenter. Someone was always after him to do a remodeling job on their houses and this work usually required the services of a helper. Dad had an impeccable work ethic and always highballed through every job he ever did. Those who hired him got what they paid for. I must admit, the money was good but I'll also admit I hated to work for him because he was such a hard driver!

On the side, Dunk Hukill always needed help with his roofing tar business and, if things got real desperate, Mrs. Evell's yard needed tending and Old Pop Lundy always bought any scrap copper I could lay my hands on.

One thing is sure. A little hard work never hurt anyone, not even a kid.

Chapter 4
My First Rifle

I RECALL IT WAS IN GRADE SCHOOL, PROBABLY SOMETIME during the seventh grade, that an interest in firearms was awakened inside me. This awakening was more by accident than by design.

In the 1950s, in Juneau, there were a number of old row apartments along Willoughby Avenue. Many of these were typically tiny, low-income rental units built on pilings over unfilled tidal basin. In the past it had probably been cheaper to drive pilings to build on rather than fill the hole. The tide rose and fell twice each day under these dwellings, seeping in and out from Gastineau Channel through the surrounding rock fill.

Older retired people, most of whom were held prisoner by limited income, occupied many of these apartments. Somehow or other I had become acquainted with one of these elderly residents, a gentleman needing some work completed but lacking the funds to pay for the service he needed.

As was fairly common at that time, for heating and cooking he used a wood-burning kitchen range. He had a little woodshed adjoining his rental, which held slightly over a cord of wood, a cord being a pile measuring 4 feet by 4 feet by 8 feet. His wood had been bought from a firewood supplier but the order had been delivered as sawed log chunks. These were unusable to the old man. They had to be split into pieces that would suit his little woodstove. Not only did the whole pile need splitting and piling, but a portion of it had to be further split into fine kindling, smaller pieces needed to kindle, or start, fires in his woodstove.

I tried desperately to get away from this situation, which I could only view as a bunch of heavy charity work.

Chapter 4— My First Rifle

I had almost pulled free when the old gentleman dangled an irresistible carrot in front of my nose. If I split the wood for him, including the kindling, he would give me in trade, he said, his favorite 30-40 Krag rifle. The offer was no more than mentioned when he dragged the old firearm out and placed it in my hands for inspection.

During this rifle's obviously long life it can hardly be said that it appeared to have been well cared for, although at the time I knew preciously little about the finer points of any firearm. For the last five years of my tender young life I had been removed, by the death of my father, from the influence of a man who would probably have cared about my training in the subject of weapons. I was to learn later in life that it was not impossible that this rifle, properly referred to as the U.S. Magazine rifle, Model 1892, could possibly have been used in the Spanish-American War, during the Philippine Insurrection, or perhaps have even seen service in the Boxer Rebellion in China; all of which took place in the late 1800s and early 1900s! This rifle was not a youngster!

The best and most immediate indicator of this rifle's condition was half an old copper penny that had been brazed onto a notch on the top back of barrel where, at some time in the past, a rear sight must have been located. A tiny hole had been drilled through the top middle of the half penny. This contraption had been concocted to serve as a peep sight!

All the metal parts had a dull brown patina of rust and grime and the barrel rifling, what was left of it, had definitely seen better days.

Still, I was instantly smitten by the possibility of owning my own weapon offered in the old gentleman's proposition for a trade. With Mom's permission, I concluded negotiations, split all the pile of cut logs to my bartering partner's satisfaction, including the kindling, and the rifle was mine.

For a number of years I put more wear and tear on that old firearm cleaning it periodically than I did using it in the field for shooting. For one thing, ammunition was too expensive. I bought a few boxes of shells but I guess I chose, in most cases, to do other things with the money rather than spend it on bullets. I was still too young to go out and do any serious hunting on my own and not well enough connected to anyone interested in taking a kid along on a hunting trip.

I have to admit here, there were a few scary times when I got up enough nerve to go into Rusher's Hardware and swipe a few rounds out of full boxes of 30-40 Krag ammunition. I would only palm a couple of bullets—and did this only a few times. I never had nerve enough to steal a whole box. The risk was too great and the consequences of being caught too frightening to allow it. But that regretted bit of thievery is also another story.

I had the rifle in my possession until my family suffered a disastrous house fire in Skagway during the late 1950s. We were all away from home when the place caught fire, the cause being a faulty floor furnace. We lost everything that afternoon except the clothes each of us had on our backs. All that was left of the old Krag, and of several other precious old weapons I had managed to accumulate, was a scorched, seized-up magazine and barrel.

And that is the story of the beginning of my hopeless, lifelong slide into the hinterlands of hunting.

Chapter 5
An Apology to Miss Rodland

I SUSPECT THAT ALL OF US LIVE WITH SOME REGRET FOR a past deed, or deeds. Such is the case involving my behavior during my seventh year of elementary school in the Juneau public school system. An apology is necessary.

Miss Rodland was my teacher in Juneau during that second half of the seventh-grade year. I had just transferred from White Cliff School in the Ketchikan school system sometime in about the middle of that year.

A teacher by the name of Mr. Ford had taught me during the first half of that grade. He was a large, imposing person, but a most fair and reasonable man and one of gentle temperament. I remember he wore his hair in a crew cut and always wore a tie, white shirt, and a tweed sport coat. Due to his size, and his gender I suppose, he cut a figure to be reckoned with and I never gave him any trouble.

Miss Rodland, on the other hand, was to be the recipient of every rotten trick I could possibly devise while under her charge. I have no idea why. Mostly because I was mean enough to do so, I suppose, and because she was there and I didn't really want to be.

She was a new teacher, probably not more than a few years out of college. A tiny woman, blond and blue-eyed, she may have been of Scandinavian origin. I know she had people who lived in Petersburg, the Little Norway of Alaska.

Grades were of little or no concern to me. I rarely did homework and seldom took part in class activities. The only bright moments during the school week, it seemed, were once-a-week art classes, when Mr.

Louis, the roving grade school art teacher, came to give art classes, and the times we were allowed to listen to the Standard School Broadcast, an elementary school educational program, for half an hour in the morning once a week on the radio.

I recall spending a good part of many days standing alone in the coatroom outside class, where I had no opportunity to further disturb Miss Rodland and the other students.

I considered myself a master of sabotage. It was a simple thing, for instance, to rig the pencil sharpener to fall apart all over the floor when the next student used it, or for handles to be suddenly pulled off file cabinet drawers, or coats to fall on the floor when an attempt was made to hang a garment on a deliberately loosened coat hook. It was not long before all eyes, and blame, would fall on me when *any* mishap affected the class. In most cases the instant judgment was justified.

One of my favorite pastimes was playing hooky. When the urge struck me, I acted like I was off to school in the morning, for Mom's benefit, but instead I headed for the federal building and met up with my favorite "note to the teacher" writer. Both the Juneau High School and the Fourth Street grade school were located just up the hill from the federal building at that time. High school students would loiter and smoke in the warmth of a back corner of the federal building's post office lobby until it was time to head up the hill to class. My high school friend, dependable Darlene, had handwriting that looked just like my mother's and she was always willing to pen me a note requesting Miss Rodland to please excuse my recent absence—for whatever reason seemed like a good one at the time. No one ever caught onto these forged notes, supposedly written by Mom. (Even in later years I never confessed to my mother that I had done this!)

Another ruse I used to get me out of school for the day was the old liquid soap trick. During the early morning at school I hung around class trying as best I could not to look well. Soon I asked to be excused to go to the bathroom. In the bathroom I squirted a little green hand soap under my tongue. Not really a pleasant-tasting thing but the most essential element of the farce. It took a great deal of control not to swallow that horrible stuff or begin drooling. Next, I told the teacher I didn't feel well and could I please go see the school nurse? The first thing the school nurse did when a student didn't feel well was stick a thermometer in their mouth. For a technical reason I cannot explain,

Chapter 5— An Apology to Miss Rodland

that green hand soap under a tongue causes a rise of at least a couple degrees on a thermometer. It never failed; I was excused to go home sick, and after spitting out the detergent, was free to proceed with a better plan for the day than sitting in school.

There were times that I got caught being a bad boy. Not too many, but life is not always a bowl of cherries. It seemed, boys being boys, tempers could easily flare to the point of a duke-out during recess. On one such occasion two of us got nabbed by the schoolyard attendant and carted off directly to the principal's office. Mr. Dryden (nicknamed Dragonfly!) a tall, gray-haired, rather athletic fellow, who always wore a light blue business suit, had a zero-tolerance policy toward his students fighting. He laid the law down to both of us—and a bit more than that! In those days if you had a paddling coming nobody called home and asked permission—they just did it. The sentence for fighting was three whacks on the bare behind and, to add insult to the assured injury, the school nurse was obliged to be present to witness the proceedings. The other guy got his first. I had to stand outside the office door listening to the sound of the three-foot paddle meeting the bottom of my adversary. When it came my turn, I resolved to put up as brave and devil-may-care a front as possible. After the first strike, however, all I could manage was to grit my teeth and tightly close my eyes. Mr. Dryden had a major-league swing.

Near the end of the school year Miss Rodland laid it on the line. My work would either significantly improve for the remainder of the term or I would be taking the seventh grade over again. The threat of being held back did not appeal to me. *Now* I know I could never have improved my grades enough, at that late point in the school year, to actually pass the grade. This was a last desperate attempt to get me, at the very least, to finally do some schoolwork. I knew this was no idle threat on her part and a feeling of great dread came over me. The thought of suffering the seventh grade over again was too much to bear. I took her at her word that if I did the work, even at that late date, I could move on through into the eighth grade. The handwriting was on the wall so, completely out of character, I hit the books.

To this day I am plagued with a recurring dream. In this dream I am always trying to take a very important test and, in the dream, due to a variety of circumstances beyond my control, I am never able to complete the exam. As each episode unfolds, I am increasingly filled with a miserable feeling of failure. A ticking clock is always evident. If it was my seventh grade experience that marked me for life with this bad dream it was through no fault of Miss Rodland!

In the weeks that remained, I proved what I suspect my teacher knew all along. I was perfectly capable of doing the work. I had just been too lazy, too mean, and too wrapped up in my boredom to do so.

On the last day of class Miss Rodland passed out report cards and, one by one, turned all the other students loose. She looked at me briefly, smiled, wrote "Passed" at the bottom, then signed and handed the report card to me. I let out a genuine whoop and headed for the door. A bookcase along the way was just too much of a temptation. Purposely delivering her one last miserable insult, on the way by I elbowed some books off onto the floor and kept on going.

Miss Rodland, I am truly ashamed and I apologize. God bless you wherever you are.

Chapter 6
Recreational Gold Hunting

I HAVE ALWAYS BEEN INTERESTED IN RECREATIONAL gold hunting. I say gold "hunting" because traveling around looking for traces of placer gold with a gold pan, a sluice box, or even a small diameter gold dredge is not gold mining—it is gold hunting. People who use front-end loaders and caterpillar tractors and pump thousands of gallons of public water through huge commercial sluice boxes are the folks who are "mining." A moose wading a stream raises more sediment in the water than most small gold dredges; and God, when he makes it rain heavily, and raises a stream's depth significantly, creates more muddy water than five hundred recreational miners, yet God appears to be exempt from the mining regulations.

I grew up in Skagway, in Southeast Alaska, an area generally void of the geologic upheavals and the proper rock formations necessary for the presence of gold. You don't find a lot of the yellow metal in mountains made of granite. I panned every stream in that country and never found a fleck. This is both ironic and frustrating, considering that just a few miles across the Coastal Range from Skagway, the Atlin and Tagish country in the Yukon is shot through with gold deposits, both hard rock and placer, much of which, I am sure, is yet to be discovered.

To the south of Skagway, along Lynn Canal, are a number of old hard-rock mines, such as the old Comet Mine, which produced gold up until World War II, when nonessential industries were shut down to conserve fuel. The soaring price of gold has sparked mining company interest in these old mines. The proposed Kensington Mine, north of Berner's Bay in the Juneau vicinity, is one new proposed hard rock-mine, although environmental groups are currently using all means available to fight development of this mine to a standstill. The Kensington mine has become a Southeast Alaska "environmental" poster baby.

Other parts of Southeast Alaska have a good smattering of gold. There are a number of other old mines on Lynn Canal, other than the Kensington, there are old and new mines north of Haines, historic low-grade gold mines at Juneau, on Windham Bay, on Admiralty Island, and on Chichagof Island—but there is not a trace of gold near Skagway, at least none that I was ever able to find.

Of course, there are stories of lost placer mines and a few tales about hard-rock gold deposits found and then lost again. If information found in an old book about southeast Alaska is true, I am certain I have ascertained the location of a stream, somewhere within the Misty Fjords National Monument, where the gravels of a certain creek are shot full of course placer gold.

It was not until I moved to the Anchorage, Alaska, area in 1969 that I found myself in country where I could actually pan fine gold from a number of area streams. I recall the first flake I found was from the East Fork tributary of the Eklutna River, on the back (east) end of Eklutna Lake, about 45 miles northeast of Anchorage. I was moose hunting in the area at the time and dredged a small sample of sand from the river bottom with a cut-open pop can tied to a long stick. I took the sample home and panned it out later. The cup of sand yielded one lovely flake of gold a bit larger than a pencil dot. But that was it! I was hooked on recreational gold hunting on the spot!

Don't rush off with your mining equipment figuring to satisfy your lust for gold by mining the South Fork. This little tributary drains into Eklutna Lake, now the main source of water for the city of Anchorage. The entire Eklutna watershed is protected. Mining activity is limited to a shovel and a gold pan. No other equipment is allowed, not even a small hand sluice. Also, the whole of the Eklutna Lake system is inside the borders of Chugiak State Park. An old road along the north shore of the lake is a popular summer hiking and mountain biking destination. Motorized ATC traffic is currently authorized only on certain weekdays. This road is patrolled by a motorized Chugiak State Park ranger who is there to, among other things, assure that no one plays too hard at recreational mining in any stream draining into Eklutna Lake!

A better destination in the Anchorage vicinity for the recreational gold hunter would be the Crow Creek Mine. This mine is located in the Girdwood area, south of Anchorage 30 miles or so via the Seward Highway. The mine is a privately owned summer recreational concession, accessible by a good-quality gravel road, where for a modest daily fee gold seekers are allowed access onto patented mining claims along Crow Creek to hand-mine to their hearts' content; and they may keep all the gold they find. Camping spaces are available near the mine entrance for a modest nightly fee. Hand-mining tools—a shovel, bucket, gold pan, and a small sluice box—are provided by the operators as part of the entry fee. Mineral detectors are welcome.

The attraction working the gravels of Crow Creek is the size of gold that can be found. If a person works hard and moves a lot of material, the pieces of gold recovered are typically of a larger size than what is found in other gold-producing streams, like those farther south along the Seward Highway on the Kenai Peninsula. The gold at Crow Creek tends to be "chunky," unlike the finer gold dust typically found in the Kenai streams. Also, mining at Crow Creek, on private, patented mining claims, allows recreational people the opportunity to dig into stream banks and generally excavate where they choose on the property in their search for the yellow metal.

Most gold-producing streams on the Kenai Peninsula are located on land managed by the U.S. Forest Service. Recreational mining activity is regulated and confined to the active streambed. No permit is required at this time for panning or for using a portable sluice box. A permit from the Alaska Department of Fish and Game is required for operating gold-dredging equipment in any stream supporting a run of salmon. Dredges are limited in size and to the time of year during which they may be operated. Dredging is prohibited in some areas on certain streams. Care should be exercised to assure that the proper permit is obtained, that the stream to be mined is open to dredging, and that there is no conflict with an active mining claim.

Pieces of fine gold, or "dust," can easily be found with a gold pan in a number of small streams on the north end of the Kenai Peninsula. Bertha, Spokane, Granite, Silvertip, Canyon, and Six Mile creeks are all accessible by the Seward Highway or the Hope Cutoff road. With some diligent panning, any of these streams can produce small amounts of fine gold.

Chapter 7
The Dunking of E. Waneta Coring

SOMETIME IN THE MIDDLE OF MY HIGH SCHOOL CAREER the beginning of my junior year as I recall, the Skagway public school system was blessed with the addition of two new high school teachers. They were E. Waneta Coring and Connie Conard. The two came as a pair, imported, like most things needed in Alaska at that time, from somewhere down in "America."

The two newcomers were infatuated with Alaska and filled with a desire to rub noses with the country. We were in the middle of our short fall. The bottom of Skagway Valley is covered in cottonwood and their yellow leaves were already turned and falling. The days were cool and blustery, stirred by a north wind rolling down over the mountains out of the Yukon. All these are sure signs of approaching winter.

A favorite seasonal haunt of mine was the clear, ice-cold streams north of town at the end of what was generally referred to as the "san" road—*san* being short for *sanatorium*. First an army hospital was built out there during the war years. This was taken over after the war and operated as a tuberculosis sanatorium by the Territory of Alaska. The old sanatorium had been closed and then torn down long before I arrived in Skagway in 1955.

The cold creeks in the area were feeder streams off the Skagway River and the spawning grounds for a small run of chum, or dog salmon as they are irreverently nicknamed. Along with the chums came a respectable run of Dolly Varden char in pursuit of the larger salmon's eggs. Most of the chums were red in color and spawned out, so the char were

Chapter 7—The Dunking of E. Waneta Coring

the object of most interest. These sea-run "Dollies" were as beautifully colored as a rainbow trout and some ran in size near to that of the salmon. Dollies caught in freshwater tasted just as good as any of their species pulled fresh from the salt of the ocean.

There was no local fish or game warden at that time. I took the small amount of fish I wanted with a crude gaff made from a halibut hook nailed on the end of a long, thin pole. The trick was to sneak up on a fishing hole, slow and quiet, ease the gaff into the water downstream behind a fish, bring the pole and hook up slowly on his far side, then jerk the pole toward me. I often scared fish off while approaching where they lay on the bottom but if a fish allowed me to get into gaffing position I rarely missed it.

Misses Coring and Conard were fascinated by my fish stories and asked for a demonstration. So, one cold morning found us out at the san, sneaking through the alders toward my favorite fishing spot. On the way we crossed one small stream, not more than 10 feet wide and 6 inches deep, just deep enough that I had earlier placed some large rocks across the channel to use as stepping stones. I always wore ankle-length leather boots and loathed wet feet. On the trip in, the ladies did well crossing the somewhat tippy rock bridge.

Sneaking up on the fish hole was a masterful demonstration of competence on my part and I was quick to pull a 3-pound Dolly from the icy water. Thrilled by the experience, and chattering up a storm, we headed back through the alders to the car. As I recall, Miss Conard re-crossed the intervening creek on the shaky rock bridge first. When it came Miss Coring's turn she did fine until about midstream, where she misplaced a foot off-center of one of the stepping stones. The rock rolled slightly and, arms flailing violently in a vain effort to regain her balance, she fell, in what seemed like slow motion, backwards, flat on her bottom in the middle of the creek. Miss Coring was a rather large, healthy woman and the toppling climaxed with a tremendous splash. My first thought was worry that she had hurt herself, but that fear was quickly dispelled by the roar of laughter immediately following the dunking. I waded in to help her, but she was laughing so hard she was nearly helpless. I was finally able to get her on her feet and out of the water, but all the way out through the alders to the car she never ceased that near hysterical, bellowing laughter.

This was a great cap to a fine day of fishing. The new teachers had a good story and took the spoils home with them and had a fresh trout dinner that night.

Miss Coring, the dunkee, is gone now. Miss Conard, long retired, still lives in Skagway at this writing.

After all these years, until now, I have never had the heart to advise either of the ladies of the fact that, long ago, they had been accomplice to poachers!

Chapter 8
Alaska Statehood, A Big Night!

THE EVENING OF JANUARY 3, 1959, WAS A BIG NIGHT IN the Territory of Alaska for on that day "we were in." The Territory ceased to exist and we were now, officially, the State of Alaska, admitted to the Union as the 49th state.

On that evening the city of Skagway, where I lived at the time, blew wide open in one of the most unbridled celebrations I had ever seen in Alaska, or have seen since. The best-remembered Fourth of July, Labor Day, New Year's Eve, or Christmas pales in comparison. Every bar on Broadway, the main street through downtown, threw the doors wide open and in a celebratory frenzy served any person entering the establishment. If you were tall enough to reach the top of the bar you took part in the celebration. The local police chief went home for the night and stayed there. For a multitude of legal reasons he would have had to arrest half the town that night had he been down there.

No one, to my knowledge, suffered for the big celebration, save for some tremendous hangovers the following day. In view of the importance of the date, and the wild enthusiasm with which statehood was heralded, it is wonder to me why Alaskans fail to pay more special attention to January 3 each year. The date was made a state holiday. a holiday which generally passes by without much fanfare.

Chapter 9
Working for Nick

I TURNED SIXTEEN IN FEBRUARY 1957. FOR A BOY LIVING in Skagway, Alaska, and attending his first year of high school, this particular birthday was a landmark, more like a rite of passage. Like so many other young lads before me, reaching sixteen meant that the following summer I would be old enough to apply for a seasonal laborer's job on the White Pass & Yukon Railroad.

The WP&YR is a historic, narrow-gauge railroad extending from tidewater at Skagway, on Lynn Canal, at the upper end of Southeast Alaska's Inside Passage, to Whitehorse, Yukon Territory, approximately 125 rail miles due north, on the banks of the Yukon River. This railroad was built because of demand from the 1897/1898 Klondike gold rush and, until my birthday in 1957 at least, it had been in continuous operation every year since, hauling material, food, and fuel north into the Yukon.

Everyone who lived in Skagway either worked for the railroad or depended on its existence, one way or another, for their livelihood. This source of employment made Skagway a rich little town by Alaska standards. Work was dependable and generally year-round, rather than seasonal. The transportation economy didn't depend on the vagaries of market supply and demand like the mining, fishing, or timber industries, which support so many other Alaska communities. If you were known for providing a day's work for a day's pay, and mostly kept your nose clean, you generally had a job if you lived in Skagway.

The railroad put on extra help each summer. Of importance to me was their practice of hiring a crew of seasonal employees to work on the

Chapter 9— Working for Nick

tracks up and down the line. About every job on the railroad had a title. There were longshoremen, engineers and fireman, train crews, carmen to keep the rolling stock repaired, painters, blacksmiths, and bridge and building crews, to name just a few. One of the hardest jobs, and because of that fact the least desirable, was working on the section gang. This work was dawn-to-dark hard labor. Men who worked on the tracks were, and still are, known as gandy dancers. During the summer the section crew's main job was to work up and down the line on the railroad bed, mainly pulling and replacing rotten, worn-out, or busted railroad ties, a continuous, year after year, never ending chore. Ties are timbers which reside under the rails, buried in the gravel railroad bed. The rails are held in place by being spiked to these ties. Working on a section crew, at that time, meant a repetitious, backbreaking job every day. But I didn't care. I was young and strong and planned to live forever. I wanted to buy my own car that summer and this job would pay for it.

When summer vacation began, I was hired, and as the date approached for me to report on the job, I was ready for any hardship that working the tracks could throw at me. The only sense of dread I felt came from being assigned to work on section one, the section of track which extended from Skagway north for about the first 15 miles or so of the line. The dread had nothing to do with the toughness of the job—it was due to the fact that I would be working for the most notorious of the section foremen, Nick the Greek!

Nicolas Arson was a first-generation Greek. He had apparently come over from the old country as a young man and had spent most of his working life on the tracks of the Great Northern Railroad. When he came to work on the WP&YR I don't know, but he had been there a considerable time before my family moved to Skagway in 1955. Nobody knew for sure how old he was, but I believe it would be a safe bet to say that by 1957 a number of years had passed since his sixty-fifth birthday. He was a little, wiry guy with yellow-gray hair, black, beady eyes, and a brown, ruddy, weather-beaten face with more wrinkles and lines than a busy road map. Other trademarks were his felt fedora, an old battered one for working and a new one for dress, and his heavy, checkered wool shirt, which he always wore to work, come scorching summer or freezing winter. He was a gentleman of the old school and had earned his living the hard way all his life. On the job there was no time for foolishness. He had reportedly made the statement a number of times that all he wanted to see when his crew was working was assholes and elbows. You either did the work or you were gone. He set the tone for all of us when we reported for work that first morning. We four young new hires had arrived early and were cowering in the plywood-covered back of the flatbed section gang truck when Nick came out of the railroad depot, walked around the back of the rig, looked inside, and swore out loud to himself. On the spot, he told one of us, whom he apparently knew something about, to go home. "I don't want you," he said. And that was the end of that.

It didn't take long to settle into a section gang summer routine. First, we loaded and hauled railroad ties up and down the line and distributed them along the tracks at places where replacement was needed. There were no roads parallel to the railroad right-of-way so we moved on the rails with a motor-driven car, a boxy little plywood and wood vehicle. It is proper to call this machine either a motorcar or a "Casey," in railroad terms. Having the Casey on the tracks, or tearing out ties from under the rails, created some obvious safety problems with numerous trains coming and going. We had to set the motorcar off the tracks and in the clear on temporary, makeshift sidings we had to construct near where we would be working. Work was timed between trains, typically a northbound in the morning and a southbound late in the afternoon, and around several roundtrip tourist trains which provided scenic rides into the mountains for tourists on days when the tour boats hit Skagway. We could tear up only a limited amount of track per day, having to time what we did to allow for safe passage of the freight and passenger trains. We started work at 8 a.m., had a fifteen-minute coffee break at 10 a.m., a half-hour lunch at noon and quit work at 4:30 p.m. The only other breaks we got during the day were the few minutes required for a train to pass by. Nick always acted like this extravagant bit of down time was a personal favor from him. "Aw light (all right), boys," he would say when we could hear the train coming, "take a smoke." If you lit a cigarette, you never had enough time to finish it or you smoked while you were working again, for the moment the train passed the first words out of his mouth were, "Aw light boys, les go to work."

Once we settled into a work routine together as a new crew we were able to change about one hundred ties per day, all by hand, with no mechanical devices, just picks, shovels, crowbars and spike mauls.

Chapter 9— Working for Nick

(These days machinery does most of the work.) Toward the end of the season, we were putting in between 125 and 150 ties a day with a six-man crew of mostly boys driving themselves to work like men. There was never any thought of trying to deliberately slow the pace, because the watchful eye of Nick would have caught the plot immediately and there would have been hell to pay. He knew every day how much work we did and, if less work was completed the following day he was never bashful about telling us about it.

Here was how a typical day went: We began the morning by digging out the ends of the ties to be changed that day. Nick marked the ties to be removed. At the same time, a couple of us began pulling the railroad spikes out of the rotten ties with huge crowbars. Doing this kept us plenty busy until about 9 a.m. when Number 1 (the northbound regular daily train) passed and cleared out of the way. If there was a tourist train, it generally came through shortly behind Number 1. As soon as the morning trains were in the clear, we began pulling the spikes in earnest from the remaining ties, jacked up the rails with track jacks, and pulled and dumped the soggy, 200-pound rejects over the side of the roadbed, by hand, into the clear. We could pull only so many ties before we had to stop and begin replacing them behind us. At least every other tie that had been pulled was replaced, the gauge, correct spacing between the rails, was checked and adjusted, and the rails were spiked back down onto the new ties. At a certain point no more bad ties could be pulled. To wind up a day's work, the whole crew then had to drop back to replace and finish spiking the remaining ties that had been removed earlier. The foreman then checked for low spots in the rails and the level of the track was adjusted in places, as required. Once this was done, all hands hit the short, square-pointed shovels and roadbed gravel was tamped (pushed and packed) under and around the new ties to solidly set them in place. Tamping ties for most of an afternoon every day was definitely the most bitter and backbreaking part of a 1950s' gandy dancer's job. Once that was accomplished, the track was dressed up (smoothed and made pretty!) over the course of the short remainder of the afternoon.

All these steps, with the exception of dressing up, had to be timed so that the tracks were buttoned down and safe by the time Number 2, the southbound regular daily train, passed through and into town, usually about 3:30 p.m. Nick always timed it so we would be in town at the motorcar shed where we put away the tools and parked the Casey for the night, just in time for quitting at exactly four thirty.

This schedule put me home at my parents' house about 5 p.m. Usually I headed into my room and crashed on top of my bed until Mom woke me for supper at 6 p.m. Many times I recall being so wasted that I refused the chance to eat, preferring instead to wash up a bit and crawl under the covers for the night, resting my exhausted body until six the following morning, when the same daily routine started all over again.

Looking back now, I can see that the hard work never hurt me. As much as I have painted the old Greek as a tyrant, his tyranny consisted mostly of insisting each of us who plagued him as summer help do a day's work for a day's pay. In fairness to his memory I need to say that for all the instances when he *was* a bit mean, the crew never passed on an opportunity to repay him in kind and it is probably debatable to say for sure who ended up ahead in the contest.

I don't know how many times one of us cornered a mouse while working along the tracks and sneaked it into Nick's lunch pail. The result was predictable. There would be a long list of colorful expletives, followed by the banging and crashing of Nick dumping his lunch over the side of the railroad grade. He never could figure out how in the hell a mouse was able to get inside his latched metal lunchbox!

We were quick to learn that Nick detested the sound of a loud burp, prompting most of us to bring along large bottles of carbonated soda for lunch every day. This facilitated the production of huge belches for his listening pleasure. We succeeded so well at this that he rarely sat close to the crew, preferring instead to lunch a defensive distance up or down the tracks by himself. Even then, the belches were deliberately loud enough so he could still hear them. I cannot put the language in print that Nick used most times when someone cut loose with a good one.

There were the times when one or the other of us would kick the Casey out of gear going up the grade when Nick turned his head too far away from the controls. This caused the rpm's of the engine to roar and run wild and Nick to cuss and holler about the perceived ineptness of the foreman of the railroad's gas shop, Benny Lingle, to properly fix "his" motorcar. "Got dam Benny Lingo!" he would say.

There were also the times when we had to "line track." That is, to push the track one way or the other using huge bars on the insides of the rails and a lot of back power. This required one man, always Nick, to back away,

Chapter 9— Working for Nick

sight along the rails, and tell us to bar the track over in whatever direction was required—thus we were "lining track." If he wanted the rail moved a lot he said, "Hit it, boys." We did this lining work with the heavy bars in unison. One of us would say, "Ready—heave!" On "heave" we all leaned into the bars at once and, hopefully, moved the track, ties and all, with the combined effort. If Nick wanted us to move the rails some distance he would holler "Hit it." If he wanted to move the rail just a small bit he would instruct "Joos a sheck it." (Just shake it.) Every so often, on signal, we threw the rails hard on "Joos a sheck it," or fake it in unison and not move them at all when he wanted us to hit it hard. These little tricks while we were lining track always made Nick a bit crazy.

Nicholas was not known for being a teetotaler and his overdoing with whiskey caused him considerable grief on occasion. One summer night in the Igloo Bar, a well-known Skagway waterhole he favored, he got pretty tipsy, fell off a barstool and cracked several ribs. Because of this, he was quite subdued for about ten days with a painfully taped chest. All you had to do to pull a good bad joke on him was to point a stiff finger at his ribs and act like you were going to poke him. This happened repeatedly.

I worked on the section gang for two summers. In the third work season of high school I graduated to the bridge and building crew for summer employment and never again had the pleasure of working for Nick. In the fall of my senior year he retired from the WP&YR, and his work life. When he had talked about himself, which wasn't often, several times he had mentioned Weiser, Idaho, a place where he had apparently lived in the past. His plan after packing it in was to return there to live.

It is surprising how many of us kept our ears to the wall regarding his departure. True to his old-school ways, Nick would never have considered leaving on an airplane. There was a terrible party in the Igloo Bar the evening of his departure. It wasn't planned, but a whole crowd of us who had worked for him in years past showed up to escort the intoxicated old Greek down to the city dock and pour him onto a steamship southbound for Seattle. When we tenderly eased him down the gangplank and handed him over to the ship's personnel for some much-needed help to his stateroom, there wasn't a dry eye on the dock. The boat backing away and his departure marked the beginning of a new era for him and the end of an era for the young men of Skagway. We never heard of him again.

Chapter 10
The Local Jacket

LIVING IN A SMALL SOUTHEAST ALASKA COMMUNITY during the early 1950s required a lot of patience. The few stores we had in Skagway at the time were typical. Try as hard as they might, it was just not possible to carry an inventory, without breaking the business, that would satisfy the needs of everyone, all of the time, in such a small community. If whatever was needed was not in stock, the standard offer was, "I can have it for you from Seattle in fourteen days." Either you depended on the accommodating nature of your local businessman, or you ordered what you needed from either the Sears or Monkey Ward's (Montgomery Ward) catalogs yourself. If you ordered the item yourself, there was still a two-week turn-around waiting for what you needed to arrive on a mail boat by parcel post.

Being patient was a two-way deal, for both the somewhat frustrated businessman *and* the frustrated customer in need. My future mother-in-law, Rex Hermens, owned and operated a general merchandising business, Keller's Store, in Skagway during that time. The following is a classic illustration of how one local businessperson coped with small-town impatience, while still maintaining a sense of humor.

On entering the store one day a particular customer, not well known for being one of the most pleasant people, spied a nice jacket hanging in the men's section. It was a smart-looking garment and fit the man perfectly. Looking at the attached sales tag, he noted a sale price of $29.98. "I can buy this jacket in Seattle for $18.98," he noted sourly. Without batting an eye the wily store owner replied, "I'll sell you that jacket for $18.98." Rather startled by the generous offer, the fellow replied that in that case he would take it.

Ms. Hermens brought out a box, folded the jacket and placed it inside. She then quickly covered the box in wrapping paper, taped it tight, wrote his name on it and placed the package high on a shelf behind the counter. "Now" she said, "That will be $18.98 for the jacket, plus a fee for postage and handling, a modest profit for my business, and some small change for city sales tax. Give me $29.98 and you can come in and pick up the jacket in fourteen days when the next mail boat carrying parcel post mail comes to town."

She never had a problem with that customer again.

Chapter 11
Hunting Mine Mountain

IT IS EASY TO SAY, "WE ALL HAVE TO START SOMEWHERE." But it is a matter of fact that I was not ready, or properly prepared, to bow hunt, to wish the consequences of my general ineptness with archery tackle on an animal the first time I tried. Still, that first time, I elected to go bowhunting anyway.

The year was 1965. My wife, Sharon, and I took a break from college at the University of Alaska in Fairbanks during the 1965-66 school year. Sharon was pregnant and our plan was to lay off college for a year, have the baby at home in Skagway, Alaska and work at banking up some money to return to school for a final semester in the spring of 1967. Until the baby came, Sharon would work in her mother's general merchandising store, and I had a job working as a bridge and building carpenter on the White Pass & Yukon Railroad.

I owned an old Fred Bear, glass-backed, semi-recurve bow I had plinked around with for years. I couldn't shoot it very well and neglected the practice I should have been working on before fall rolled around. Ready or not, I planned to try to take a Rocky Mountain goat in the mountains around Skagway before the snow flew.

In those days there was no such thing as camouflage (camo) clothing. *If* you could find arrows with hunting points, they were sold out of a big cardboard box and you had to pick through many to find a few cedar shafts that were nearly straight. Aluminum, fiberglass, and graphite arrows weren't even thought of yet! There was no such thing as inserts or auxiliary blades, only single-blade broadheads. Fred Bear's

Chapter 11— Hunting Mine Mountain

Razorheads were not available yet, at least as far as I knew at the time. The best backpack of the day was the Trapper Nelson, a backbreaking canvas pack bag mounted on a wood frame. Carry much weight too far with that rig and you paid a hefty physical price! I wish I still had that pack. You rarely see one anymore, but somewhere along the line it got away from me. Tents were canvas and most often leaked, keeping campers in constant prayer that God would not make it rain—but it seemed he usually did. The top-of-the-line sleeping bag was the duck feather World War II army-type mummy bag; it was either that or a newer, bulky, and terribly heavy, canvas-covered bag with an inside flannel lining. That was the general state of affairs for sporting goods in 1965.

Fall rolled around and, ready or not, a hunt was planned. I had scouted several places for goats and settled on Mine Mountain, a granite monolith located about 10 air miles, or 30 to 35 winding railroad miles, north of Skagway. The advantage of this location was that it gave hunters a good look at those parts of the mountain, the south-facing front and the east side, where goats like to live. A hunter could check for goats on the mountain as he rode up along the railroad right-of-way seated in a comfortable chair on a northbound train. The train did all the climbing for anyone hunting there. All that was necessary was to take careful note of where the goats were from the comfort of a railroad parlor car as the train passed by. After passing the south-facing front of the mountain, the railroad grade then climbs roundabout and upwards through a west-to-east valley, gaining altitude steadily until it loops back and passes by across from the east side of Mine Mountain, providing a good look at any goats that might be on that side.

On this trip we noted there were two goats on the mountain, just around from the south face, on the east side, a little below the top. They were at least ¼ mile or so south of an old defunct mining camp high on the mountainside, the old mine from which the mountain got its name. The camp still had some remaining dilapidated buildings, one still had a decent roof and served as a base for anyone goat hunting in the area. It was a greatly appreciated shelter when rain and clouds closed down over the top of the mountain—which happened frequently.

The east side of Mine Mountain and the railroad grade are separated by a deep, narrow valley which had earned the name Dead Horse Gulch during the 1897/98 Klondike gold rush. Many hundreds of horses and other pack animals (some people estimate thousands) perished down in that valley bottom while negotiating a miserable winter snow trail and carrying or dragging gold rush supplies. If an animal fell or was hurt along the trail, it was promptly shot on the spot. This miserable state of affairs went on until the White Pass & Yukon Railroad was constructed in 1898. Passage into Canada over the mountains on the railroad thankfully ended most of this pack animal cruelty.

Dead Horse Gulch and the railroad grade climbed steadily uphill toward the north until the Gulch ended and Mine Mountain and the mountain the railroad tracks were on converge at a narrow gap named White Pass. Here we got off the train. At this spot we were near the top of Mine Mountain and a diesel locomotive had done all the work! All we had to do now was climb a few hundred feet from the railroad tracks, then walk back along the near-level spine of the mountaintop to the mining camp, a straight-line distance of slightly more than 2 miles. Starting from the mining camp we would be above the goats and hunting downhill after them.

The trick to this hunt was to be the first party of the year to chase goats on the mountain. It was necessary to get there before another hunter ran all the animals out of the country and up onto the higher adjoining peaks in this coastal range, where they would be much more difficult to get to. The main local competition for being first on the mountain was one of the Sullivan boys, Richard, a Skagway longshoreman, ex-marine, and a tough hunter. The first time I hunted Mine Mountain, years before, had been with Richard.

This trip, I was hunting with a young fellow, Denny Story, who worked with me on the White Pass Railroad bridge and building crew. He had never hunted goats before and, hearing of my plans, asked to come along. Denny would be my backup. If I failed to take a goat with the bow, or, God forbid, wounded one, he would take over with the rifle. He had no weapon of his own and so was carrying my 30-06 rifle. We were agreed that this was a bow hunt first and a firearm hunt only after all chances with my archery tackle were exhausted. Denny was young, a professional logger working for the railroad in the off-season, and tough as nails. He was a good choice for a hunting partner and we were the first hunters on Mine Mountain for the 1965 season.

It required a little about two hours to hike down along the top of the mountain to the mining camp. We dropped our gear in the cabin

Chapter 11— Hunting Mine Mountain

and headed south again along the top until we reached a point where we estimated we must be above and a bit south of where we had last seen the goats from the train. It had already been hours since we had last seen the animals and the lay of the terrain prevented our spotting them from any distance, or them spotting us, except by accident. In either case a first encounter would probably be sudden and at very close range. We dropped down the mountain, spread out about 40 yards apart, and started to slowly sweep our way north along the steep mountainside. Denny was above me with the rifle.

In a short time we came to a fairly wide, level rock terrace running along the side of the mountain. Off to my left I could see Denny as he crept along even with me, rifle at the ready. Moving slowly and quietly forward I came to a low rock rise immediately in front of me. It was high enough to obscure everything ahead. As I moved forward up the rise, the tips of two black goat horns came into view behind the very top of the rock bump. The animal could not have been more than 20 feet in front of me. I stopped and crouched down. Off to the left Denny was looking ahead and creeping forward. I frantically waved my hands trying to catch his eye and warn him of the goat, but could not get his attention. I knew immediately when he saw the animal by the surprised expression on his face. Then, all he could do was look at me and poke a finger toward the goat, which by now had spotted him and was up and running.

Denny generally stood between the goat and escape uphill, so the animal did the next best thing in its mind, it sought a getaway by going down. The side of the mountain dropped off steeply at the outside edge of the bench. Bow in hand, I ran to the brink where it had disappeared. It had obviously not been really spooked as it was standing on a little rocky ledge, below, looking back up at me, about 25 yards away. The angle down to the animal was very steep. This, in addition to my being unpracticed and a lousy bow shooter anyway, caused me to overshoot the first shot by several feet, then overcompensate and undershoot with a second arrow. The goat started at the sound of the shafts smashing to pieces in the rocks around him but still did not flee. He stepped over curiously and sniffed at each of the shattered arrows. A third shot went high again by about a foot. With that, the goat had had enough and took off.

About that time Denny arrived by my side. Judging that the goat was now spooked for sure, and any further chance with the bow was gone, I told him to carry on with the rifle. Out at about 70 yards the fleeing animal stopped for one last curious look back and, with the loud crash of the 30-06, my first try for a big game animal with a bow was over.

In 1976 The Klondike Gold Rush National Historic Park was created. The park is a corridor containing the two Lynn Canal routes to the Klondike goldfields. One trail wound up to White Pass, north of Skagway, and the other route up the Chilkoot Trail, to Chilkoot Pass, from tidewater in Dyea Valley.

Creation of the national park ended all goat hunting in any of the coastal range mountains located between Taiya Inlet (Dyea) River on the west, the White Pass Railroad right-of-way on the east, and the Canadian border on the north. There would be no more goat hunting on Mine Mountain.

The year 1965 was a long time ago and times are a-changing. I guess that's not necessarily a bad thing.

Chapter 12
Don't Eat the Putshki!

PUTCHKI (A RUSSIAN NAME PRONOUNCED PUSH-KEE), or Indian rhubarb, or, more properly, cow parsnip, is not a plant to mess with.

In Arthur R. Thompson's book, *Gold Seeking on the Dalton Trail*, a Chilkat Indian guide advises the party he is guiding over the Dalton Trail—over the mountains to the Klondike goldfields out of present-day Haines, Alaska—that cow parsnip is "good muck-muck," or good food in the "Stick Indian" (pidgin English) language of the day. Such advice should be taken with a good deal of caution.

This is the same advice I got about eating the plant from some Tlingit Indian kids I grew up with. Their practice was to peel the young stalks of cow parsnip, like pulling the fibers out of celery, and eating the tender inside. I did this one time along with them and paid a terrible price. The result was that much of my body broke out in a rash which then turned to horrible water blisters. The blisters soon broke, leaving itchy, weeping sores which I did not dare to scratch. These sores lasted for a week or more before finally drying up. As a result, I was left with a lifelong sensitivity to any contact with cow parsnip. One touch of the juice of the plant now is like coming into contact with poison ivy or poison oak.

The culprit, according to information available on the Web, is a substance in the sap, or latex, of certain plants, among them cow parsnip. The sap of such plants reacts with sunlight to cause sunburn-like sores on the skin. Technically, these sun-induced burns are referred to as *phytophoto dermatitis*.

Why my Tlingit friends were not affected by contact with the plant, especially by eating it, is a mystery to me. Perhaps some people are immune to the substance in the plant that reacts with the sun to cause the burns. I, sadly, am not one of them. I must give putchki a wide berth for the rest of my days—a difficult thing to do as it grows everywhere in Alaska—or pay a horrible price for every touch.

Chapter 13
UofA Engineers Day

"OH WE ARE, WE ARE, WE ARE, WE ARE THE ENGINEERS, we can, we can, we can, we can drink forty beers." This was an oft-heard refrain, always sung with top-of-the-lungs gusto at the Malamute Saloon, at Cripple Creek, during Friday nights in the mid-1960s. The Malamute was a beer-and-peanuts establishment (the peanut shells and sawdust floor mix was sometimes inches deep!) located several miles west of the campus of the University of Alaska (UofA), Fairbanks. The establishment catered to the weekend crowd of the more lively students attending UofA. On Friday and Saturday nights it was usually crowded to capacity and *always* very noisy. There were few such places like this in the Fairbanks area where a pitcher of beer was cheap, as were the peanuts, and management would most often put up with revels of the student clientele. Singing of any kind (even by engineering students!) was encouraged.

The University of Alaska, Fairbanks, was originally established in 1922 as the Alaska Agricultural College and School of Mines. Over the years, the originally intended curriculum of the school grew beyond agriculture and mining to be more inclusive to meet most of the state's advanced educational needs, eventually leading to its designation as the University of Alaska.

Over the years UofA continued to maintain a reputation as a fine engineering school, a fact engineering students seemed driven to crow about whenever an opportunity allowed, with obvious pride and haughtiness, especially on Friday or Saturday nights at Cripple Creek!

But oh, how the mighty can fall!

On the same winter day, for years, the UofA, and its surrounding miles of countryside, had been abruptly awakened by a dynamite blast in the center of the campus. This blast marked the beginning of Engineers Day, a special day touting the resident engineering establishment, including both faculty and students. During the fall of 1966 or 1967, I don't recall exactly which year, this dynamite charge was set in the vicinity of Woods Hole. Woods Hole, nicknamed in honor of then university president William R. Woods, was a large circular fountain under construction at that time in the center of the huge grass-covered mid-campus plaza. A number of buildings housing the various academic disciplines surround this plaza, most facing directly toward the plaza center and Woods Hole. The most prominent of these buildings, at that time, was the Bunnell Building, a huge multistoried, glass-fronted, structure housing numerous classrooms, an auditorium, the school library, and most of the university offices.

Whoever was in charge of setting off the explosion that morning evidently did not consider that the outdoor temperature was well below normal—even for Fairbanks. A cold blue frost covered almost everything. Either the charge was too large, the cold temperature magnified the effects of the explosion, the temperature effected the strength of glass in the surrounding buildings, or there was an unfortunate combination of these possibilities. The result was that a *considerable* amount of glass facing the plaza that Engineers Day perished when the charge was touched off. One would think that engineers, whom I had been led to believe were supposed to know everything, would have known better.

I don't recall an accounting of the damage done that day, or who ended up paying for it, or who, perhaps, should have ended up with a black eye over the matter. The unfortunate accident was quickly and quietly forgotten. I am sure that had, say, the business administration faculty and students pulled such a trick they would all *still* be in jail! Neither do I recall the incident making a measurable reduction in the haughty attitude of UofA's engineering students. I don't believe it had any effect at all.

Chapter 14
Trouble Bruin
First printed in *Bowhunter* magazine, titled
Bear Trouble August-September issue, 1972

A FLUSH OF EXCITEMENT RAN THROUGH ME AS I approached the tree stand. On several previous occasions, I had spooked a black bear at this point, sending it off through the alders in a panic. My disappointment at not immediately seeing anything was momentary, for as I topped a small rise overlooking the bait station, the sounds of a fleeing animal farther up the hill reached me. Once again it had caught me approaching and fled. I remember how mad I had been the first time I chased a bear off this bait, cursing at missing the chance for a shot. I had long since learned that this was standard procedure with *this* bear. He was smart, but for sure a hog for a free meal. He would be back again before dark. I had been baiting and studying this guy for weeks at this point and pretty much knew what he would do.

When the rustling and snapping sounds faded into the woods, I began to move toward the bait pile to dump the 30 or 40 pounds of meat scraps I had carried in with me. I hadn't moved more than a few steps forward when new sounds of breaking brush startled me. There was a second bear in the alders. It was only a short distance away and coming toward me very fast!

I was standing half hidden behind a big birch tree when the animal broke out into the open about 30 yards away. It was a big sow, and like the bear I had just run off, one I was very familiar with. She had been onto the bait pile several times with her cub. Actually, she was a nuisance since she was illegal to arrow because of her cub, and on two occasions I had seen her chase legal bears away from the bait. Right now she was looking for an intruder with fire in her eye, swinging her head from side to side and popping her teeth in warning.

Reaching down with my right hand, I released the hammer strap and upholstered my .44 Magnum pistol. The shock of suddenly being faced with this situation caused some shaky knees and a very dry mouth. I did not want to shoot the old girl. For one thing, she had a cub. Shooting her would mean ending both their lives. Second, my usual secure feeling because of my heavy pistol had completely deserted me. I carry the pistol as a backup for going into the brush after an arrowed bear. Against this bundle of furious motherhood the weapon suddenly seemed woefully inadequate.

The infuriated sow halted her headlong charge a few yards out into the small semi-clearing that surrounded my tree stand. Rising up on her hind legs, she peered in my direction, trying to locate me with her notoriously weak black-bear eyes. All the while she tested the air for my scent, pulling in quick whiffs through her long brown muzzle and popping her teeth with every exhale.

She wasn't a particularly large bear. I judged she weighed about 175 post-hibernation pounds and measured something barely over 5 feet, nose to tail. However, the thought of this bundle of enraged motherhood charging across the narrow space which now separated us left me chilled. I did not wish to settle any argument with her at this time.

Our standoff continued for about ten minutes. In that space of time she continued to test the wind, moving about on all fours at the edge of the clearing, occasionally rising up on her hind legs for a visual check. With the immediate threat of her charging straight into me now somewhat lessened, I slipped out of my bait-laden pack and quietly eased it to the ground. A quick check of the surrounding trees produced no sign of a cub up a tree, so I reasoned she must be running a rear-guard action, allowing her cub time for a ground getaway. Hopefully, she would retreat with her cub. But just about the time her departure should have taken place, she chose to lie down, facing in my direction.

It seemed the next move was up to me. I wanted to get up a tree, but the nearest thing I could climb was the big spruce that supported my tree stand. That tree stood about 20 yards away and slightly downhill from the spot where I leaned against the birch tree, cowering in respect of the sow's anger. This big birch was no good to use for escape. Its nearest limb was 10 feet above my head. I reasoned that if I tried to

Chapter 14—Trouble Bruin

escape by shinnying up the trunk, the sow would probably be waiting for me at the top!

My only course of action, outside of waiting this bear out, would be making a dash for the spruce tree. By now time the sow obviously no longer considered me a threat. She began pawing at her ears, licking her paws and generally relaxing.

Carefully leaning my bow against the birch, I holstered my .44 Magnum, preparing for a quick sprint to safety. There was slightly less than 20 yards of shin-tangle and potholes to negotiate to the base of the tree, then about 10 feet of dead limbs to climb up the trunk before I would be in the clear. If I could reach that point I would be fine, and woe unto Mrs. Bear if she tried to climb the tree after me. If she really wanted me, she had about a 35-yard dash downhill, over some terrible terrain, to cut me off before I reached my tree.

Ready to run, I waited until the old girl seemed particularly engrossed in licking her paws, then I bolted from behind the birch and headed downhill toward safety.

About halfway through the mad dash I chanced a quick glance over my shoulder. Expecting to see the sow in hot pursuit, I was surprised to see her black rump disappearing in the opposite direction, evidently more scared of me than I was of her. The sounds of her crashing retreat faded quickly and the woods were silent again. Satisfied that she had really left, I quickly returned to the birch to retrieve my bow and pack. Then, after dumping the fresh bait on the pile, I climbed the spruce to my shooting platform.

As I said, I had been after one particular bear over this bait for almost a month. By this time he was getting fat and sassy, feasting daily on the many pounds of meat scraps, bones, and tallow I had carried in each weekend to add to the pile. Several other bears were feeding on this bait as well, including the sow that had just treed me; but I had set my sights on one medium-sized bear with a jet-black coat.

Up to now he had eluded harvest by never quite giving me the target I wanted. On a number of occasions I could have taken an imperfect shot but preferred instead to wait for a better setup. Also, this bear had the annoying tendency of waiting me out until it got too dark to shoot, with what appeared to be a deliberate stall tactic. In those cases, I would have had to climb down and leave for home through the woods in the dark, leaving him to lunch on the bait pile overnight at his leisure.

He was a smart one, but his one weakness was the predictability of his eating schedule. I could count on his coming to the bait any evening around seven o'clock. He always came from the same direction, down an alder-choked gully off the mountain and to the bait along a moose trail through an alder and cottonwood thicket. I often thought of laying for him in a ground blind along that trail, but enjoyed our little game so much I decided against the trick.

I had taken a smaller bear off this same stand the previous spring, preferring the condition of the fur after the end of winter to the animal's pelage in the fall. I had found that bears come to bait more readily in the spring, just out of hibernation, thin from a winter's sleep, and at a time when less natural food is available in the woods.

I live in Anchorage, Alaska, and at this particular time, May 1971, I was hunting in the foothills of the Chugach Mountains not far from Palmer, Alaska. There is a healthy population of black bear in this section of southcentral Alaska, as evidenced by a legal bag limit of three animals. With a little scouting, it is easy enough for a bow hunter to find a spot to place a bait. I like to use commercial meat scraps when I am baiting. It took some hard looking in those days to cultivate the friendship of a few local meat cutters. Other people who hunt black bears using bait often prefer to use old bakery products. Using that source for bait is cheap and generally much easier to acquire than meat scraps. For some reason, people who don't like the idea of *anyone* hunting bears over *any* kind of bait are particularly offended by the use of bakery goods. Attacking bear baiting by conjuring up lurid descriptions of donuts and Twinkies scattered across the landscape is a favored practice used by people to support their anti-baiting positions.

My tree stands are typically simple platforms of four 2-by-4 boards lying across the limbs of a large spruce tree. To avoid giveaway squeaks, I pad the 2-by-4s where they contact the spruce limbs and tie the boards down securely with nylon cord. For added support, I string wires from the outer ends of the limbs back up to the tree. I build these platforms about 15 feet up from the ground and place my baits about 10 yards out from the tree, ideally so a bear can approach the bait pile through thick cover until the last few feet. Some trimmed limbs, a hand line, and an old wood box for a seat complete my tree stand improvements.

The afternoon wore on into evening. The sun had just disappeared below the horizon and I began to wonder if, true to form, my friend

Chapter 14—Trouble Bruin

was going to appear. Already, at the end of May, the longer Alaska summer days were becoming obvious. It was approximately nine o'clock when darkness began to set in.

As I contemplated climbing down and heading for home, the sound of rustling leaves from up the hill brought me cautiously to my feet. From out of nowhere, here he came again.

There was an unusual urgency in his pace, which puzzled me. He moved rapidly down out of the ravine and into the cottonwoods almost at a trot. He dispensed with the pauses and wind tests usually performed in the cottonwoods and moved right ahead along the moose trail to a point about 10 yards in the brush from the bait clearing.

I wasn't prepared for this. Usually, I had plenty of time to watch him and calm down while he went through all the antics of circling, leaving, returning, smelling, and so forth. Now, here he was, 25 yards away before he even paused to check the wind. This was completely out of character for him.

Rising up on his hind legs, he looked the clearing over, *then* began testing the wind, poking his black nose straight up in the air and moving it from side to side. With that brief test, apparently satisfied the coast was clear, he dropped to all fours and advanced toward the bait.

As he moved out into the clearing I slowly began to inch a Micro-Flight arrow back to full draw. I held my breath and little exhausts of air quietly puffed from my body with each heartbeat and in the flush of excitement the 55-pound pull of my old Shakespeare Neceda recurve bow was hardly noticeable.

To get at the bait the bear had to walk around a brush pile I had placed as an obstacle. This would turn him broadside or, hopefully, quartering slightly away from me for the ideal lung shot I wanted. Like clockwork he moved around the brush pile and turned a complete left broadside toward me. Shooting downhill, I held my 20-yard sight pin just a tad low on his chest as he did so.

Suddenly, it was obvious that he knew he had made a mistake. Inches from the bait he paused, then turned quickly to retreat the way he had come. This placed him quartering away from me along his right side. At this angle, undecided, he paused again, and I released the arrow.

There was no doubt about the quality of the shot. The high-precision broadhead caught him high in the chest and, angling downward, the shaft buried itself to about one-half the 29-inch length of the arrow. Almost as if unharmed, the bear continued on his exit course off through the alders. As soon as he was out of sight there was a muffled crash and then the woods were silent.

Fifteen minutes later, as I climbed down out of the tree, it was almost dark enough to require a flashlight. There was not a sound from the woods. I knew this bear was down and out, but I had not brought a flashlight with me and the memory of my run-in with Mad Momma that afternoon prompted me to leave recovery until the next day. For me, this would not be a restful evening.

I returned early the following morning and found my prize about 40 yards back in the alders. Later examination revealed that the arrow had passed down through one lung and pierced the heart dead center, an ideal shot. My estimated his weight near 200 pounds and the hide, when tanned, measured 5½ feet nose to tail.

For just plain smarts, I'll place the black bear against any North American animal. It has excellent hearing, an even better nose, and almost human intelligence. Like the whitetail deer, the black bear is very adaptable. He can literally live in your backyard and most of the time you won't even know he's there.

To anyone planning to hunt black bear with a bow I recommend bait and a tree stand, provided baiting is legal wherever you choose to hunt. Spotting and stalking this animal on the ground, though more healthy for you than sitting in a tree, can either be very easy or very hard, depending on circumstances and luck. Dogs are used in some locations (at this writing use of dogs is illegal in Alaska) but I imagine unless you have a good friend with trained bear dogs, that could be an expensive way to hunt.

I treasure my black bear bowhunting experiences and plan to be in the woods again next spring (1972). We utilize all the meat and, when I accumulate enough hides, I plan to have a winter parka made, which I feel will be unique, using only hides taken with a bow.

To those who are interested and lucky enough to live where black bear may be hunted, or possess the means to travel to where they may be found, I refer you to Mr. Bruin. Hunting him is a real challenge, making the reward for success all the more sweet.

Chapter 15
My First Client

THIS IS AN ACCOUNT OF HOW I ALMOST GOT A CLIENT in trouble with a brown bear. It is easy enough to have the occasional brush with a bear. Almost any guide who has been in the business awhile working the big bears has a good story, but this was my first client on the first day of my first hunt as a contracting big-game guide!

Prior to retirement from a real estate appraisal career with the State Department of Natural Resources in 1997, I had tested for and obtained my Alaska big-game guide license. I first began working on experience credit to obtain this license during the fall of 1989. To be eligible to sit for a written test for this license, a candidate is required to work a certain number of years for registered Alaska guides in order to gain experience. During that time the candidate must guide so many clients per year for at least so many years. The application submitted when applying to take the guide exam must be accompanied by a list of hunters—including names and addresses—that the candidate has worked with while serving as an assistant guide. During the application phase, the Alaska Big Game Commercial Services Board uses this list to contact hunters to inquire about the candidate's performance in the field.

After "going through the chairs" and getting my ticket, I was ready and eager to head out into the guiding world. First, I needed a decent place to take a person on a hunt, then I had to find a client. Finding a decent place to guide in 1990s' Alaska, some country with decent game offering a reasonably attractive remote-Alaska experience for a client, was not an easy thing. The choice places in those days, mostly on federal refuges or on Native corporation lands, were effectively plugged by old-timer guides and it was all but impossible for a new kid on the block to break into the concession club. Without being a sorehead, that's all I'll say about that.

I have a camp on the beach on Raspberry Island in the Kodiak area. I bought the place back in 1982. There are lots of deer and a fair number of brown bear there. Sitka black-tailed deer, although numerous on Raspberry, did not fit the bill for my idea of guided hunting. It would have to be brown bear.

Client Rudy Senefeld looks at the point where we encountered a sow and two cubs. The bear family was asleep on the flat grassy spot at the end of the point.

All brown-bear hunting on Raspberry Island at that time was conducted on a drawing permit basis. Hundreds of applications were submitted each year for a drawing for about eight to ten Fish and Game bear permits. On Kodiak Island, inside the Kodiak Wildlife Refuge, permits to hunt brown bear are issued to guides owning federal guiding concessions. Permits are not issued to other guides operating in area around the Refuge. Some Raspberry Island drawing permits were available for the spring and some for the fall. All anyone had to do was enter the drawing, pay a $10 filing fee, and submit an application. Either residents or non-residents could apply. If a resident's name was drawn, all he needed to do was purchase a hunting license, buy a relatively cheap resident brown bear tag and go hunting. If a nonresident or a nonresident alien's name was drawn they had to purchase a nonresident hunting license, buy a pricey nonresident brown bear tag, and submit a copy of a contract showing they had hired the services of a qualified big-game guide to accompany them on the hunt. It was not necessary to buy the license, the tag, or obtain a contract with a guide until *after* the nonresident's name was drawn for a permit. Working with someone who drew a permit was the only way I could guide out of my Raspberry Island camp for brown bear.

At that time it was legal to submit an application for another person—as long as the application fee was paid and all information on the form was complete. I knew a number of people who had surprised relatives by submitting applications for them and having them drawn for bear hunts. Under certain conditions nonresidents were allowed to hunt brown bear, sheep, or mountain goat in Alaska when accompanied by a close blood relative. Otherwise they were required to hunt with a registered guide. (Nonresident alien hunters must *always* be accompanied by a registered guide.) My plan was to contact a number of out-of-state clients I had guided in the past and offer them a deal. I would submit an application for them. I would pay the $10 application fee. If they were drawn for a permit, they would use my services as a guide and we would hunt out of my Raspberry Island camp. For that 1996-97 drawing I submitted applications on behalf of three potential clients, including a German fellow named Rudy Sennefelder. Rudy got lucky and pulled a spring permit in the lottery. We scheduled his hunt for the following April—and I was in the guiding business!

I met Rudy at the Kodiak airport the morning of April 14. We took care of all the paperwork at the Kodiak Fish and Game office and were sitting in my cabin at Onion Bay on the west end of Raspberry Island drinking coffee by early afternoon of the same day.

We made a plan. The morning of the first day we would hunt the hillsides and the beach to the south and east of camp along the rugged coastline of Kupreanof Straits. The hills there in the spring are the typically open, grassy, salmonberry-brush and alder-patch country found on much of Kodiak Island. Moving about on foot is generally easy and glassing the mostly open slopes of the hills on that part of the island makes for easy hunting. Most of the waterfront behind the beach consists of vertical cliffs, 50 to 70 feet high, dropping to either a jumble of seaweed-covered rocks or open, cobblestone beach. Several miles of this treacherous shoreline would not be a good place to unwittingly become trapped against the cliffs by a rising tide! The high bluffs offer a good view down onto the beach but it is impossible to climb up the cliffs from the beach, except in very few places.

A 1½-mile walk from camp early the next morning placed us on the low side of a huge bowl in the side of a mountain. Here we sat in the gathering morning light glassing the steep slopes above and the narrow plain, which extended out from the base of the mountain to the top of the bluffs above the beach. We glassed for several hours, having a whole lot of country in view. There were a hundred places in the 300-plus-degree sweep of land in front of us where half a dozen bears could be feeding, hidden from view, or bedded down in the brush sleeping. We found deer all over the place and a couple of cow elk up high on the mountainside, but no bear.

It is difficult to get a new brown bear hunter into a proper spotting frame of mind. Guide consensus holds that the best method to hunt the big bears is to locate on a good, high spot, get comfortable, set up a spotting scope and glass the country with binoculars, sitting still and quiet until either you find a bear to take a run at or it gets too dark to see. Clients who have never done this kind of hunting soon tire of the hours of staring through binoculars, and begin to fidget. It is best to sit still and glass, rather than thrashing about in the brush, stinking up the country. Brown bear have excellent noses, especially for the smell of humans. Rudy proved to be an impatient one. He was a tough, medium-sized man, a professional baker who owned his own business back in Germany. He had arrived for the hunt in good condition, and it was soon obvious that he preferred a more active hunting style, despite my assurance that it would be best if we stayed put and spotted. Wanting especially to please my first client, of *all* clients, I finally accommodated him with the suggestion that we move down the coast along the top of the beach bluffs, keeping a sharp eye peeled up above on the hillsides and on the beach below us.

We had gone less than a mile when we came to a rugged rock point jutting out from the bluff. The top of this point itself was grassy but the uplands immediately behind it were wooded with a dense grove of wind-blown, very old spruce trees. We approached the head of the point through the spruce woods and found a large hole through the

Chapter 15—My First Client

trees, not unlike a huge cave opening, out onto the level, grassy top of the rock point. I wanted to get out to the end of the point and glass down the beach for bear sign. I exited into the open, more interested in the beach off to the southeast than in the point itself. The point was about 40 yards in length. About 15 yards wide where it joined the beach bluff, it gradually narrowed to a tip about 4 yards wide at its outer end. I looked down to the beach on both sides. It was easily 50 feet straight down to seaweed-covered rock on both sides.

About 10 yards from the end, I began to get keenly aware of my footing. A fall down into the rocks off either side would result either in death or, perhaps even worse, in a long and miserable life if surviving such a fall was possible. I recall I was looking straight ahead, toward the end of the point, when a huge bear head raised, looking at me over the edge where the end of the point dropped off. I instinctively readied my rifle in defense and hollered at Rudy, who was several yards behind me, "Brown bear!" The words were no sooner out of my mouth when a smaller head raised up behind the larger one. The smaller one was, obviously, the head of a cub and the other was, just about as obvious, the head of a big sow. All I could think to do was holler again, "No! Don't shoot! It's a sow!" With that I turned and beat a fast retreat behind Rudy along the top of the point, back toward the opening in the trees. There was nowhere else to go. I never looked back, fearing the nightmare view of a charging brown bear and the choice of either killing her on the spot with a lucky shot or yielding the top of the point to her with a deadly leap into the seaweed covered rocks far below. Just as we reached the portal through the spruce, Rudy tripped on shin tangle and went down. I reached down, grabbed him by his pack frame and lifted him to his feet. I did hazard a glance behind us at that moment. She wasn't coming, but I knew she would—and soon. "Hurry," I said. "She will charge!" In a few more feet we were into the spruce grove, and, in another few yards each of us held up behind a large spruce tree, rifles at the ready. I had a clear view from behind my tree directly out of the opening and along the top of the point. It was only a few more seconds when, as expected, here came the charging sow. Every time her front paws hit the ground an ungodly sound came out of her, fair warning of exactly what she was going to do when she reached us. It looked very much like we were going to have do battle with her at close quarters there in the spruce trees.

The huge sow came storming through the opening. Halting a few yards inside, she turned slightly sideways at an angle to our right, pointing off through the trees. She was light blond in color, as big as a sofa, and stood only a few yards from where the two of us cowered behind our trees. Behind her from off the point came *two* yearling cubs, running full bore. The cubs passed through the opening, ran past on the far side of the sow and away in the direction through the woods that her nose pointed for them. Within a matter of seconds of the cubs' disappearing, the sow followed on the run. She was out of sight in a few bounds.

In one sense, I gave thanks to the hunting gods for the notoriously poor eyesight they gave to the brown bear. In the heat of the moment I expect she never saw us just a few feet away behind our trees. In another sense it seemed to take too long a time for her to muster a charge. I would have expected her to have overtaken Rudy and me on our retreat to the treeline! Is it possible that the huge sow took time to weigh the consequences of being cornered, allowed us time to get out of the way, and took a chance on fleeing rather than fighting, perhaps for the sake of her cubs. Standing almost broadside to us she had never turned her head our way, which seems out of character for so wary an animal, especially for a mother with cubs. Could it be she had not made eye contact on purpose? For if she had she had done so, I suspect, something would have died in that spruce grove that morning.

We would learn later after cooling our heels and regaining composure, that the sow had apparently chosen a small, level grassy bench, just below the end of the point as a spot for her and the cubs to sun themselves and take a nap, a spot no larger than a closet where any one of them would likely have perished in the rocks below had it rolled over even a little in the wrong direction in its sleep.

This was as close as Rudy would get to shooting a bear on this hunt. We hunted hard every day for ten days, even during several days, at Rudy's insistence, when the weather was as foul as Kodiak is capable of making it. But his harvesting a brown bear was just not to be.

It is necessary to work at guiding a number of German hunters to even partially understand how seriously they take their hunting and how devastating it is for them to go back to their homes and their hunt clubs without a kill. I shall never forget the pained look on Rudy's face when we finally parted company back in Anchorage.

This was also my one and only season for guiding a hunter out of that camp on Raspberry Island. Rule changes for lottery drawings the following year effectively precluded submitting names on behalf of other people for a lottery permit. The new rules required that in order to enter the drawing an applicant must also provide proof of having purchased an Alaska hunting license. The cost of a nonresident hunting license at $85 and a nonresident alien license at $300 (at that time) pretty much discouraged people from out of state from taking a chance on the lottery drawing; and at this writing there is a plan afoot to raise the cost of *all* hunting licenses even more.

That is the story of my first guided hunt.

Chapter 16
Land Otter Man
This treads heavily onto one of the ancient beliefs of Southeast Alaska's Tlingit Native people. In no way is it meant to disrespect either their beliefs or their culture.

FOR EONS, THE DOMINANT NATIVE CULTURE OF NEARLY all of south-coastal Alaska was the Tlingits'.

In ancient Tlingit lore the act of drowning was considered the most horrible of deaths. This must have made life stressful, considering that these people made their living mostly from being on or around the sea. When a tribal member was drown, and the body was not recovered and properly cremated or otherwise prepared for an afterlife, it was suspected that the unfortunate person had been "rescued" by otter spirits who lived in a world under the sea. This was the work of Kushta ka, the Land Otter Man, or of the Land Otter People as a group. To Native people of the south coast, perhaps even during the time frame of this story, it was apparently taunting bad luck to even mention the name of this dreaded undersea spirit. The belief was, once a person was captured by Kushta ka in the water, or even sometimes on dry land (Kushta ka had the power to lure intended victims away from the safety of land with a friendly appearance), his or her charmed body would then be slowly transformed in stages, eventually assuming the form of a land otter.

Early one morning in the late 1950s, after an evening of partying, two young men elected to depart Skagway by outboard motor skiff for Juneau, Alaska, a distance of about 125 miles. I knew them both well. Under the best of conditions this is a trip not to be taken lightly in a small boat. Lynn Canal, the only route for water passage between Skagway and Juneau, can be a risky, treacherous piece of water for small craft. Typically, during the summer months the Canal is usually

Chapter 16—Land Otter Man

calm and pleasant during the night hours and early morning, seldom forecasting what kind of weather is coming from the south later in the day. There are few places along this route to tuck in and safely ride out a blow. Traveling south from Skagway or Haines, once clear of Sullivan Island, where a reasonable shelter for a boat during a violent southerly is usually available, a traveler by boat is generally committed to one of two things if the weather goes bad—either turning back up the Canal and riding the storm on a heavy following sea, or pounding ahead toward the south into the weather to Berner's Bay at the north end of the Juneau road system. The shoreline along the canal offers few decent beaches for an emergency landing. Most of the coast looks very much like the steep side of a mountain.

The two young men from Skagway became missing, following a typically rotten Lynn Canal blow, and a search for them was conducted. The wreckage of their skiff was located and one of the bodies recovered. The second person could not be found. After a considerable time the hopelessness of finding the missing man alive, or of even finding the body, became evident to authorities and the search was abandoned.

The mother of the missing man, ever hopeful that her son might by some miracle still be found alive and well along the rocky expanse of the Canal, pressed for continued search—but to no avail.

What followed was thousands of years of Native lore, not to be denied even in the late 1950s, briefly colliding with thousands of years of motherhood. A rumor reached Skagway of a man, naked and covered in red hair, (the missing man had red hair) being seen running along the shore somewhere on Lynn Canal. The inference of a connection between Kushta ka and the missing son in the rumor was undeniable. This did little for the mental health of a distraught mother still clinging to whatever desperate hope remained that her son might yet have somehow miraculously survived.

This agony persisted for weeks. The missing body was never found and the rumor of involvement of Kushta ka in the incident slowly faded away into almost forgotten history.

Chapter 17
Twins for the Pot

First published in *Selected Hunting and Fishing Tales,* Volume Four, 1976. This was an annual hunting and fishing publication of *Alaska Magazine.*

I WAS ABOUT A MILE UPRIVER FROM CAMP WHEN I HEARD the shot. The report of the heavy caliber rifle rumbled down out of the mountains from the direction in which my hunting partners, Dave Crosby and Ron Swanson, had gone earlier that morning. The two had struck out just before sunup after a bull moose I had spotted up in the willows on the side of a narrow valley across the river from camp.

I had spotted the bull from a bluff behind camp while on my way heading upriver to hunt in the opposite direction. I returned to camp, told Dave and Ron about the moose, and then carried on with my own bowhunting plans for the day.

Before the echo of the first shot subsided there was a second, then a third report, then silence.

Satisfied the shooting was over, I once again turned and backtracked to camp. If the guys had a bull down the hunting fun was over and there would be little but hard work from here on out. I toyed with the possibility that they might have two moose down, but considering the sequence of shots ruled that out as unlikely. By agreement, today was to be the last day we could harvest two moose, provided we could locate any moose at all. After today, the distance to the highway and the time available to haul out the meat with pack horses would limit us to one moose. We were all pressed to be back at work on fast approaching dates.

It was late September and we were a long way from home. The three of us lived and worked in the Anchorage area, where we were all employed by the Alaska Division of Lands.

Chapter 17—Twins for the Pot

Several weeks before the hunt, Dave, who owned and operated Snow Cottage Outfitters, asked if I knew of a decent place to hunt moose with pack animals. He was interested in a winter's meat supply, which none of us had yet, and he also wanted to get some experience with two new pack animals he had just purchased from a local horse guide.

My first suggestion was a valley in the Mentasta Mountains of the Alaska Range in the central part of the state near Tok, Alaska. Dave and Ron agreed and a hunt was arranged for the end of September, the last week of season. Our camp would be in a spot I knew along the Little Tok River, about 10 miles off the Tok Cutoff highway over some pretty rough terrain.

This morning, after returning to camp, there was some doubt in my mind if a moose had been shot at all. We had all agreed that one shot would be fired five minutes after downing an animal. This would mean "Moose down. Come help." There had been no confirming shot.

Glassing the willow patch where I had spotted the bull that morning disclosed two dark forms in the brush. It was two moose. I continued to watch and was dumbfounded as more and more animals began to appear around the first two. Two, four, seven, ten and finally twelve animals in all! Out of that many moose one of them simply had to be a bull!

I could tell that for certain that eleven were cows. The twelfth animal remained partially obscured behind a spruce tree. It seemed to take forever for the animal to browse its way into view, but when it finally did the huge white antlers were unmistakable.

In a flash I ran into camp, grabbed my pack and was off across the river and up into the valley. All the while I was wondering what had become of Dave and Ron. Had they missed the bull I was seeing in the brush? Had they shot another moose and were unaware of a second bull and his cows in the willows?

A small creek lined with big timber and light underbrush followed the valley floor. Immediately, I was on a well-traveled moose trail following the creek. *If I had roller skates, I could move faster,* I thought. If we did get moose back in here, getting them down to camp along this trail would be easy, especially with the horses.

As I moved up the valley I whooped every so often in an attempt to locate my partners. The shouts were lost in the timber and side canyons, producing nothing. So as I neared the willow patch where I had seen all the moose I stopped yelling.

A single thought nagged like a toothache. What if the guys had two moose down? In view of our self-imposed limit I would be a mighty unpopular guy if I filled my tag with a third animal.

As I moved along, the large spruce tree cover gave way to alders and then chin-high dwarf willow brush. Judging from the bald rock bluff landmark I had made note of, I was nearing the spot where I had last seen the moose. I began slowly working my way uphill from the creek bottom. Another 100 yards farther found me in chest-high brush on a relatively open, sloping hillside.

Suddenly, from out of nowhere, frantic cow moose were thundering away from me in all directions. I froze, so did they, and we had a standoff.

Three large cows stood less than 20 yards in front of me. I could see two more through the brush above me and three more below and to the right. All stood frozen still, watching me. The big question was, of course, the whereabouts of the bull. I hoped he would show himself, but for the moment he was out of sight. As the standoff continued, the panic exhibited by the cows was gradually replaced by curiosity. Several of the closer cows now moved even closer for a better look.

In an effort to break the standoff I decided to try grunting at the bull, hoping this would bring him out for a fight. My guttural challenges appeared to have little effect on the herd master, although I was definitely impressing several of the more amorous cows.

About the time I was beginning to get concerned about how close one of the cows was getting, my attention was drawn to a clattering in the brush below me. I took only a few seconds to realize that this was the sound of branches clattering through antlers. Once you have heard that sound you will never forget it. It was also clear that he was not coming uphill to fight. He was running down the slope away from me.

I quickly moved about 5 yards downhill to a solitary, stunted spruce tree. Bracing against it I held my rifle, half-aiming, waiting for a target to come into view on the uphill slope of the opposite side of the narrow valley. My sudden movement had put the cows in panic one more time, sending them scattering and breaking brush in all directions.

I watched tensely over the rifle scope as a lone cow charged into view about 150 yards or so below me. She continued at a run up the hill, followed shortly by a second cow. There was a short pause in the action, then the bruising hulk of a bull moose burst up out of the brushy creek bottom.

As I found him in the rifle scope, I let out a loud grunt. On hearing the challenge, all three moose stopped and turned for a look at the

Chapter 17—Twins for the Pot

intruder. The bull turned perfectly sideways, offering the best possible target. As he did so, I aligned the crosshairs of the scope on the lung area behind his front leg and squeezed off a shot.

The Remington .270 recoiled against my shoulder with a roar, but the shot appeared to have no effect whatsoever on the bull. It looked like I had missed! The three moose milled around the hillside, confused by the rifle report and uncertain of which way to run. The bull paused a second time and I fired again, this time more deliberate and less hurried.

Again the shot appeared to have no effect. I began to visualize my winter's meat supply disappearing over the mountain. The second shot produced the same result as the first, sending the three animals milling around in the willows. Still uncertain of which way to flee, the bull paused a third time, offering another excellent target. If he was hurt he certainly didn't show it.

This time I would hit him or it would be the fault of the rifle! Bracing the weapon so hard against the tree I wondered if the barrel might bend, I squeezed off the third shot. At first it appeared that this shot had no more effect than the first two. I swore aloud as I bolted the fourth round into the Remington's chamber. What now? Where were the blasted bullets striking and where should I aim for the next shot? I paused briefly, watching the bull. I was about to shoot again when suddenly the huge animal faltered, staggered wildly for several steps, then abruptly crumpled to the ground. I watched the spot where the bull disappeared for several minutes. He did not rise and the brush was still. The two cows, gaining their senses after all the shooting, fled over the mountain, pausing only for a moment to look back from the crest.

Finally, deciding the bull was down for good, I began working my way in his direction. I hadn't moved five paces when a far-off voice taunted from high on the hill behind me, "You'll be sorry you shot that big dude!" It was Dave. He was on the crest of the next ridge toward camp. It turned out he also had a big bull down, almost identical twin to mine. He had been the one responsible for the shooting earlier that morning and in the excitement had forgotten to fire the promised signal shot. He was really in a mess as his bull had gone down in heavy alders and, to make matters worse, had collapsed belly down in a bathtub-sized hole.

Over the distance which separated us, Dave thought I was Ron. The two had parted company early that morning and he had not seen Ron since. It turned out Ron had returned to camp alone later that morning after failing to find the source of Dave's shooting earlier in the day. He also heard my shots but wisely stayed in camp until Dave and I stumbled in late that afternoon.

Dave and I spent the next ten minutes hollering back and forth along the side of the valley at each other before going to work. The time then was about 11 a.m. It would not be until after 5 p.m. that we would all finally get together and really hash out the day's events. First, each of us had to skin and quarter an 800 to 1,000-pound moose and prepare the meat as best we could for the night.

We would return the following morning, bone out the meat and haul it to camp with the horses.

Two tired and hungry hunters stumbled into the warm light of Ron's campfire that evening just before dark. Details of the hunt, already shared between Dave and me, were aired a second time for Ron's benefit over the remains of the evening.

The next four days were spent shuffling meat and our camp back to our trucks out at the highway. Regrettably, we had to leave the antlers where the moose fell. Despite our desire to bring them out, their weight, the amount of meat and gear to haul, and the distance to the highway dictated otherwise.

Should we ever hunt that area again, which is likely, we will surely try to locate the 60-inch antlers and bring them out. That is, provided the grizzlies and porcupines have not mauled them too badly, which is likely.

Meantime, we all had a winter's supply of good meat, some horse-packing experience, and, perhaps best of all, the tonic of a week in the Alaska wilderness.

Dave Crosby shuttles meat from our two moose into camp across the Little Tok River.

Chapter 18
The Kids at Skwentna

I STILL LIKE TO TELL THE STORIES ABOUT WHEN I WAS a kid about growing up on a ranch in central British Columbia, Canada, and all the wild things I got to do at that time. I was about seven years old and, many days, I did the work of a man around the place—or at least thought I did. Mom cooked for all the ranch hands. Whatever Sis and I could do to contribute to the never ending work that needed to be done on a ranch paid in some part for our room and board.

I remember my sister and me skidding logs for the resident sawmill with two huge draft horses. If you needed lumber on a ranch at that time you put up a gypo sawmill and cut it yourself. I also remember how the horse team, old May and June, liked to head for the barn at the end of the day. The ranch owner, Billy Morris, would give us hell thinking we gave them their head to run hard for home at the end of the day. Each of us rode on the back of one of the team, both horses still in harness, up the country road to the ranch. Try as we might, it was impossible to rein those giant horses back and slow them down. They knew that rest, feed, and a comfortable stall waited for them at the end of the run.

I had long thought that those days were gone forever. For years I had it in mind that kids just weren't what they used to be. What had happened to the independence, toughness, and responsibility our youth once possessed? Had it all disappeared into the softness of modern living? I held that thought up until just a few years ago when some grade school kids from the community of Skwentna, a dot on the map along Alaska's Skwentna River, passed by under my nose causing me to reconsider.

We had been on a guided raft hunt on the upper end of the Skwentna River, two German clients, my assistant guide, and I. We were after moose and hunting had been bad, mostly due to wolf kill but partly to rotten weather. Rain and early snow had put a damper on things. We had only one small black bear to show for the entire ten-day hunt.

This river float hunt ended at the community of Skwentna, the first bit of civilization encountered downriver from the mountains. It was still raining when we landed at the little patch of beach on the river end of the gravel road which led north to the Skwentna Airport, Skwentna Lodge and the local elementary school. It's not much, but that about describes most of the community of Skwentna.

We had trouble getting my two big Aire Catarafts ashore. The sandy little landing area, normally deserted, was plugged full with a fleet of small jonboats—flat-bottomed outboard motor-powered river craft. Not wanting to offend any of the locals, we worked around the troublesome armada, first unloading, then hauling the rafts up on the bank where they could be deflated and taken apart in preparation for transport back to town by aircraft.

We were no more than halfway through the dismantling job when a noisy train of four-wheeler all-terrain carriers pulled into the middle of our project. Classes were evidently finished for the day and here came the kids from the local grade school. The adults running the machines dropped off their loads and promptly headed back to where they came from. This was the Skwentna school bus system! The youngsters headed for the river, backpacks and lunchboxes flying. I looked around for more adults who surely must have been waiting here somewhere to motor the kids home, but there were none. The kids untied the boats, piled in, fired off the outboard motors and backed out into the rain-swollen river. Some went upstream and some went down. Half the craft had two kids aboard and the other half just the motor operator. In a flash they were all gone and we were left standing at the landing with our mouths hanging open. I am sure there was not one youngster in that whole bunch older than ten or eleven and, although it obviously doesn't matter, most were young girls.

Remembering this little event is always refreshing and makes me back up a step in thinking about how rough and tough I thought my life was at their age. Living the city life all these later years, I had long ago lost track of the fact that there are kids all over Alaska that live and function perfectly well like this, little independent people who must contribute what they can to make life in the Alaska bush a bit easier for everyone. They live on the tail end of the last frontier of America, and judging from what I saw that soggy afternoon at Skwentna, it is a pleasure to report that they appear to be doing it quite well.

Chapter 19
Sheep Fever
First published in *Bowhunting World, Extreme*, **Vol.6, 2005**

SO YOU WANT TO HEAD NORTH AND BOWHUNT DALL sheep? You had best get vaccinated with sheep shots before you do, provided you're able to find a sports doctor who can locate a serum.

I pose with my hunting partner's Dall sheep in the early fall of 1971. I hunted with a bow and he with a rifle. He won the coin coin flip to see who would make the final stalk.

Sheep fever, for short, is a dread disease caused by a bite from the sheep bug. Symptoms of the malady are a craving for high places and for long horns with big bases, accompanied by a siren-song ringing of the ears. Side effects are known to be a chronic disregard for both body and pock-

Chapter 19—Sheep Fever

etbook and a near total disregard for hunting any other big game. The fever is regarded as incurable. You may not die *from* it, but, once contracted, you will certainly die *with* it. I have lived in Alaska for over half a century. My strong natural immunity, inherent laziness, and general reluctance to climb high mountains where Dall sheep—and the sheep bug—live, have apparently combined to ward off the affliction.

Being armed with knowledge of this disease could be helpful. You might spare yourself from this plague by reading on.

Sheep hunting requires hard work from the get-go. No matter how hard you train, you are always in the shape when the hunt is over that you should have been in when the hunt began. It is unusual if you don't start the hunt by packing for miles deep into sheep country up some remote drainage before you ever start a stalk up a peak after *Ovis Dalli*.

Then, after harvesting your trophy, there is still the long pack home. Early sheep season is generally pleasantly warm, and when the hunt is over the guide *and* the successful client usually find themselves packing hard for an aircraft pickup point, heavily laden with rapidly perishing sheep meat, the horns, a cape, and all the camp they can carry.

Don't waste time wondering why hunters are typically stingy about offering you a taste of sheep meat. Hands down, it's the best game meat there is and after you get it home and in the freezer, provided most of it doesn't spoil first, it's much too valuable to give away to the villagers.

Memories of a successful sheep hunt are usually topped by the experience of eating sheep ribs roasted over a willow brush fire. If I could be granted one wish to share with every sportsman in the world, it would be for everybody to sit down and eat a feed of those sheep ribs with me.

Hunters with sheep fever, and in particular chronic sheep guides—the underpaid guys who drag a client behind and chase up the mountains every fall—are a weird breed. I know a number of Alaska resident hunters who hunt this animal every fall without fail. A hunter hard bitten by the bug will have it no other way. These are dyed-in-the-wool purists. Every season they spend at least a thousand-dollar bill on bush charter airfare, and grunt their way up into the talus looking for a bigger set of horns than the pair they took last year. A guy with sheep fever may walk and climb for days, spend hours bellying up on a full-curl ram, judge the animal as, maybe, an inch shy of last year's, and then pass on shooting. And if he never sees another sheep the whole trip, there's not an ounce of remorse!

Suffering is mandatory. Some I know are content to operate for days on a diet of chicken-flavored couscous—lightweight pasta, full of carbohydrates. Others are known to have their hair cut short and tear shirt labels off to save on weight. Comfort is secondary; finding a big head is the primary goal. If camp is ripped to pieces by a grizzly, they buy a whole new one for next year. An expensive pair of mountain boots usually lasts about one tough sheep hunt. Either they are ruined, or it's not worth the risk of their failure in the middle of next year's hunt. Water, or lack of water, can quickly become a problem. Like a Bedouin, you learn to get by with less—or find yourself doing without for long, dry periods. Find a waterhole in high places and chances are you will also find sheep.

To the sheep purist, total dedication is an obligation. I had a good hunting companion who repeatedly stated that when he died he wanted it to be while climbing up a mountain after a Dall ram. Of all the animals he could have chosen as the object of his prophetic statement, it had to be a sheep. Several years ago, he died in a drowning accident on his way to a moose hunt. He may not have been chasing a ram, and he probably wouldn't agree with me, but I like to think his final hunt was probably close enough to say that in the end he got his wish.

Unlike many of my friends, I was never clobbered by the virus. As a resident, I had just too many different animals to chase in Alaska, and my goal of harvesting one of each with a bow and arrow (along with getting into the game-guiding business), has taken up a lot of time. As a consequence, I have been able to squeeze in only four sheep hunts during my fifty plus years of living here. All four times I was bowhunting. On every occasion the opportunity was there, but luck was not.

My first hunt was into the headwaters of Goat Creek, behind Pioneer Peak in the Chugach Mountains north of Anchorage. I lost a coin toss and my partner, dressed in white camo, crawled up on the lone ram we took that trip and ground-sluiced him with a rifle. He shot it at 20 yards. I could have thrown my hat and hit that ram. It would have been an ideal setup for a bow hunter—but I lost the toss fair and square. That was so long ago, August 1971, that a three-quarter-curl ram was legal at the time. At this writing, to be legal a ram must carry a full curl.

Another hunt was a permit-drawing deal for a trophy ram in the Tok Management Area. That was in 1981. This sheep management

Chapter 19—Sheep Fever

area is about 130 miles due south of Fairbanks, in the Alaska Range. These are hundreds of square miles of good sheep mountains, managed to produce trophy Dall rams. Even in 1981, there was a full-curl restriction in effect in that area, long before a full-curl regulation was established everywhere else. These days, 100 to 120 permits are drawn by lucky hunters each fall season. The drawing is a no-nonsense deal. You put your name in the hat with everybody else and you're drawn— or you're not. A nonresident must buy or provide proof of applying for a nonresident hunting license to be eligible to apply for the Tok Management drawing. Remember, if you're a nonresident and draw a permit, you will be required to hunt with a guide. Rest assured, if you draw a permit you will be contacted by mail by several registered guides offering you their services! Information regarding the Tok Management drawing can be obtained by calling (907) 267-2347 or online through Yahoo, inquiring for "Dall Sheep permits, Tok Management Area Alaska."

My partner and I hit a lucky streak and drew permits the first year we tried. We were both bow hunters and any animal taken by our camp was going to be a bow kill or nothing. It turned out to be nothing, but it wasn't due to lack of trying. I lost track of the number of rams we slipped up on. In one instance, I crawled to within 20 feet of four full curls, the largest of which would have made a purist drool. They caught me as I was rising to shoot and I clean missed the biggest of the four as they ran off uphill. The big one stopped a moment, 20 yards away, staring at me in my white camo. By the time I gathered presence of mind and nocked another arrow, he was running again and out of range. I could have shot him easily with my sidearm but that was not the game plan. We packed out empty.

After waiting the mandatory four seasons before being eligible to enter the Tok drawing again, would you believe it, we drew permits a second time! (Two hunters can apply on one application for a "party hunt." If that permit is drawn, both hunters get a permit. If you want to submit an application for a party hunt, be sure to ask for a party hunt application when you contact Alaska Fish & Game for information.)

It worked out that my customary partner couldn't pull free so we could hunt together on that hunt, so I packed back into the management area and hunted alone; the desire not to waste the permit overcame reason and good sense. I knew that hunting alone far back in wild, remote country, especially in sheep country, is a game for the foolhardy, but I went anyway. Maybe I *do* have a touch of the fever!

Again, I crawled up on big sheep, but again, harvesting one with the bow was not to be.

That solo hunt was one of my most memorable. I'll never forget the black, broomed horns of one particularly beautiful old ram. I glassed him for three days, each day from positions at less than 100 yards, but he never gave me the chance to get close enough for a bow shot. And I will also always remember how I sat up all one night on that trip rattling rocks in a pan to keep a wheezing grizzly away from my tent.

My last sheep hunt was in the Talkeetna Mountains in southcentral Alaska, in 1985. A more than competent pilot friend put two of us up on a dry glacier bed at the 6,000-foot level above the Talkeetna River. We landed flying uphill onto the mountainside on a slope so steep the pilot had to stand on the brakes while we unloaded the plane. To leave, he spun the aircraft around and, falling off the mountain, was airborne in a heartbeat.

The advantage here was that we were on top and avoided a big climb. An even bigger advantage was that our pilot placed us 500 feet *above* two full-curl rams!

We observed the mandatory "no hunting the same day airborne" law, camped overnight, and the next morning hunted downhill after the sheep.

My new partner (again!) won the coin toss and made a stalk. He got caught about 75 yards from the sheep and spooked them up toward me. Just when things looked good for an ambush, they dipped out of sight a second, changed direction, and then ran past about 50 yards away. It was too far and happened too fast for a bow shot, and the rams fled to safer country.

Two days later I located what looked like another big ram. He was down the other side of a huge, long mountain valley and miles away. I could tell he had good horns, but he was too far off through mountain heat waves to determine if they came around to full curl, even with a good spotting scope.

My hunting partner and I split camp and I shoved off after the ram. It took the better part of two days to get to him. He was, indeed, a full curl and then some. I probed him for another day waiting for an opportunity before the tail end of a Pacific typhoon rolled in and obliterated the mountains with a scud of clouds, sleet, and then snow. I tried

Chapter 19—Sheep Fever

for him in the fog, but in a bush league move, I lost the wind. He had caught a whiff of me because, from the tracks leading out of his bed, he had left in a big hurry. To my surprise the ram didn't really spook. He moved off about a mile along the mountain, joined up with some smaller rams and settled down again.

Long story short, the weather cleared and I dogged the big sheep for another day without the chance of a shot. I could easily get to within less than 100 yards of him, at most any time, but never into bow range. Finally, the big guy went where I could not follow, up into a hanging glacier cirque. I don't believe I could have reached him with climbing equipment.

In the nick of time, our pilot spared us a long pack down out of those mountains by plucking us off the old glacier bed before a *truly* rotten snowstorm hit the last day of our hunt. So much for sheep adventures with a bow and arrow.

Probably the main factor in my never contracting the fever has been the fact that I have never killed a sheep, with a bow or a rifle. Everyone I know who has fallen victim to the bug has harvested at least one. A Dall ram is one of four remaining Alaska animals I have yet to take—hopefully with a bow. (There are ten huntable big-game species, not counting wolf and wolverine.) I am sixty-five as I write this, and I figure my sheep-hunting days are numbered. But who knows? I know that, against better judgment, I will put my name in for a Tok Management Area ram permit again this year. I may hear that siren song yet!

Chapter 20
A Day Worth Spending

THERE IS A RULE, I HAVE BEEN TOLD, BY PEOPLE TALKING like they know, that if it is cold enough to freeze the beer, it's too cold for ice fishing. I don't subscribe to that, because if I did, chances are I would never get to do any winter fishing. Not because of the inconvenience of frozen beer, but because I like to ice-fish!

A limit of landlocked silver salmon made the day worth spending.

The rule creates a dilemma! When you ice-fish in Alaska, when is it *not* cold enough to freeze the beer? Early in the season, when it may be a bit warmer, the ice isn't ready. It's too thin and you risk a hypothermic death by venturing out over water on something that won't support

Chapter 20—A Day Worth Spending

you. In the spring, as the temperature warms, the ice is slowly and dangerously rotting and the fish, after a long season in near-freezing water with limited oxygen, are lethargic and not the best thing to fish for anyway. Wait for spring thaw, open ice along a lake edge, and fresh supply of oxygen in the water, and *then* the hungry fish you seek will bite on a cigarette butt.

I have repeatedly appealed to what I consider the hardiest of friends to go fishing as soon as the ice will safely hold us. All my appeals fall on deaf ears. The lure of a strategically drilled hole in the ice and a feed of fresh fish are just not strong enough to draw any of them away from a warm house. If I ice-fish, it looks like I must do it alone.

In November 2007, following Thanksgiving, after patiently waiting for word that there was probably enough ice to support my little 300- pound frame, I headed north from home base at Peters Creek to Talkeetna to give it a try at Christiansen Lake. Christiansen is a landlocked lake which has been stocked by the Alaska Fish and Game people with both rainbow trout and silver salmon. Season is open the entire year and the daily limit on the landlocked salmon is ten fish. For the stocked rainbow, the catch limit is five. The silvers are small, tending to run about 8 to 10 inches—in this lake a 10-incher is a nice one. The rainbows will generally run larger. In the past, I have caught bows from 12 to 14 inches and lost a number that tore up my light gear, usually scraping apart the light line on the jagged ice at the bottom of the hole. I suspect these were much nicer fish. I have seen 14- to 16-inch bows caught by other people. The regulations give a fisherman a chance for a fifteen-fish limit on a lake he can drive to. Not a bad deal!

I won't mention any names (I don't know them anyway!) but one day, years ago, a friend and I arrived at Christiansen—a rare day when I had a partner—to find two sweet older ladies on the ice already fishing. We had neglected to bring along a copy of the regulations and we were not positive what the limit was. I walked over and asked the two women how many fish we could keep. Their reply was "ten fish, plus however many more you can stuff in your hip boots." I don't know for sure how many fish those two ladies caught, but they had been there well ahead of us and fishing was exceptionally good all that day. We watched as large numbers of fish were landed and thrown into a 5-gallon bucket. Finally they had enough, I guess, and pulled out and left. I don't think the comment about stuffing your hip boots was a joke.

After a quick breakfast at the Sunshine Restaurant, at the Parks Highway and Talkeetna Cutoff junction (early-bird fishermen should be advised that during the winter this restaurant does not open until 9 a.m.!), I was at the lake ready to fish just before eleven o'clock. There was not another soul in sight and not a sign of a drilled hole. It looked like I was the first fisherman of the ice season and the whole lake was mine.

In the past, a little shoveling had been required to clear a fishing spot. Not this time. There was not a flake of snow on the whole lake and the ice was as clear as vodka. From the look of cracks, which ran in all directions, the surface was frozen down to a depth of 14 to 16 inches. To me it is always disconcerting to walk on clear ice. My sense of self-preservation rebels. I always feel as if I am walking on a thin sheet of glass over water and, at any moment, I might suddenly break through and plunge straight down to bottom. I must have had that experience at some time in one of my previous lives! Knowing the fish would probably see me, I guess, I walked out onto the lake to a point where I could no longer see bottom through the ice. There I drilled a hole, put a line down to bottom, and set up my comfortable folding camp chair. God! What a great place to bring some kids!

My fresh raw shrimp bait worked like a charm and I was soon landing little landlocked silvers. Before I knew it I was nearing my ten fish limit (and I wasn't wearing hip boots!) and there had not been one sign of a rainbow. I tried using bigger bait (the bigger the bait the bigger the fish?) but the hungry little silvers tugging at the end of my pole soon wore me out. In addition, an afternoon breeze driving ten-below-zero air across the lake soon helped me make up my mind that maybe I had had enough for this trip. A can of beer would have frozen before a person could drink it!

I drove home to Chugiak in sunglasses, with an almost-warm southern sun shining in my face. I will go up there again later and try for a few of those elusive rainbows. Who knows? Maybe they were just too smart to allow themselves to get caught, looking up at me above them through that clear ice.

To top off the experience, for breakfast the next morning we had a feed of pan-fryers. All in all, it had been a winter day well worth the spending.

Chapter 21
The Weather Spirit of Birch Creek
First published in *Backwoodsman* magazine, November/December 2006

I HAVE DONE SOME PRETTY WILD AND CRAZY THINGS during fifty years of hunting in Alaska but few can match my one and only canoe hunting trip. We did this in the early 1970s in Alaska's interior. In a nutshell, on that adventure the local weather spirit was truly kind.

Previous to this, the sum of my canoe experience had been an hour or so fooling around on a small lake near my home in Eagle River, Alaska, and one brief lake crossing while sheep hunting on the Kenai Peninsula. Bruce Atkinson, my hunting partner, had little more experience than I did with double-enders. We both admitted to low-key misgivings about being ready for a trip as ambitious as the one we were headed into.

The weather closes in on us on Birch Creek. No need for me to try to look cold posing for the photo. I am Cold!

There we were, making camp in the dead of night in a gravel pit off the Steese Highway some 100 miles north of Fairbanks. Off in the darkness we could hear the faint rush of Birch Creek, the objective of this little safari. This was late September 1973. We had come to float this creek in hopes of harvesting a moose for a winter's meat supply. Beef prices that year had run off the chart, so our little adventure was as much driven by economic necessity as by the pleasure of hunting or a sense of adventure.

We had selected Birch Creek for one main and several lesser reasons:

> First, it was one of the few streams a person could float where the trip began and ended on the Alaska road system.

> Second, this float is so lengthy that few people would choose to use it for a short-term hunt. The stream is generally too shallow over the first 50 miles to accommodate an outboard motor. Once you start down the creek, you are committed to go all the way through. We were correct in assuming that these access problems would pare back hunting competition somewhat. The trip was 120 map miles from beginning to end. We would need to cross five USGS inch-to-the-mile map sheets to complete it. The distance involved and our general lack of canoe experience were definite pucker factors.

> Third, we had arrived at the creek on September 26. At that time, in that game management unit, the hunting regulations provided for opening a one-week cow moose season beginning October 1. If we had not harvested a bull moose by October 1, we would be free to take any moose on the creek we could find.

The all-day drive from Anchorage had been a long one and things quickly got quiet in the gravel pit that night after we ate supper and rolled up tight in our down bags.

Rolling out again at first light, I pushed back the tent flap to find 2 inches of new snow. This was very bad for morale, but things improved quickly when the sun came up and the new white stuff quickly melted away.

We each had 17-foot Aluma-Craft aluminum canoes. First, we had to drag the boats and supplies about 400 yards across the tundra to a small tributary, then half-float and half-drag the loaded rigs another quarter mile down the little feeder stream to the main channel of Birch Creek. After a short last-minute check, mostly to assure ourselves we indeed really wanted to do this, we were out of sight of the highway and into remote Alaska within minutes after shoving off downstream.

Chapter 21—The Weather Spirit of Birch Creek

For the next seven days we would not see another human being, not even anyone flying over in an airplane. This was the ideal canoe hunt we had been looking for!

In the space of the first 15 miles from the highway and some first-hand experience with sweepers and log jams, I quickly learned how to read the river and generally how to handle a canoe. The gentle flow of Birch Creek was an accommodating place to learn.

By early afternoon we were well past Harrington Fork, a main tributary draining a range of hills lying to the west of Birch Creek. This robust tributary nearly doubles the flow of the main channel below this confluence.

Soon after Harrington Fork, the north-south course of the creek valley turned straight east. As the sun dipped off behind the hills we put in on a wide gravel bar covered with dry firewood, and made camp near the mouth of a small stream. That night we lay awake a long while after dark with the tent flaps open, staring up at a hill-rimmed sky ablaze with northern lights. We could almost have hunted that night by the light of the aurora.

We broke camp late next morning. After a big breakfast we were on the creek just before noon. We had blown some prime early-morning time for spotting moose along the creek, but we didn't care. After several hours of floating, I was in the lead on the water. Bruce had lagged back several hundred yards enjoying the warm early-afternoon lazies. In the heat of the day, neither of us was expecting action of any kind. I slowly rounded a wide right turn in the creek to find a huge bull moose in mid-channel, wading across the stream in front of me. Bruce was well out of sight behind me at the moment. As the bull continued slowly across the creek I picked up my Super 8 mm movie camera and began filming him. He arose from the stream on the right side and stood on a gravel bar looking me over. Gallons of water streamed off him and he shook himself. I continued filming until I was almost even with him on the bar. At that point I laid down the camera, drew my .44 Magnum pistol, took careful aim behind his shoulder and fired. He was less than 20 yards from the end of my pistol barrel. Three shots echoed around the narrow valley that afternoon. Each time I shot, the bull spun halfway around, exposing his opposite side. With the third shot he went down and immediately died. Our hunt for the one moose we wanted was over.

That night there was a celebration at suppertime with moose rib steaks and a bottle of victory wine. When we turned in that evening it was very still and there was a cold chill in the air. I snuggled into my down bag and fell asleep immediately.

The next thing I knew Bruce was quietly shaking me. He whispered that he could hear chewing sounds coming from our moose parts, which were laid out on tarps in the open air by the river to cool. I thought I could see a dark form, silhouetted by starlight off the creek, but when we turned a flashlight on the scene, both of us armed to the teeth, the meat thief turned out to be imaginary. I was almost asleep again when the first of a pack of at least four wolves began howling nearby from the surrounding hillsides. We lay in our bags for a good hour staring up at the stars and listening to the chorus. By tomorrow night, we guessed, this pack would probably be profiting from the leavings of our kill.

Those who have harvested one of our Alaska moose know that the rest of the story is mostly a matter of logistics. From the moment you shoot a moose until it is in the freezer, you are either butchering it, packing it, keeping it clean and safe, or worrying about it. Because of the increasing cold, our meat would be in excellent shape for the duration.

Come morning the country was blue with hard frost and the creek frozen 4 feet out from both shores. We were a long way from the end of the float and this was our first warning of an impending freeze. The message to get on downstream, with some degree of urgency, came home quite clearly. If we paddled hard, at best it would take a good four days to get back to the highway by water. The Weather Spirit of Birch Creek had begun to assert itself. From where we were at the moment it was a 15-mile hike over rolling hills to the Steese Highway. If we became frozen-in here we would need to abandon our equipment and canoes, and the moose meat, and hike out of there overland; and the farther downstream we traveled from here the greater the overland distance to the highway became.

Along with a worried eye toward the weather came the realization that a canoe loaded with an additional half a moose handles far differently than one hauling just half of a light two-man camp. Because of the cold, the creek had dropped overnight. The lost water would be replaced, we hoped, by several large tributaries flowing into the main channel farther downstream. But for today, and still for much of the remainder of the trip, we would spend a lot more time pulling and

Chapter 21—The Weather Spirit of Birch Creek

dragging the heavily laden canoes over a multitude of bars and riffles we would have floated over just a few days ago.

In addition to the cold, we were to suffer some other pain during the trip. After a few days, the ends of our fingers began to crack open and bleed. This was obviously caused by aluminum oxide from the canoes. Our hands were a constant dull gray metallic color and we had no hand lotion with us to replace the natural oils dried out of our hands by the oxide. The only relief was to wear gloves and keep them constantly wet—not a real comfort, especially during the frigid early-morning hours. Also, after hours of forced paddling every day, we were both afflicted with burning "canoe muscles" between our shoulder blades. The only cure for that is rest, but we could not afford the time.

On the morning of the sixth day we awoke to find another 2 inches of new snow and the creek frozen 10 feet out from shore on both sides. It was then that little intelligence details about Birch Creek, which we had failed to comprehend before the trip began, really started to come home to roost.

The Fish and Game Habitat officer in Fairbanks I had called had canoed Birch Creek a number of times. He had been very helpful, but either he failed to caution us about a potential September freeze-up, or I had failed to listen.

Up front, we had left our pickup in the parking lot at Eagle Creek Lodge, several miles up the highway from our put-in point. We planned to hitchhike back to retrieve the truck from the other end of the float. We now recalled comments made by Don Bennett, the lodge owner, about the weather, which neither of us had particularly picked up on. It was something about our attempting this float so late in the season…

Unknown to us, the weather during the end of September, up to this point, had been unseasonably warm. We would not understand until the last few days of our adventure just how lucky we were that the temperature held and that we had not been forced to walk out of there.

By the seventh day, less than 10 miles short of the end, the creek had deepened considerably and we met two local beaver trappers coming upstream by riverboat. They were amazed to see us still on the water, advising that this creek had been frozen solid enough to walk across by the twenty-sixth day of September the previous year. We passed them midmorning on October 1.

Two years prior, we would learn later, a canoeist on lower Birch Creek, between the Steese Highway and the Yukon River, had become iced-in on the creek in late September and spent over a month slowly starving, subsisting on snowshoe hare, before he was finally missed, located, and rescued by helicopter.

Late afternoon on October 1, we happily arrived at the highway, retrieved our pickup from Eagle Creek Lodge and were loaded and headed home down the highway—through a blinding snowstorm! Nobody else was foolish enough to be on the road that night. I recall, when it was my turn to drive, holding my head out the open pickup window in an effort to keep track of the road surface in a complete whiteout.

We had our moose and it had been one hoot of an adventure. But looking back, when it was all over there was no doubt in either of our minds just how lucky we had been and how unwittingly we had taunted the weather spirit of Birch Creek.

I still have the 8mm movie of that huge bull moose crossing the stream ahead of me.

> Author's Note:
> Since 1973, Birch Creek has been added to the federal National Wild and Scenic Rivers system. An access road has been constructed to a launching area on the creek on the upper end and a well-marked landing area, with an access road, has been built on the lower end.
> We have never been back there for another hunt.

Early on in the hunt I pose with our Birch Creek moose. This was before the weather started to threaten.

Chapter 22
Little Tok Grizzly
First published in *Traditional Bowhunter* magazine, October/November issue, 2003, under the title "Stalked on the Little Tok"

FEW OF MY HUNTING EXPERIENCES RIVAL A HUNTING trip I took during the late 1970s. I never harmed an animal hair on that trip. What made it so special was the feeling, which came out with me at the end of the adventure, that I had been the one being hunted—not that I had been the hunter!

A good friend of mine, Gary Hebert, taught school in Tok (pronounced "Toke" as though it rhymes with "Coke"), a tiny community in the Alaska interior located at the junction of the Alaska Highway and the Tok Cutoff. Gary owned his own aircraft, which gave him access to an almost unlimited number of places to hunt. We had chased moose together during several previous seasons. I was trying to take a moose with my bow at that time and Gary was busy at work preparing for a new school year. Although he didn't have the time to accompany me, he agreed to spend some flying time getting me back into good moose country and drop me off to hunt. He would pick me up the following weekend. After a harrowing landing on a small bush strip along the Little Tok River, about 50 miles southeast of Tok, Gary flew off and left me standing on the riverbank.

I had the comfort of a small cabin located a few hundred yards back in the woods off the river. I arrived to find the front door ripped out of the wall. The scene told the story. Judging from his tracks, a very large, very strong bear had punched his claws into the top of the entrance and pulled the door, frame and all, right out of the wall. He had then wrecked the interior of the cabin, biting into all the stored canned goods inside and breaking everything else he could find. It was obvious that he had cut the bottoms of his paws on broken glass in the process, probably flying into a rage when he stepped in spilled salt and rubbed that into his cuts. Every pot was bitten and the woodstove had been turned over and the sooty stovepipes batted all around the cabin. It took most of the day to reinstall the door and clean up the mess.

I began hunting the river bars for moose the next morning. On the third day, while following generally the same route I had followed the previous morning, I found pie-pan-sized bear tracks over the top of my footprints. From the size of the prints I assumed this was the cabin wrecker. He had trailed me through most of the river bottom I had hunted. His tracks covered mine soon after I had departed the cabin and turned off my trail within about 100 yards of my return.

For days we repeated this process. Every day I hunted, the next I found his tracks over mine. How far he had been behind me the previous day I never knew; maybe hours but perhaps just minutes. But one thing was sure, this bear was tracking me every day.

The cabin along the Little Tok River where I stayed while a grizzly haunted me.

All week we played cat and mouse and it took only a short time before his predictable presence had me spooked. At night I had come to leaning folded metal chairs against the door for an alarm. If he pulled the door out again I had a shotgun across a stool by my bed pointed in that direction. Every waking minute of the day and night, from going to the river for water, to going to the bathroom, that bear was on my mind. I pictured him behind every tree and willow patch, poised to attack me. At night I imagined him silently circling the cabin, waiting, just on the other side of the log walls.

By the following weekend, when I was picked up, I was psychologically fried. This had been excellent country, with loads of old sign but I had not seen a moose. I hadn't really given myself a decent chance to look for one. I was too busy, spooked, and constantly on my guard watching for that bear.

Later, in October, Gary sent me a letter advising that two weeks after I left another pair of hunters had killed a large bear where he had dropped me off. It had been shot right in front of the cabin, from the front door. His teeth were worn and he was skinny. Obviously, this was an old bear that probably could no longer effectively hunt for himself and had turned to cabin robbing.

If he was the same bear, and I think he was, I find it difficult to fault him for ruining my hunt or even for stalking me, if that was the case. His reason for being there was infinitely more valid than mine. The hunters who ended his life probably did him a favor, by sparing him the misery of starvation or the insult of freezing to death outside a warm den where he should have been by the time he was killed. I'm glad I was not the one called upon to do him the favor.

Chapter 23
Dyea Beach

Blades of grass bend north and flit about a wind that's always blowing.

Far up the beach the cottonwoods moan a song about the past,
when they were young behind a smithy's barn.

A slivered skiff that once held men of dreams lies rotting on its underside.

Down toward the grey canal a drunken seagull reels to beach, exactly on the
spot he chose – just to pad in discontent from what he found.

In alternating blues and grays the sky whips round the upper peaks.
The mountains sit in timeless pain while Mother Nature slowly tries to tear
them down, filling milky streams that make the sea run pale.

A gnarled pine clings defiant to a rocky point around the bay.
A veteran of a thousand storms the stunted tree would rather
break than bend, and lives from day to day on granite dust.

A row of grey piles, imposing down the beach,
has fought the test of time and lost.
Like wagon wheels, and men with muddy boots who met an age in flower,
the planks are gone, off to where it is that bleached white driftwood goes.

The scars of man have all but disappeared.
With every passing season less is seen of what a dreamer's lust for gold could do.
Only glimpses are left to ponder.

Chapter 24
The Other House

IT IS DIFFICULT FOR ANYONE WHO HAS NOT LIVED IN remote country for a time to relate to one of the simplest and most basic of conveniences—the outdoor biffy.

Books have been published about the Alaska outdoor toilet, most often humorous, although the subject itself is serious business. There are even catalogs on the market these days offering a wide array of supplies and accoutrements to both the ordinary and the discerning outdoor toilet user.

The pit privy, as it is sometimes called, serves one of the most basic of human needs. To many these days it is still as important to the well-being and health of the user as clean water, shelter, or decent food.

Here in Alaska the outdoor toilet has a considerable following. This is due mostly to economic necessity and the lack of electricity and running water in many of this state's far-flung remote areas. It is also partly due to a matter of choice, where the intended user may often have the wherewithal to solve power and water problems but

The Dutch doors of our new outhouse allows an excellent view while assuring the proper amount of privacy.

elects instead to keep things simple. Few things are as simple as or more functional than a reasonably comfortable seat out of the weather, and a roll of good-quality toilet paper when the need arises. These days, satellite telephones carry information that was once brought by dogsled and mail boat, and the Coleman lantern has given way to propane lights, but so far nobody has come up with a good, cheap, workable idea to replace the simple convenience of the outdoor biffy.

We bought a piece of land on the beach on remote Raspberry Island in the Kodiak Island area in 1982. At that time, there was an existing outdoor toilet that was in even worse condition than the old cabin that came with the purchase. In its heyday the old toilet had obviously been quite the thing. One of the previous owners, a retired navy man named Murphy, had lived on this remote property year-round. Murphy had been an electronics kind of guy in the navy and was quite handy with wiring up gadgets. He loved his football and baseball—whatever he could get on his Trans-Oceanic radio at that time—and he apparently hated to miss any part of a game. Accordingly, he had his radio wired to an external speaker in the outhouse so if he had to suddenly make a call the game was continuously being transmitted to the biffy and all he missed of the sports event was a short time in transit, a problem easily solved by judicious use of commercial messages and timeouts.

Since we bought the place we have recreated at Onion Bay most every year and, with minor repairs and occasional painting, nursed the little outbuilding along until it became such an embarrassment that my wife began to make threats. My vote was for an addition to the cabin first for more room, comfort, and convenience, as I put it. "Not so," my financial manager advised. It soon became evident that no cabin addition was likely until the outdoor facility showed some remarkable improvement. Of obvious necessity, a plan to replace the aged biffy began to evolve.

Much discussion occurred over siting of the new structure. Looking at the pluses and minuses of where to build, we finally settled on the existing site. The old pit, dug years before, was still substantial, far in excess of what we would ever require during our lifetime; and after twenty-three years we had become very used to the existing beaten path.

One thing was certain, if we were going to build a new outhouse it was going to be the classiest of such structures as existed along the entire west Kodiak shore. It was to be finished and trimmed, inside and

Chapter 24—The Other House

out, have an opaque roof for good interior light, and an attractive set of Dutch doors, allowing the user a view benefit while still affording an appropriate amount of privacy. The floor would be tiled and accoutrements, such as door handles, coat hooks, toilet paper dispenser, flower vase and magazine rack, were to be of the first order. The crowning touch would be a south-facing stained-glass window. After months of searching we located a suitable piece of stained glass (reportedly from an old demolished English church), but in the end we had to compromise and substitute the opaque roof with plywood. When it arrived at the bay, just prior to the building project, our order for clear acrylic roofing turned out to be flimsy greenhouse stuff that would never hold up when a storm rolled into our bay off Shelikof Straits. Probably we will remedy that important design change at a later time.

Our neighbors in the bay, all of whom have outdoor biffys, have viewed our pretentious outhouse excess with good humor. One by one they came by, to be treated to on-site inspections, if not, in some cases, a test drive. The stained-glass window prompted one clever and irreverent friend to dub the structure the Sistine Crapper. If it has to have a name I would be more inclined to call it the Flying Nun in view of its excessive roof overhang. It has remained in place for two years now but I still have the uneasy feeling that it may take flight one of these days during one of the powerful gusts of west wind which periodically blow down our bay.

I suspect it will be many years before Onion Bay sees a flush toilet. So far, *our* camp at least, has even resisted the ubiquitous propane lights, preferring instead the comforting hiss, the brighter light, and familiar smell of a Coleman lantern. I guess we are just children of the fifties and that is part of us.

With a good radio, and a high antenna, we probably have better reception these days than old Murphy ever dreamed of, even with his Trans-Oceanic, the Cadillac of radios in those days; but we are not sports fans and will probably never bother to wire the airwaves out to the new outhouse.

Some things change and some things never do.

Chapter 25
The Goats of Victor Creek
First Published in *Western Bowhunter* magazine, March/April, 2003

MALCOM "MAC" McCAIN AND GARY HOAGLAND, MY two hunting companions, stood huddled under the brush several yards down the trail, waiting for the rain to let up.

This was the first day of a seven-day goat hunt. We had been packing up the trail about three hours when this freak downpour struck without warning. I stood, looking at my partners, as drops the size of grapes splattered on me off the alder I pointlessly hunkered under for protection.

The plastic bag I had taped over the feathers on the arrows in my bow quiver was long gone, pulled off somewhere down the trail in the tangle of alders and thorny devil's club brush we had pushed our way through. The only protection the fragile fletching now had was a coat of Dri-Tite waterproofing. I had twelve arrows taped together in my bow quiver—if the feathers went, so did any chance I'd have for a goat this trip.

Early that morning we began packing up the Victor Creek drainage, off the Seward Highway, on what had been represented to us as a Forest Service "trail." This mountain valley is on Alaska's Kenai Peninsula. As the crow flies, it's a tad over 50 air miles southeast of Anchorage, where we all lived and worked at that time.

This was early August 1973. Back then you could hunt Rocky Mountain goats about anywhere you could find them in Alaska. Now you either need to be drawn for a permit or take part in a sign-in/sign-out registration hunt. There are also a few Dall sheep back in Victor Creek. We had hopes of lucking onto a three-quarter curl—which was legal

Chapter 25—The Goats of Victor Creek

horn size at the time (legal sheep anywhere *these* days must be full curl), but the odds of a legal sheep were slim at best. This was a goat hunt. I had harvested a number of goats with a rifle but I was here trying to harvest my first one with archery tackle.

I was the only bowhunter in the party, and always treated, to some extent, like the village idiot. The general attitude of my rifle-hunting partners toward my choice of weapons was more one of quiet tolerance than disdain. On our usual annual moose or caribou hunts I had always been afforded every consideration, and most times an offer of the first shot. Following that, the rifles always took over. I was then allowed to assist in carrying meat back to camp. In that regard, I always did my share. On this hunt, the practice of my taking a back seat to the rifles in camp was overdue to end.

Prompted by impatience, I stepped out of the alders and into the rain, pointing out to my companions that we were soaked to the skin anyway, so why not move on up the valley?

As we sloshed along, the rain stopped as abruptly as it had begun and the sun came out warm and welcome. We climbed higher and broke out above timberline into the open. Dampened spirits brightened and our earlier snail's pace easily tripled. We passed a bewildered black bear, leaving him behind without thought of a shot, which might have alerted the other, more valued valley inhabitants. Afternoon was well along when we climbed up over the lip of a level, grassy bench where Gary recommended we camp.

Gary was our guide this trip. He was the only party member who had hunted here before and he was still nursing a trick knee for that distinction.

From camp, the mountains rose to near vertical on both sides of the narrow little valley. It was a dizzy nightmare of pitched emerald fingers cut by slate-gray slide chutes. One had the feeling that everything here was falling, or about to fall. Occasionally we would hear the crash of ice and boulders, as pieces, loosened by the rain, broke free and ricocheted down the canyons. Nobody needed reminding that being caught in one of those funnels at the wrong time could mean an untimely death. There was a constant rush of tumbling water, cascading down chutes on both sides of the valley. These feeders joined with Victor Creek, which mumbled its way past camp, deep under the eternal snowpack which completely bridged the stream for 100 yards up and downstream from camp. Off to the west, part of Kenai Lake was framed, low in the notch formed by the mouth of the valley.

Setting up camp ran in fits and starts. Every few minutes someone would spot a likely white spot on the opposite mountain and send everyone scurrying for binoculars. Finally, the chores done, we set about the business of serious glassing. We would scout the area that afternoon and be ready to hunt the next morning, opening day of season.

We located three goats and a Dall ram across from camp that evening, studying them carefully with the spotting scope. They were all good size and probably billy goats. The sheep caused quite a ruckus but he turned out to be an inch or so under legal size. He plagued camp for the remainder of the trip with frequent appearances at different locations. New sightings never failed but to send camp in an uproar. Later that afternoon we located two more goats. These were up high on our camp's side of the valley.

Opening day dawned bright and clear. After a quick breakfast, we were off up the mountain behind camp. We planned for Mac to take one of the goats we had spotted behind camp the previous evening. He had never harvested a goat before; both Gary and I had.

We spent most of the day in a confused search on the broken mountainside, looking for the only goat we could find that morning. We lost the animal on a bungled stalk, and climbed high above it before locating it again. We then backtracked down the mountain and Mac did himself proud with a 300-yard, one-shot kill with his old 300 Savage lever gun.

With the head, cape, and meat of Mac's big-bodied goat in three packs, we inched our way down into camp before dark. After a dinner of goat liver and some victory cheer, no one needed prompting to turn in early.

A high wind came up and howled all night, snapping the tent so violently we feared the seams would fail. Most of the storm blew through by morning but a stiff, cold wind lingered, which did little to accommodate spotting.

We found one lone goat on the mountain opposite camp. I was elected to try for it with the bow. Gary would stay in camp with Mac to flesh and salt his goat cape.

Before departing, signals were arranged which, I hoped, would aid in locating my goat. I put on winter white camo so a spotter in camp could easily track me up the mountain.

Chapter 25—The Goats of Victor Creek

It was 10 a.m. Late start. I dropped down to the creek, crossed the snow bridge, and began picking my way up the other side through the maze of slate chutes. In time I could see the entire mountain behind camp. I signaled the guys that the remaining goat of the pair we had hunted the day before was still on the mountain. Gary soon headed out up the other side after it. I watched him off and on for the next hour before he disappeared in the scenery.

I continued up my mountain, working toward a rust-colored bluff chosen as a landmark near my goat. From camp, Mac kept signaling me up and to the west in that direction. I had the wind and knew I was somewhere at least two major canyons east of the animal.

I climbed and side-hilled all afternoon. Stopping for a drink from a trickle at the foot of a snow patch, I glanced up as two goats appeared, above and west of me, along the skyline, 500 to 600 yards away.

I dropped out of sight and maneuvered to where I could glass the animals. Both goats bedded down, facing off into the valley. At least 500 yards of truly miserable mountain terrain separated us. There were no fewer than four canyons, who knew how deep, in that direction and all of the ridge tops along the route were fully exposed to the animals.

I was now eight hours out of camp. It was 6 p.m. but I still had a good five hours of daylight to spare, thanks to the famous Alaska midnight sun. Still, it would take hours of careful stalking to reach these goats. I didn't have enough time to get over there, do all that was necessary, and then get back to camp before dark. It was a bad deal all the way around.

The solo goat I had started after this morning had to be somewhere parallel to me on the mountain, or perhaps now even below me. I had passed my landmark bluff some time ago and opted to ignore the two latest goats as undoable and look for the lost billy. I spent another hour scouting but found nothing. Turning to Mac, back at camp, I raised my arms in the "Where is he?" signal. Camp was so far off I had to use my binoculars to read his reply. "He's gone. You blew it." Not exactly what I wanted to know.

I lay in the moss watching the two new goats on the mountainside. Both finally meandered off back around the ridgeline to the west and out of sight.

I was about defeated and ready to head for camp when suddenly a nice-sized goat walked into view around the mountain to the west of

103

me. He was at about the same level on the slope as I was. Behind him came another, followed by a third and then a fourth animal. All were moving along the face of the mountain—in my direction.

The four were joined by yet a fifth animal and the group moved out of sight into the largest canyon that separated us. If they showed on the next closer ridgetop, the distance between us would be narrowed to less than 300 yards—reasonable striking distance!

The sun dropped behind the mountains to the west and the alpine air began to rapidly cool. There was enough time yet to make a move, provided the goats eliminated one big canyon between us; but no matter what, I knew if I took a run at them I would probably never get back to camp before dark.

I return to camp on Victor Creek with the second and last load of my goat meat.

Soon a goat appeared over the closer ridgeline. It walked downhill a few yards and lay down on a grassy ledge, at the foot of a huge, square boulder. It faced west, away from me. *You're on,* I thought to myself, and eased out from protective cover into the open ground that separated us. All he needed to do was turn his head and he had me.

I had moved about 50 yards when a second goat appeared on the ridge above the first. It was about the same size as the other animal, but more inquisitive. I leaned back against the mountain and froze as he looked directly my way. Either my camo had me looking like one of the gang—or I resembled a pile of snow. His gaze brushed past me. Lowering his head, he grazed back over the ridge and out of sight.

I continued across the open mountainside, never taking my eyes off

Chapter 25—The Goats of Victor Creek

the bedded billy. Soundless movement through the loose slate was agonizingly slow, but I was finally able to work my way uphill to a point where I had the huge boulder between the goat and me. There I shed my pack and binoculars.

I was sure at any second another goat would walk over the ridge and catch me, but another thirty minutes put me 30 yards up the spine of the ridge above the boulder screening me from the goat. The other animals had simply vanished.

I removed an arrow from my bow quiver and nocked it.

The mossy rocks on the spine of the ridge provided quiet footing. I closed the distance comparatively quickly, to 20 yards, then 10 and, finally, to about 15 feet.

The problem now was to get the animal on its feet, without alarm, and somehow out into the open.

I was contemplating throwing a stone to make him move when, suddenly, he stood up. I could see the tip of his nose around the side of the boulder. He was obviously alarmed—rigid and looking.

I have always believed animals have a sixth sense about danger and here that belief was staring me in the face. I had not made a sound and I still had a mild uphill west wind in my face. I knew there would be only a few feet of open space for a shot once he discovered me and struck for the canyon. Coming to half draw, I could feel my heart trying to pound its way out of my chest as I waited for the move I was sure would come.

Suddenly the white muzzle I had been focused upon moved forward, exposing the head, neck and front quarters of the animal and I found myself staring into the eyes of a very startled billy goat.

As if in slow motion, he lowered his head and moved forward, bent on the canyon. As he did, I came to full draw and released at a spot behind his shoulder. The Microflight spit out of my old Herters bow and struck were it was sent. The bodkin-tipped arrow passed completely through him and kept on going. At this range there was little marksmanship involved.

Following a 60-yard run, the goat collapsed on a slate slide, his last act a kick, which sent him down into a steep creek ravine. I had to rope down to reach and dress him—standing in small pool of water halfway to my boot tops. Luckily, he had come to rest in that pool. Beyond there the water fell off hundreds of feet almost straight down. A tumble of a few more feet and there would have been nothing left, near the bottom of the mountain, worth recovering.

Skinning the goat in ice water, and the pack down off that mountain was a nightmare. I stumbled into camp in the dark, just before midnight. I was fried, but I had finally broken the jinx between bows, rifles, and me in the same camp.

The goat had over-8-inch horns and scored a fraction above forty Pope & Young scoring points, well above the thirty-five-point minimum to qualify for the bow book at that time. The scoring minimum was later raised to forty points, so he is still in the book.

Our merry little group moved on to other hunts and new adventures. We never returned to Victor Creek. The memory each of us had of packing full loads of goat meat for hours down that talus trail and out of there always turned off the idea of another hunt—although the memory of that not quite legal Dall ram had us dwelling on it for a few years!

Chapter 26
Who Speaks for the Salmon?

THE COW PARSNIP ALONG THE FAR SIDE OF THE CANYON are turning yellow. The late August mornings were becoming progressively cooler. There has been a need for an early fire in the little cast-iron cabin stove over the last few days to knock the corners off the chill, and for some reason the perking morning coffee smells much better than usual. All our friends owning commercial salmon-fishing beach sites have closed their camps and left to take up their jobs back in the other world and the bay, and the entire west end of the island, now belong to my wife and me.

We have 5 acres on the beach in Onion Bay, on the west end of Raspberry Island. Raspberry is a long skinny wedge of land squeezed between Afognak Island on the north and Kodiak on the south. We are drawn to this remote place each fall to sharpen our dulled city senses, gorge on wild salmon and thank the gods we sought out and bought this remote place more than twenty years ago. Years of hard work and eventual retirement have combined to allow us to be here.

An old, dilapidated cabin came with the land. It looks as worn and tired today as it did when we first saw it in 1982. Still, after all these years, it is as much home to us today as home itself.

The bears here are wild. No human watches or photographs them as they go about their business. We see them only in glimpses and by accident. Man is just another animal here that is an enemy to be avoided or confronted, as a bear feels is required. Humans must be wisely attentive, especially of bears imbued with motherhood. These animals also come to the creek that borders our property to gorge on salmon—along with us, the eagles, river otters, and foxes.

Now is not the time that bears are the most important creatures here, nor are people, river otters, or foxes. At this time it is the lowly little salmon that are both king and queen. The cycle of their lives entwines tightly with most animals that use these Kodiak islands.

To sense when the salmon's return is close at hand one need only watch the tall beach grass along the lagoon and around the mouth of the creek we border. All summer it is unspoiled and pristine, waving in the wind like green wheat. Then, suddenly, one early fall morning, impatient trails and trampled banks appear everywhere. The bears have been here in the dark, seeking, inquiring. We never saw any on the creek this year, as we have in the past, but we heard them talking in the night several times, their moaning calls mindful of an African lion. That you don't see them means nothing. It could be they have already received word that a good run is coming and they choose to wait for it in the greater privacy available upstream.

It takes some years of watching to pick up on the rhythm of the local run. First come a few jumpers. With no obvious plan, they enter the bay, announcing their arrival with an occasional leap, typically leaving the water with only a single bound. Jumping activity occurs so seldom at this time that what does occur is easily missed. Within a week or two, activity intensifies and, with new arrivers, leaping salmon are now seen all around the entrance end of the bay. The number of jumps seems to increase with the number of jumpers. It is not unusual for a single fish to leave the water as many as six or eight times in succession. To see this, I believe, is one of the few times a human observer might be convinced that perhaps a salmon is capable of expressing great joy. Prior to ascending the creek the fish stop jumping en masse and circle in the brackish water in the lagoon at the mouth of our stream, entering and retreating again as their eggs ripen with each tide.

The year 2005 was a banner year for the pink salmon here. On schedule, the second week of August, five hundred or more came into the lagoon to the mouth of the creek—more than usual and probably too many for this little drainage. But the key to salmon survival is to produce a greater number of young than the environment can destroy, so every few years it probably pays to get ahead of the game.

One school at a time, participants await their turn at ascending the

Chapter 26—Who Speaks for the Salmon?

little brown-water stream. With each change of tide a new group replaces most of the last. They pause in the rising brackish water and swim slowly in a huge, lazy circle in the mouth of the creek; one last moment of ripening as they wait for the highest point of the tide to help them the first few hundred feet upstream.

Watching their water ballet reveals a lot about the tribulation in their lives. Everything is their enemy. They must have little peace. Amid the school of sleek bodies a good number are scarred with white gillnet marks, a testament to good luck and freedom rather than bad luck and the inside of a can. Good luck relative to a salmon is a matter of how one thinks and where one resides. A fisherman has one point of view, the fish another.

Seals and other sea predators have cleaved a number of the circling bodies. The injured ignore their horrible wounds and continue the dance with the others. Their genes are undamaged, and they are determined. There are big fish and small ones. Some are perhaps returning late and some too early. Who knows why each has chosen this year to join in the dance?

Eagles hunt them when the tide drops and the lagoon goes near dry. I was quietly offended when our last-to-depart neighbor's dog would come by to chase the fish in the shallows. She is a fine pet but for the fish's sake I was glad to see her leave. The little pinks have enough problems without adding to them the elation of a young Labrador retriever.

The resident mother-and-child pair of river otters must be in hog heaven, evidenced by the partially eaten bodies of would-be spawners along the banks of the better fishing holes. The foxes, seagulls, and ravens profit from the otter's leavings. Nothing is wasted in this pageant.

They spawn in water here that is rarely deep enough to cover their bodies. Could this be the reason the female turns on her side to spew eggs in the hole she has dug in the gravel? The male that fought hardest to be her partner moves in instantly to fertilize what she deposits. Then, all that remains of their life's work is to refill the hole and bury her seeds. Throughout the entire process there is no room for escape if doom steps down over the edge of the bank.

Late next July we will surely be at the cabin again. It won't take long for me to slip down to the creek and have a look in the big hole just above the mouth. If it was a good season it will be full of tiny fingerlings, busy making a living under the cut banks, avoiding the resident kingfisher who claims this stream. If times were tough there won't be so many fish. In view of this year's run, and with luck, there could be hundreds, maybe even thousands I don't see, waiting to go off to wherever it is these tiny fish go on the journey of their lives. Then, if the ocean is kind, there will be another bumper return in three or four years. But who knows? Who can speak for the salmon?

Chapter 27
Mom's Broke Leg

YOUNG PEOPLE GROWING UP IN ALASKA DURING THE 1940s, '50s and '60s missed many things taken for granted by kids who lived down in America. There was no swimming pool, let alone one that was Olympic-sized. Not having an Olympic-size pool these days causes many Alaska parents terrible heartburn.

In my town, the Skagway public school didn't have a football program. There was no track, we didn't play hockey and we rarely played baseball, except for makeup softball games on the 4th of July. If you didn't play basketball during those days, you didn't participate in high school sports. Through most of my high school tenure, 1956-1960, average public high school attendance was about forty to forty-five students. Nearly every male with a warm body and a pulse spent his winter playing on the Skagway Panthers basketball team.

In addition to sports, there were many other things we did without in town. There was no TV and we didn't have a radio station. If you had a good car radio you could hook onto a makeshift antenna up at the Point, to the west and above town, and receive music from KINY in Juneau—provided atmospheric conditions were right. There was no road to Skagway then and there were no state ferries in southeast Alaska. Ferries didn't show up until the mid-1960s. To drive to America then you had to load your vehicle on a White Pass & Yukon Railroad flatcar, ship it to Whitehorse, Yukon Territory, and drive down the Alcan Highway to the U.S. border through Canada.

One of the sad and very dangerous inadequacies of living in Skagway during the late 1950s was the lack of a doctor. A nurse was on call at the Skagway Hospital but patients needing medical services beyond what a nurse could provide had to wait for weekly visits from a traveling doctor from Juneau. Emergencies were handled between the resident nurse and the doctor by telephone, a circumstance which was destined to place me in a position where I definitely did not want to be!

Late one afternoon during that time I was at the family home of my girlfriend (and future wife) a few doors down and across the street from my parents' house. Answering a violent knocking at the front door we found my stepfather, Alf Kalvick, in a near-frantic state. My mother had fallen over at home, he said, and it looked like she had broken her leg. Knowing I was just across the street he had left her where she fell and run to me for help. Could I come and assist?

Mom was on the floor in the utility room, a windowless and poorly lit little room often used for passage between the master bedroom, at the back of the house, and the kitchen. She had tripped and fallen in the darkness. Her leg was obviously broken. My first reaction was to remove her from the floor and get her into the bedroom and on the bed—a move I was to catch hell for from the nurse. I was later lectured that I should have left her where she lay and called the hospital. What does a seventeen-year-old know about a broken leg his first time out?

An ambulance was called and on-duty nurse Alice Selmer instructed me to follow them to the hospital. Little did I know of her plans for my assistance.

Mom was placed on a gurney in a large white hospital room with many lights. Alice was quickly on the phone to Juneau discussing the situation with a doctor. It was not possible for a doctor to fly to Skagway that afternoon, she was advised. She would have to set the leg herself. Alice looked at me and told me I would have to help her—there was no one else. I felt all the blood drain from my head and knew I was in danger of fainting. "I can't do this," I told her. "This woman is my mother!" "Yes you can," she snapped. "I repeat, there is no one else!"

Alice Selmer was a large and very commanding woman. She was unusually tall, only slightly shorter than my 6-foot-2-inch height and the grey braids she wore wound tightly on the top of her head made her appear even taller. She was big boned and carried herself like a lady who was proud of who and what she was. Nurse Selmer was not a person to be trifled with. "What do you want me to do?" I asked.

Chapter 27—Mom's Broke Leg

Ms. Selmer prepared yards of gauze and plaster of Paris and began slathering the mix around Mother's leg. As gently as possible I held and supported Mom's ankle and foot. Mom could not hide the fact that she was in misery. At a certain point, cued by the doctor standing by on the telephone, Alice looked at me and told me that I was now to slowly pull on the leg. This would straighten out the break and hopefully set the broken bones in the correct position. Once this was done I was to continue a steady pressure to hold the limb straight while she carried on forming the plaster cast that would immobilize the leg.

If you have ever seen this done in the movies you will recall how when the leg is pulled the victim screams and passes out. This is exactly how it happens, the only difference being this victim happened to be my mother.

The plaster cast set quickly. Mom was then wheeled into an x-ray room where the break was photographed. As luck would have it, the bones were all correctly aligned and properly immobilized. The job was done and mending the break was now up to her healing powers. This required months to accomplish but she did it well and suffered no aftereffects.

My blood still runs cold when I think of that moment when I had to pull that leg straight—not an easy thing for a young son to do. This would be an unlikely thing to happen in most places today although in Skagway, even with thousands of tourists passing through town every week during the summer season, in the new millennium there is still not a resident doctor in Skagway! With improved transportation and communications, things are little better than the 1950s, when, as Nurse Selmer had pointedly put it to me, there was no one else.

Yes, we missed a lot of advantages growing up in Alaska during that time which I never regretted. But this was definitely one thing I could have lived without had it never happened.

Chapter 28
The Three-Legged Deer

THE MOST EFFECTIVE WAY TO HUNT KODIAK AREA DEER is by placing at least three hunters online and driving, or "beating the brush," for them. Sooner or later, somewhere along the line, an animal (sometimes a brown bear!) will jump up in front of one of the drivers.

It was early November and three of us had been sweeping the hills for hours out of my Onion Bay camp on Raspberry Island. We had seen a few deer that morning and we had shot a number of times at fleeting forms, but harmed nothing. Not seeing a goodly number of animals for an extended period is not all that unusual, although during good times we will often see fifteen to twenty deer in a day's hunting. They were there all right, it's just that on some days, for their own reasons, they hold tight and don't show—either that or you're just not in the right place at the right time. Usually, with perseverance and hard hunting, one minute you have nothing and the next you have all the venison you would care to carry off the mountain. This was just one of those slow days.

The morning had moved into afternoon and a decision was made to make one last drive. We would sweep down off the mountain to the beach on Kupreanoff Straits and then walk back to camp along the shore. In the descent of the steep slope toward the beach were a number of small spruce patches, favorite hiding places for Sitka black-tailed deer. Approaching one of the small groves along the way, I swung over to the far edge to cover the chance of any deer trying to sneak out the back door. Rounding the edge of the patch I spotted an animal about

Chapter 28—The Three-Legged Deer

30 yards downhill, standing with its neck and head in the trees. It had obviously heard one of our party going down the mountain on the other side of the patch and was curiously watching the far side through the trees. I pulled up my rifle, shot, and immediately killed the deer. After I shot, a nice forked buck jumped out of the same trees and into the open. He froze, staring at me from about 30 yards' distance. I quickly ejected the spent cartridge from my little .45-70 and took sight on this second deer. Pulling the trigger I was rewarded with nothing but a loud click. My rifle was empty and, brilliantly, my spare shells were in my backpack.

My nearest partner on the drive was Ed Hartig. He was standing about 40 yards away, near the top end of the spruce patch, where he had halted in place after I fired the shot at the first deer. The buck stood there looking at me, paralyzed, either out of curiosity or in fearful confusion. I hollered at Ed to come quick, explaining I was out of ammo and had a deer facing me a short distance down the hill and in the open. From where he was he couldn't see the animal because of the trees. He needed to move in my direction at least 20 yards before he could view it. The buck stared at me, as if hypnotized, and I pleaded with Ed to hurry over and shoot. Finally, he reached a point where he could see the deer and quickly dispatched it with one shot. Now there was lots of venison to show for the day and we congregated over the fallen buck with a lot of excited conversation and backslapping.

After observing all the comrade amenities, I told my two partners to dress out the buck and I would go over and work on the other animal which, I correctly assumed, was a doe. Regulations for the Kodiak area at that time of year allowed for the taking of five Black tails per person, either sex. Close approach to the deer confirmed that it was, indeed, a large doe. I reached down and grabbed a front leg to roll it on its back to begin skinning. Never suspecting anything, I was shocked to find there was only one front leg. God! I had shot a three-legged deer!

The doe was fully grown, fat, and healthy, and her ability to survive and prosper on three legs was not subject to question at that point. This little inconvenience had obviously been with her since birth but had apparently not deprived her of leading a life just like any other deer. Still, her years of healthy living seemed a bit of a miracle on this bear-infested island. The fact that there were no other deer predators here, other than man, probably helped some.

115

It has always been our camp policy that does accompanied by first-year fawns are not to be harvested. Rather than put the fawns at risk, without the guidance of a mother, we prefer to wait until the following year when the fawns are nearly full-grown, mature deer. Numerous new mothers have made it safely away from out in front of our drives because of this policy and our collective share of island venison has never suffered because of it.

Looking back, the survival of that three-legged doe, until the day I shot her, is definitely an inspiration. I am a meat hunter and make no apology about animals that die to feed me, but I am sure, had I been able to read between the lines of the story of that amazing little deer on first seeing her, half concealed in those trees, I would have let her be.

Chapter 29
On Keeping a Diary

UNLESS YOU ARE BLESSED WITH A PHOTOGRAPHIC memory, my advice is to keep a diary of all your hunting and fishing experiences. If you are like me, without a lot of thought and counting of fingers you can't remember where you hunted in, say, 1990, *what* you hunted, or whom you hunted with.

As a retired big-game guide, and part-time writer, I am constantly falling back on my diary records for information on past clients— memories that long ago became fuzzy. Even as an assistant guide I maintained a diary of every hunt. Usually on the first day in camp I imposed on the hunter for his full name, mailing address, and his home and business telephone numbers to log in my book. On hunts these days, I also ask for fax numbers and e-mail addresses. Although I am careful to log this information in my computer at home, my diary remains the primary source of the hunting experience I had with each client or friend.

I try to faithfully record the events of every day of each hunt. Details such as weather, temperature, what we did during the day, the time we arose and went to bed, what we ate, and who we saw (if anyone!), are all recorded in the book. In a busy camp it is difficult to faithfully make an entry every day—but I try. If I cannot make an entry every day I make it a point to pause as soon as possible, later, and update the book. Delaying making notes during a busy hunt is not a good idea but easy to do. I have found that delay often results in lost information and produces an inaccurate record. If the only time I can find to do this chore is in the bunk at night, then that's when I do it. Probably a majority of my diary entries were made in my sleeping bag, when camp was quiet, by flashlight.

One never knows when these notes will come in handy. Recording the color and, if possible, the numbers on a passing aircraft could turn out to be a record of its last known position in the wilderness, useful information during a later search if the plane comes up missing. With passing years the details of a hunt turn hazy. We can often recall the big stuff but the details tend to slip away. A diary is especially useful if you're interested in writing. It is fun to read the thing years later to shake awake old memories of a hunt. However, it is essential if you need details for a story. My written record has settled a number of arguments about how, when, or where certain things happened.

On a side note, it is always a matter of interest to clients and friends when they see me writing something in my diary, especially when they sense I may be writing something about them! Some guides I have worked for have become particularly irked when they observed me keeping notes. This is a diary and, as far as I am concerned, something personal. In the past I have allowed clients (but *never* other guides!) to read my entries; but only when it became obvious they were spooked about what I might be writing.

To begin a diary, find a nice style of entry book, one that looks good, is a size that works for you and is constructed well to hold up under field conditions. Years ago I located the book I liked and bought a half dozen of them. I now have a uniform set, which won't go out of print, a supply that will last until I won't need them anymore, a set that is smart looking and fits conveniently in either my camp bag or later in a bookcase. My selection has a tough cover that travels well and will not dog-ear with use.

When we grow old, and we all will, these books full of adventures will be a pleasure to browse through, perhaps even a treasure that can be handed down to another generation.

Chapter 30
Alaska Range Moose
First published in *Bowhunting World – Extreme* magazine, retitled *A Moose-Sized Problem*, Vol. 55, No.6, 2006

"HEY," I SAID OUT OF THE BLUE, "WANT TO SEE A NICE set of bones?" The remark startled my hunting partner, Ron Swanson, who, like me, had generally slipped into the early-afternoon sleepies, propped against a spruce tree in the warm autumn sun. We had been spotting for moose since first light and the lack of activity during the morning, and the comfort of the warm early-afternoon temperature, was lulling us away toward a delicious nap.

Quite unexpected, the shiny antlers materialized as I scanned the maze of low birch hills off to the south of the high ridge we were spotting from.

We have a moose down and the highway is located at the base of those mountains, ten miles away.

I had glassed that area dozens of times over the course of the morning without a sign of moose. Now, suddenly, there he was, bedded down in the dwarf willow directly behind the skinny trunk of a solitary spruce tree.

His antlers appeared as though they were nailed to the back of a tree and probably would have been passed over again as tree branches, or an upturned root mass, had I not been using the 20-power spotting scope. He had probably been lying there all morning with his headgear turned at just the wrong angle to reflect the early-morning light. The brighter afternoon sun now betrayed where he lay.

I centered the rack in the scope and gave my weary eyes a break while Ron had a look. All around us the white-topped peaks of the Mentasta Mountains stretched out of sight. Long fingers of fall color streaked up each mountain gully from timberline. In the twelve days we had been back in these hills the short central Alaskan fall had nearly run its course. The birch, poplar, and willow, almost solid green just ten days ago, were now vivid yellows, oranges and golds, and their leaves showered to the ground at the slightest breeze.

It was becoming increasingly easier to spot game in the thinning cover, particularly from our vantage point hundreds of feet above the surrounding terrain.

We were nearing the end of a fourteen-day bow hunt for moose. Time had passed so quickly it seemed only a few days ago that we had loaded our gear into the pickup and headed north from Anchorage, where we both lived and worked, to the interior Alaska community of Tok. There we teamed up with an old high school friend of mine, Gary Hebert, for the rough tractor trip back into the Little Tok River drainage in the Alaska Range.

Gary lived in Tok. At that time he was principal of the public school there. Anxious to secure his winter supply of moose meat, he had already completed a scouting trip with his plane. The Little Tok River was the place to go, he reported. The animals were up high, near the timberline, he had found. They would be tougher to hunt this season. We had hunted from this same ridge the previous year. Despite the physical punishment of climbing up and down this high spot we had decided to camp up here again. The site offered a commanding view and the successful hunt we had experienced the previous season made "Tenacity Terrace," as we had named the ridge, the undisputed choice of hunting spots once again.

Chapter 30—Alaska Range Moose

The tractor trip up the Tok drainage had taken almost a day. We set up a comfortable camp in a wooded dimple on the very top of the ridge. Our spotting point, a rock outcrop barely 40 yards from camp, afforded a good 300-degree view of the country. From here we looked down into two drainages. Toward the south the Little Tok River passed through the landscape, flowing from east to west. A smaller tributary stream passed by our ridge on the west side. It flowed down out of the mountains from the north to a confluence with the Little Tok.

The iron rule, adopted the previous year, was that we stuck to spotting from dawn until dark, or until an animal was located we could make a stalk on. Standard practice was to be up at first light. Game movement was most likely during these early hours. If a bull was found we would keep the glasses on him until he bedded down to escape the rising morning heat, usually about 10 a.m. or so. Half an hour was allowed to assure he would stay put, then one of us, usually the person who spotted the bull, had first chance at a stalk.

Ron and I were on this trip strictly to bowhunt. Each of us carried a handgun, for emergencies, but the only moose either of us would harvest would be with an arrow. This was the understanding we had with Gary. We were guests in his camp, enjoying the convenience of transportation for ourselves and our camp on his tractor rig. He and his usual crew of friends, mostly teachers from Tok, came first. They all sought a winter's meat supply and were big-time serious about the matter. While Ron and I certainly appreciated the value of a moose in the freezer, at the time we were more interested in bowhunting than economics. I had been trying to take a moose with my bow the three previous seasons—with many close calls but no luck.

We always made certain we were useful around Gary's camp, when help was needed, and that we paid our way. A barrel of fuel for Gary's rig usually came with us from Anchorage, or we paid to buy more expensive gas in Tok. To further demonstrate our gratitude for being allowed to participate in the hunt we were always on hand come skinning and hauling time and were at the head of the line for any camp chore. An advantage Ron and I had was that we were state employees. We had a choice of when we took our vacations and we could store up annual leave for moose season. Gary and crew, on the other hand, were all teachers and once the school year started they had to be there. The beginning of school generally coincided with the opening of moose season so the main group had to be in town on all but the weekends. This left the camp, and the woods, to Ron and me during the week. This great moose country was literally all ours to bowhunt!

At first we hunted as a pair but soon found that method generally unsuccessful. We found that two people tend to make three times the noise as one so we gave up doubling and hunted alone. Unless two animals were located at the same time, which happened several times, one hunter remained on the ridge. That person kept spotting for other moose while keeping an eye on the first moose of the day and progress of the stalk. Hand signals, established early in the hunt, saved us a lot of grief. We constructed hand flags to use in signaling. The spotter on the ridge could direct the stalker up, down, left, right or wave him off if the animal spooked.

On several occasions during the first week we worked our way to within 40 yards of moose. Ron got caught in the act by a real book bull just a few yards from a good shooting position. I got caught less than 40 yards from a nice bull by an alert cow in the brush I wasn't aware of. Numerous stalks went sour, mainly because of the difficulty of locating the animal in the dense cover typical of the country. But still, we were having a ball!

After the first week, our great hunting weather briefly turned windy and foul and for several days the moose stopped moving. On the afternoon of the twelfth day I spotted this moose behind the tree.

"What do you think?" I asked, as Ron studied the animal and terrain in the spotting scope. "Looks like a decent moose," he replied. "I'll try for him if you don't want to."

I hesitated for a second before answering, pondering the situation.

It was almost 4 p.m. That left a full two hours until the sun would start to dip behind the mountains. The bull was less than a mile away, all downhill through wooded terrain. The going looked easy and I guessed either of us could be on a final stalk within an hour.

"Tell you what," I said. "I'll go fifty-fifty on this one. We'll flip to see who tries for him."

Luck was with me and I won the toss. My bow and daypack were within easy reach and within seconds I was off the ridge into the willows and on my way.

Reaching the base of the ridge, going became fast and easy through the big spruce on the valley floor. I put some well-worn moose trails, which wandered through the timber, to good use. In about thirty min-

Chapter 30—Alaska Range Moose

utes the character of the terrain changed from wooded and flat to a jumble of low, rolling hills; this was ancient glacier moraine. There were chest-high dwarf willow and an occasional patch of poplar but the country was now mostly open and generally free of timber. I knew I was getting close enough to the bull for him to start being super conscious of noise. I found my course to the moose right on line when I quietly eased my way over the crest of one of the bushy knobs and spotted the bright tines of his antlers sticking up above the brush ahead of me.

He was still bedded down and I was less than 100 yards from him. The wind was better than ideal. A stiff breeze angled across from my left to right as I faced the moose. The best route to him appeared to lie through the brush to my right. That path would keep me downwind of him the entire distance. Best of all, a gathering wind was producing some noise in the brush—with luck, enough to cover most of the sound of my movement.

A few more yards and I knew the dry ground underfoot was too noisy. Keeping my eyes on the antler tops I quietly shed my daypack and jacket and slipped out of my leather boots. I then took off my dark chamois shirt, pulled off my white tee shirt and put the chamois back on. I draped the white undergarment over the top of a little spruce tree, exposing the bulk of it facing in the direction of Ron up on the ridge behind me. I was reasonably certain that by now he was watching me in these open hillocks with the spotting scope. If so, surely he could now see the white tee shirt. I figured this would clearly let him know where I was as well as mark the exact location of my boots and gear. The terrain here all looked alike and I wanted no funny business later, locating my gear, and especially my boots! This accomplished, I began working my way through the brush, in my stocking feet, around to the right of the bull.

I advanced about another 10 yards, agonizing all the while that my blue jeans were just too noisy. The brush, dwarf willow, was a chest-high tangle of stiff little branches, which pulled at and scraped across everything that passed.

Judging from the posture of his antlers the bull had not detected me up to this point. I didn't want to take the chance he would. So, as quietly as possible, I shed the noisy blue jeans and continued with the stalk in my long underwear bottoms and wool sox.

In another twenty minutes I had closed the distance to the moose to about 50 yards. At that point it became obvious that the stalk was in trouble! The jumbled terrain, working so well in my favor until now, turned on me. I suddenly found myself faced with a steep gully, situated crossways between the moose and me. It was about 40 yards across at the top and a good 30 or 40 feet deep, with a bone-dry, brushy creek bed in the bottom. The bull lay in the willows on the lip of the gully, slightly below me on the opposite side. A move directly at him would expose me in the open crossing the gully. I would lose sight of him once I dropped over the edge on my side and not see him again until I would be almost within touching distance of him in the brush up on his side. Going straight for him was too big a risk. Climbing up over the gully lip on the other side would offer no opportunity for a clear shot over the 4-foot brush until I got completely up out of the gully—just a few feet from the bull. A stalk around to the left would put me upwind. I could swing wide to my right, cross the gully and come in behind him, downwind, but the brush there looked impossibly thick. Coming at him from downwind, on his side of the gully, I would still have no opportunity for an unobstructed shot until I was literally on top of him. I was stuck where I was, in my long underwear and stocking feet and the late afternoon was progressing toward darkness.

The only option available was to move as close to the moose as I could get on my side and hope for a shot across the gully. This would mean about a 40- to 45-yard shot, slightly downhill, to where he lay on the other side. This was too far to suit me, especially in view of a rising crosswind, but certainly not unreasonable. I was out of alternatives. If a shot presented itself from here, I would take it.

Moving forward to the gully edge I planted my stocking feet and stood facing the bull across the gully. The next move was his.

I stood there in the gathering dusk, waiting for him to rise from his bed. As I waited I pondered what he might do. There was a remote chance he could move closer. In my mind I pictured him dropping down into the gully, having visions of a 25-yard shot at him in the open bottom. But, I reasoned, by the same token he could rise, take two steps, and disappear in the folds of the terrain in the brush behind him.

Several times he moved his massive head and even over the increasing rush of the wind, I was close enough to hear the brush snap and rub through his antlers. Occasionally I could detect the flick of an ear through the willows but still it was impossible to tell in which direction his huge body lay in the brush. All I knew for certain was that the huge rack, which was mostly above the brush, faced off slightly to my left.

Chapter 30—Alaska Range Moose

In the midst of my pondering the antlers began to turn to the right and there was movement of the brush. He was getting to his feet!

I raised my bow in anticipation of a shot. Every heart beat caused strange little exhales of breath from my lungs and all thought of the creeping coldness of the wind, which by now had begun to tell, faded to unimportance.

I expected at any moment to see the head and shoulders of the bull rise out of the brush. Instead, the antlers dipped low and a huge posterior came into view. This was followed by the rack and then his front shoulders. He had been lying with his body aligned away from me, with his head corkscrewed to his left—in my direction. Now he was facing in the right direction to quickly disappear into the brush. A couple steps and he would be gone!

Holding my breath now, I watched as the big bull gained his footing. He proceeded to shake himself, like a huge dog, spraying moss, leaves, and hair in all directions. This had the effect of throwing him slightly off balance. As a result he moved his left hoof forward, and to his left, to steady himself. In doing so his huge shoulder and the front portion of his body came positioned perfectly quartering away from where I stood across the gully. In an instant, he was completely vulnerable. Unknowingly he had, by that unfortunate off-balance step to the left, exposed every vital organ in his body to the most ideal and lethal of bow shots.

I brought my 62-pound Herters recurve to full draw, compensated for the wind and distance, and released an arrow at a point just behind the black outline at the back of his front shoulder—which now towered above the brush.

The arrow crabbed in the wind slightly as it arched across the gully. The shaft struck a spot slightly to the right of my aiming point and quartered forward into the huge mass of the animal. When the arrow struck him he bolted and kicked out wildly with his hind hoofs, as if trying to strike an unknown attacker. As he thundered off through the brush I could see the yellow fletching of my Microflight shaft embedded to near the feathers in his side.

After spending twenty minutes recovering my gear, pants, and boots, I crossed the gully and began tracking a good blood trail. It was obvious and well defined, even in the red moss and crimson bearberry ground cover. All indications pointed to a fatal wound.

In the gathering dark I was able to track him about 200 yards, flagging the trail, before the light failed so badly that I had to break it off for the night. I returned to camp the way I had come, literally feeling my way in the dark the last few hundred yards. Ron had a roaring fire going to guide me into camp and a victory cocktail mixed and waiting. He had to put up with my nervous chatter all evening. I was consumed with the question of whether we would, or would not, recover the bull come morning. This was good grizzly country and they were everywhere. We spotted them almost daily while glassing for moose and every old kill in the area quickly had a bear on it. There was a good possibility that by being forced to wait until dawn we would find my moose buried under a brush pile with an irate claimant lying on top of it!

To add to my worry box, we were awakened in the night by a light rain pattering on the tent walls. The shower was brief but enough to raise concern about the blood trail.

Come morning we were up at first light. The squall had passed and the day dawned bright and clear. The brush was damp but, contrary to my fears, this proved to be more of a help than a hindrance in tracking the bull. Each tiny blood droplet, mingling with the morning dampness, stood out a brilliant red and speeded us along the path of the fleeing moose. He had traveled little more than 100 yards beyond where I had quit trailing him the previous evening. I found it amazing he had gone so far, considering the damage done to his vitals by the four-blade Savora broadhead.

We were nearing the end of our hunt. The remainder of the time available was spent transporting and caring for meat. Following skinning and quartering we had to pack the meat approximately ½ mile to a spot where it could be retrieved with Gary's tractor and trailer. An easy moose hunt by Alaska standards.

As it turned out, the antlers scored almost 193 points. Well above the 170 Pope & Young Club minimums and number three for Alaska/Yukon moose for that two-year scoring period. A happy ending in view of the four-season jinx that had plagued me while trying to harvest one of these tremendous animals with archery tackle.

When we departed I knew that chances were I would be back in that same drainage next September, following a routine similar to this season's but with a different objective. My partner, Ron, would still be after *his* elusive moose. I would be spotting with him and he would get first chance at any bull we found. My interest would be in the bears that show up quickly on any kill in that backcountry. So, although my motives are slightly selfish, I'll be rooting hard for Ron's success next year.

Chapter 31
Murder Lake, Fact or Fiction?

I FIRST HEARD THE NAME MURDER LAKE YEARS AGO from a kayaking friend. He had once kayaked his way through the 20-plus miles of the whitewater canyon of the Talkeetna River. That canyon, known affectionately as the "Sluice Box," has the reputation of being one of the longest continuous stretches of treacherous toilet-bowl whitewater in North America—not a stretch of river for novice rafters.

Floaters access the canyon by flying up the Talkeetna River, landing in a small lake located to the north side of the river, and then floating down Prairie Creek to its confluence with the Talkeetna. The small floatplane lake has the local name of Murder Lake, a title the origin of which has always mildly fascinated me. The book of Alaska-Yukon Place Names contains no mention of a Murder Lake. It appears to be a name used only by locals and those who appreciate being abused, mentally and physically, by the Talkeetna River rapids.

Some years ago I happened upon a story written by Russell Annabel, my favorite Alaska author. In his book, *Adventure Is in My Blood*, he briefly relates a tragic event which took place decades ago in the Stephan Lake area. Stephan Lake is a much larger lake located a short distance north of Murder Lake. Prairie Creek connects both lakes with the Talkeetna River. Annabel's story involved caribou hunting, good fishing, a poker game, and a hideous murder.

As the story goes, back in Annabel's time, while he and his hunting partner, Tex Cobb, were taking a break from caribou hunting in the area to enjoy the fishing at Stephan Lake, Cobb became involved in a poker game in the camp of some local Natives. There was a Native woman in camp who had apparently been beaten by one of the card players. Cobb sensed bad trouble was brewing inside the surly woman over her beating. He excused himself from the game and he and Annabel beat a hasty retreat from the area, back to caribou country, not wanting to become involved in any pending ruckus. Later, back in civilization, the pair was to learn that the Native lady, indeed, had brutally extracted revenge from her tormentors, this in the form of cutting the tent ropes, collapsing the tent down over the card players, and killing all the men trapped under the canvas with a camp ax. The vengeful lady, according to Annabel, later reported the killings to authorities as self-defense and nothing was ever done to her.

Was the brief account of the incident in the book by Annabel true? Or was it a fine bit of author's license spun around a bizarre local murder story?

To my knowledge there is no other record of the incident, except for the haunting name which fails to appear on any map. Absence from maps means nothing, however. There are dozens of small lakes in the Talkeetna Mountains known only to residents and bush pilots by their local names. None of those, however, have such an ominous handle as Murder Lake.

Chapter 32
Alaska Bowhunting Details
First published in *Bowhunting World* magazine, 2006-2007 Annual

MANY BOW HUNTERS DREAM OF ONE DAY HUNTING big game in Alaska. Years of hunting literature, movies, and more recently video productions, are full of hair-raising accounts of long stalks and close-up shots at the great variety of different animals available here in Alaska. Legends such as Saxon Pope, Art Young, and Fred Bear, just to name a few, years ago drew bowstrings in this country and left behind them a legacy of magic stories.

Currently, thousands of hunters pour into Alaska every spring and fall to live the dream. Many of these are bowhunters. If they come to hunt Dall sheep, brown bear/grizzly, or Rocky Mountain goat, the services of a registered guide are required. (There are exceptions to this guide requirement if a nonresident hunts with an immediate family member who is an Alaskan resident. Check the Alaska Game regulations for details.) For moose, caribou, black bear, or Sitka black-tailed deer, the remaining big-game animals nonresidents typically come here to hunt, a guide is not required. Nonresident aliens are required to be accompanied by a guide for *all* big-game hunting.

Nonresidents need only purchase a hunting license and big-game tags and they are free to pursue the last four animals noted above without a guide, wherever it is legal to hunt them. Be careful with "wherever it is legal to hunt them." Alaska hunting regulations apply on all land, including private land, but *do not* guarantee access to private land. *All* hunters are cautioned to check land ownership before hunting. If land is privately owned, and millions of acres of remote land here belong to Alaska Native corporations, permission to enter the land needs to be obtained from the owner. Land ownership patterns in Alaska are complicated. People are left to their own devices to determine where they may legally be. There is no one map a person can use to check land status. Most air-charter "bush plane" services these days are aware of ownership patterns and can usually be depended upon to drop you off on public land where you can hunt with no problem; either that, or provide you with information on where to obtain a permit if the land is privately owned. Reputable flying services will not knowingly drop a hunter off on private land without a use permit.

Most hunts in Alaska require use of bush aircraft services. Once the animal you intend to hunt is selected you should start arranging flying services for a drop-off hunt at least three months in advance of the season you select. The closer to a hunting season, the poorer your chances of being able to book the exact flying dates and times you may need to fit your schedule. Choosing a flight service for the hunt you want may require a considerable amount of research. Most substantial bush aircraft services have Web pages describing what they offer. Select a region of the state where you would prefer to hunt and search the Web for air services that are headquartered there. Inquiring for "Alaska Air Taxis, Bush Pilots and Charter Services" on the Web will get you started. Expect to pay a deposit to book your flight dates and be sure to obtain a confirmation and receipt document.

Once licenses and tags are bought, land ownership is checked, and transportation to the hunt area is arranged, the visiting nonresident bow hunter can still be hanging out there regarding a number of things.

First, use some common sense before heading out into strange country, running the risk of getting yourself lost. Every year Alaska newspapers are full of horror stories about hunters straying from camp, becoming disoriented, and wandering for days, or longer, without food or shelter before being rescued. In some cases the missing are never found, and it's not always a nonresident who gets lost! During the spring of 2004, no less than eight incidents of lost Alaska locals, just in the southern end of the state, required professional search efforts.

Always carry survival gear with you when you leave an Alaska camp. Bring a special bag along with you, made up in advance, that you can slip in your pack just for this purpose. If you do get lost be prepared to survive. Wishing you had emergency gear with you, after you're lost, won't help one bit. Provide for some light, warm clothing, a warm hat and gloves, a comfortable couple of days' worth of emergency food, a quick, efficient means of starting a fire, and something to signal with. (Remember airport security restrictions. Don't try to get on the plane bound for Alaska with incendiary signal devices or flammable material in your luggage! Buy these in Alaska.) Having a good flashlight is a no-brainer. In the fall (before it snows) half a roll of toilet paper spread round in the brush is almost as good an emergency signal as smoke or a flare—and you can still use it for other things if you don't need it for signaling! You will be very thankful for 50 feet of lightweight nylon cord, and a poncho or space blanket to wrap around you or use to make a shelter if you are forced to spend a night or two in the rain. To a wise person, these days a GPS is an equipment necessity. Enter the location in your GPS before departing camp and the unit will provide you with both direction and distance back to the front door of your tent as it guides you through heavy brush, rain, fog, snow, or total darkness. This is a marvelous piece of equipment which performs as remarkably as it is designed to at most locations in Alaska. The only potential problem is operating in mountain terrain, with surrounded by peaks which could block line-of-sight access to the number of satellites that GPS technology requires. Note that most GPS manufacturers recommend that in addition to their equipment you still carry a good compass with you in the field!

Although they are still very pricey, satellite telephones available these days work anywhere in the world, including Alaska. The first CB radios, and now our cell phones, were only crude preludes to rapidly developing satellite communications. The introduction of satellite telephones has truly marked the end of old, remote Alaska. Get in trouble almost anywhere and you can get on the "sat" phone and call for the help you need.

Once the risk of getting lost is covered, assure that you allow another safety net for yourself during your hunt here. This piece of advice applies particularly to bow hunters. Every member of your party should bring along a heavy-caliber pistol. It is one thing to chase white-tailed deer in Pennsylvania or pronghorns on the plains. It is quite another to bowhunt big game on your own in Alaska. It is impossible to overstate how important it is for a bowhunter to carry a substantial sidearm when prowling the Alaska wilds. Many may find carrying a pistol while hunting with a bow offensive. In this country it is better than a good idea to have a handgun along and worse than a bad idea if you don't. You can never be certain that you will not be confronted, say, by a grizzly when returning to a moose or caribou kill for another load of meat. It is easy to unwittingly place yourself between a mother black bear and her cub and a bull moose can be a senseless beast when bent on attacking anything it might accidentally perceive, at the time, as a competitor during rutting season. In most cases all that might be needed is a lot of violent, defensive noise. A heavy-caliber pistol will provide this. There are few greater feelings of helplessness than being confronted by an irate animal, and having nothing but your wits to depend upon to save yourself. A bow and an arrow just does not measure up in such emergencies, and neither do bear bells or politically correct, and hazardously overrated, pepper sprays. Chances are a sidearm will never need to be drawn, but if it is available when needed, no apology to yourself, or anybody else, will be necessary if it saves your bacon.

In Alaska you can carry an unloaded sidearm in your luggage when traveling, provided it is carried in a locked case, and you declare that it is in your luggage when you check your bags. Be sure to check with your local airline regarding transporting sidearms before you leave home on your trip.

If your plans call for driving to Alaska, you should be aware of the most current regulations regarding carrying weapons through Canada—*before* you reach the border. You will not be allowed to transport a sidearm through Canada—don't even think about it! Travel through Canada will require advance arrangements to have pistols shipped from a registered firearms dealer in your state to you, through a registered gun dealer in Alaska, and then have them returned home in the same manner.

There are a number of good archery supply stores in the larger Alaska cities but available supplies drop off abruptly in smaller communities. Be advised to carefully check your gear and bring *all* the archery equipment with you that you may need for your hunt. I will never forget a guided bowhunting client, on his hunt of a lifetime, who never discovered until our bush plane departed, leaving us on the bank of the river we were to float and hunt for ten days, that he had left all his broadheads sitting on his workbench back at home!

Once your Alaska hunt is over, and you fly out of the bush with your hard-earned trophy and game meat, if you're not prepared you could suddenly find yourself experiencing a very bad case of end-of-hunt sticker shock! A big expense, which is not always fully considered or adequately researched, is the cost of flying your trophy, and especially the game meat, all the way back over Canada to your home in the Lower 48. Not only must you consider transportation cost, but also the time required, after you come out of the bush, to handle arrangements. If your plan is to pack a trophy home with you, as well as the game meat, don't count on being able to fly from camp to town one day and then head for Chicago the next morning. If money is not a serious concern, you can hand the trophy over to a local expeditor and the meat to a game-processing facility. Either of these services is readily available in the larger Alaska cities (Anchorage and Fairbanks) and in a number of the smaller towns. For a price, they will accommodate you. Preparation and shipping of a trophy through an expeditor is a service well worth the expense. They prepare the cape or horns/antlers for shipping and handle all the details that you will have to attend to yourself if you elect not to use their services. With an expeditor you get on the plane and fly home and your trophy is either shipped to you, or to your taxidermist, as you instruct. Preparation and shipping of meat is the big shocker! For example, cutting, wrapping, and freezing a whole moose costs several hundred dollars and can require several days or more, depending on how busy the local game meat processors are. Prior to shipping, the meat must be specially boxed for travel to remain frozen while in transit. Because it is perishable it must be shipped by rapid, and very expensive direct airfreight. The cost for processing a moose, and then having it flown back to America can easily run from seven to eight hundred dollars, depending on where you live. If you can spare the time, standing by until your meat is processed and frozen, you can haul it with you on your flight home as excess baggage. Even at excess baggage prices these days, this will save you considerable money over same-day air cargo service. You might consider hauling only the choice cuts of your game meat home. This would save you some money and you can give away the meat away you don't elect to keep for yourself—but that should be no big problem! Alaska hunting law is specific that *all* game meat must be recovered from the field for human consumption. Although giving away meat must be done in a specified manner, per Alaska game regulations, there is nothing that prevents a person from doing so.

The points to emphasize here are to allow ample time in your return-home travel plans to take care of shipping details, and to be aware that some big costs may be incurred at the end of the trip that you may not have anticipated in your budget.

A comment is appropriate about the amount of precious business or annual leave time you plan to allow for your hunt. It is not wise for hunters on an Alaska adventure to plan on being home on exactly the day after the hunt is over—either that or the world will end! If you will need to be at a important meeting, or at in a specific place the next day or two after your scheduled departure from Alaska, you had best adjust your schedule and provide for some wiggle room. Bad weather, mechanical problems, sudden emergencies, or any number of things can sandbag Alaska travel plans and easily throw you a couple days off schedule.

For a State of Alaska "Hunters Packet," which includes a copy of the current Alaska hunting regulations, telephone (907) 267-2137. There is no charge for this information or for postage.

See you in Alaska.

photo by Charles Allen

Chapter 33
The Woodstove

A FRIEND OF MINE, WHILE FLOATING A REMOTE RIVER in central Alaska, accidentally happened upon a tumbledown log cabin in the timber off the river. It was so old, a part of its obviously well-built roof was near the point of caving into the structure. Like most wilderness cabins, it had the door latched but not locked, making it available, as was the general custom, to anyone who might be in trouble on the trail. There was nothing inside he could use to date when it had been built. It was small, as was also the custom, for the bigger the cabin, the greater the amount of wood needed to heat it. From what was in the cabin, all my friend could figure was that this was probably a deserted trapline shelter.

The only thing out of the ordinary about the camp, a perplexing thing at first, was the rusted little woodstove inside the cabin. The oddity was that the stove was elevated off the floor on a wood crib filled with sand. This raised the cabin heater over 2 feet off the floor, not a real good idea, it seemed, for keeping the lower part of the cabin reasonably warm in country where the outside winter temperature can easily reach fifty degrees below zero.

My friend solved the mystery, at least to his satisfaction, and left the cabin in the woods behind to continue its lonely journey into oblivion. The trapper, he surmised, had neglected to haul enough stove pipe to the site when he first built the place who knows how long ago. The user had to compensate by raising the stove off the floor so the pipe he *did* bring with him was long enough to reach up through the roof, a construction error he apparently never bothered to correct later.

Chapter 34
Needed, Support from America

IF YOU LIVE IN ALASKA YOU REFER TO THE FORTY-EIGHT contiguous states as the *Lower Forty-eight, Stateside, Outside,* or *Down Below.* If you mean to travel there from here, you are going Outside for a spell, and everyone knows exactly what you mean. I have a good friend who refers to the Lower Forty Eight, the place where most other people in this nation live, as "America." His distinction between Alaska and America, sarcastic as it seems, is deeply rooted in the Alaska psyche. It is partly the result of ninety-one years of long-distance management, and considerable abuse, between the purchase of Alaska from the Russians in 1867 and statehood in 1958. The largest share of this abuse occurred as the result of federal resource management or, more accurately, the *lack* of federal resource management. There just didn't seem to be any way the feds could get anything right. From seals to timber and hydraulic mining to salmon traps, with long-distance management from Washington DC, Alaska's resources were constantly subjected to exploitation and ruin. Everything seemed a case of either feast or famine, with little foresight and painfully slow reaction time when any resource found itself approaching the brink of disaster.

Generally speaking, it took a world war for the country to realize Alaska's strategic and economic importance. Following that war, for the first time in history, people began coming to Alaska with the intention of staying. Our typically transient population, which had previously come to partake of the Territory's riches, then leave ("Boomers" they were called), slowly began to get off the boat thinking in terms of building a future and staying for the long haul. These long-haulers, the

Chapter 34—Needed, Support from America

marrow and backbone of Alaska, led the territory into statehood in the late 1950s. The tool used for the job was the Statehood Act.

Without making this a civics lesson, a pact was offered by America to Alaska in the form of a federal law, the Alaska Statehood Act, of July 7, 1958, Public Law 85-508. This same law, in turn, was presented to and voted upon by the territorial population, with the outcome of the vote answering the question : Should we or should we not become a state? Territorial Alaskans voted overwhelmingly in favor of statehood.

One of the promises made in Public Law 85-508 was that Alaska would be granted management authority (on equal footing with other states) over its fish and wildlife resources. The granting of this authority under the law was complete, except…"that such transfer shall not include lands withdrawn or otherwise set apart as refuges or reservations for the protection of wildlife or facilities utilized in connection therewith, or in connection with general research activities relating to fisheries or wildlife." Literally read, as a reasonable person would read a law, Alaska's fish and wildlife resources, subject to the limitations noted, were given away to the state. This appears to be a *very* strong indication that Alaska obtained, in perpetuity—not as a loan, with strings, or subject to any other stated law—complete management authority over her fish and game resources, except within federal parks and refuges. It looked as if the control levers for Alaska's fish and wildlife had finally moved closer to home, where they belonged.

As part of the statehood deal Alaska wrote itself a constitution. The use of fish and wildlife by our citizens is briefly and profoundly addressed in that document. "All fish, wildlife, and waters are reserved to the people for common use."

There had always been the question of aboriginal rights. This issue came to the United States along with the purchase of Alaska from the Russians in 1867. With the passage of the Alaska Native Claims Settlement Act of 1970-71, all Native claims to land in Alaska, including hunting and fishing rights, were, supposedly, extinguished—forever. The Alaska Native population was handed something over $960 million dollars in cash and given title to forty-four million acres of land under the Settlement Act. It appeared that the last potential claim to fish and wildlife ownership or management authority in Alaska had been extinguished. Then, enter the Alaska National Interest Lands Conservation Act (ANILCA) of 1980!

This act is, essentially, a statement of federal policy regarding its presence in Alaska. Under the Statehood Act, Alaska had been allowed to select 102,550,000 acres of public land. 44,000,000 acres were to be deeded to the Natives under the Native Claims Act. The federal government is the owner of approximately 168,000,000 acres of the remaining land, certainly a huge interest to be reckoned with.

The grit in the ointment, however, is the stated policy in ANILCA applying to the use of fish and wildlife resources on federal land. This policy provides that the taking of fish and wildlife for non-wasteful subsistence purposes will be given a priority on federal land—over any other use. People who live in rural areas, who may depend more heavily on fish and game resources because of where they live, will have priority access to those resources, at the expense of any other use or users. This does not mean that in times of shortage, for example a low run of salmon or a crash in a game population, that rural residents *then* get a preference over everyone. It is interpreted to mean, instead, that rural locals get theirs *first*. Only after rural needs are satisfied, do other folks, urban dwellers, get a crack at what is left. Under this law a rural preference *always* applies. Small wonder that this requirement immediately caught the eye of Alaska's multi-million-dollar hunting and fishing community!

It is no secret that the purpose of the subsistence preference in ANILCA is to make up for a deficiency in the Native Claims Settlement Act—after the door was closed. It was not possible for Congress to come back after the fact and give only Natives a resource preference. Those rights had been bought and paid for under the Native Claims Bill and such a bold move would have certainly raised a fuss. But Native hunting and fishing rights, supposedly extinguished by the settlement, had to be restored. So, in place of a strictly Native preference, subsistence rights were given to *all* "rural" residents. In this manner the Alaska Native population, largely rural anyway, was essentially assured the return of rights supposedly "extinguished" under the Native Claims Act. This is a guaranteed slice of a shrinking resource pie, a pie becoming increasingly more difficult to manage every year to everybody's satisfaction—even without federal meddling. As Alaska's rural population grows, and pressure on fish and game increases even more, it is not difficult to see who will eventually end up with *all* these resources.

Many Alaskans favor some sort of subsistence preference, especially

Chapter 34—Needed, Support from America

in times of shortage. There is currently a subsistence law in the Alaska Statutes. But the federal regime views Alaska's law as far too broad and inadequate for meeting the tough rural preference as it has mandated. In the State's view, what is proposed in ANILCA is patently unconstitutional. In 1989 the Alaska Supreme Court ruled that a preference such as the federal government insists upon, based upon a zip code (rural residency), is unconstitutional. It is in violation of the equal-protection clause in Alaska's constitution, which provides for equal access for *all* Alaskans to fish and game resources. To clear the way for a federal subsistence priority to work, and to regain the reneged-upon management, Alaska would have to submit to the blackmail of amending its constitution. This must be done to change something unconstitutional into something legal!

The ointment really gets gritty when one realizes that the federal government has dug in its heels on this policy, insisting that rural residents *will* be given priority access by the State of Alaska to fish and game resources under the federal management scheme. If the State does not provide for this preference, the federal government advised, they would take back fish and game management on all federal land in Alaska and make it so.

Despite a huge amount of pressure and maneuvering in the state legislature to knuckle under, federal deadline demands for the state to comply with a rural preference came and went. Alaska stuck to its guns and elected not to accommodate. True to its promise, on July 1, 1990 the federal government seized management of all hunting on federal land in Alaska. On October 1, 1999, after many more years of threats, it also took back management of fisheries. It is an interesting point that in neither case has there ever been a discussion of a federal taking without consideration given to compensation. Was this not a taking?

At this writing, the battle over who has authority to do what has all but exhausted itself in the federal courts. Alaska had until October 4, 2001 to appeal a federal circuit court case, known as the Katie John decision, which, in essence, held that the federal government has the right to renege on who will manage the fish and wildlife resources in this state. It was obvious that the whole legal ball of wax would hinge on an appeal of the Katie John case to the U.S. Supreme Court.

Then governor of Alaska, Tony Knowles was stuck with calling the shots for how his attorney general would handle the issue. Here was a politician caught in the middle, between a powerful Native constituency, which obviously supported a strong "rural" preference, on the one hand, the hunting and fishing community and advocates for states' rights on the other. Going in the direction of supporting a rural preference, Governor Knowles could elect not to appeal the Katie John decision to the Supreme Court. Going in the other direction an appeal needed to be filed by October 4, 2001. He was damned if he did and damned if he didn't—untenable political ground.

At first, perhaps without adequately testing the political waters, Governor Knowles stated that he would appeal the Katie John decision. By mid-July of 2001, however, he began to waffle and sent up a trial balloon, offering what he viewed as a compromise, not wanting to risk offending either side in the fracas. He now proposed that he would appeal the Katie John decision, but only if Alaskans were offered the opportunity to vote on the issue of whether or not to adopt a state constitutional amendment which would allow the resource preference demanded by ANILCA. If the vote came up no he would appeal Katie John. A yes vote would be a mandate to clear the way for the amendment and the federal preference.

Reaction to this trial balloon was that neither side of the issue liked it. The word from the Native community was that they didn't want to risk a vote. Content with the status quo, they understandably viewed federal management as more user friendly. The preferred position was to have the governor sit tight, do nothing, and let the October 4 Katie John appeal deadline pass. Sportsmen and states' righters didn't appear to want to risk a vote either, and opted to hold the governor's feet to the fire for his earlier promise that he *would* appeal the Katie John case.

In the end Governor Knowles elected not to appeal Katie John and Alaska lost its best chance—such as it was—to wrest game management back from the federal government through the courts.

As of November 2002, Alaska had a newly elected governor, retiring U.S. Senator Frank Murkowski. This meant not only a new administration, but a change of political party (from Democrat to Republican) in the governor's mansion. And the new governor's position on the subsistence issue? The tried, true, and politically safe one— "Let's let Alaskans vote on it."

As of this printing, the issue remains unresolved. Everyone has done much to accomplish nothing.

Chapter 34—Needed, Support from America

The federal government has a huge presence and great ambition in Alaska. A product of Congress, ANILCA cannot be changed, or even adjusted, without broad national support to do so. Down in America, if other folks' congressmen were in office in 1980, they have voted on ANILCA. If they were not in office at that time, most of the current crop of politicians are probably not even aware of the law—or the dual-management fiasco this federal subsistence creation has brought down around the ears of a sister state.

Alaskans have good reason to be concerned over the reneged-upon promise of local control of their fish and wildlife resources. The outcome of an appeal of the Katie John decision, pro-federal pundits assure us, would have been doubtful at best, even *if* an appeal had gone forward. Thanks to Governor Knowles, we will never know the answer to that one. In the meantime, Alaskans are stuck with two fish and game management systems. Depending on where one lives in Alaska, and where that person is standing at the moment, on state or federal land, either he is competing for fish and wildlife resources on equal footing with everyone, or he has a preference working for or against him—an absurd and divisive checkerboard turf battle. A reasonable person could easily be suspicious of the mind-set of federal courts, of the credibility of any federal promise made and, certainly now, a justifiable amount of paranoia regarding any future dealings where Alaska may find itself pushed up against federal muscle.

For the moment Alaska is the only state singled out for this interesting renewable resource experiment. To people who live in sister states, this fiasco begs an answer to the questions, "If you live in another state, do you approve of how fish and game matters are managed where you live?" "How much federal land is there in your state?" Could what is going on here in Alaska become a precedent, setting the stage for mischief elsewhere?

Chapter 35
Three Culprits in Bear Country

IN THE MOVIE *MOUNTAIN MAN,* CHARLTON HESTON, playing the role of a grizzled mountain trapper, explains a fact of life to an upset camp companion. Lying in their blankets in the night the man exclaims, "There's something out there!" Heston knows that Blackfoot Indians are stealing their horses, but rather than jump up shooting, and get them all killed, he advises the man to keep still and that… "there's *always* something out there!"

Few things raise the hair on the back of your neck higher than waking in the dark of night to the realization that something is thumping around outside your tent. It can be as subtle as the sound of light breathing or as pronounced as something tripping on the tent ropes. It is then you truly realize that this thing that surrounds you, which you call a tent, is not designed to keep out much of anything except some of the weather.

People who spend a lot of time in the woods in wild country, especially those who do so for a living, accept the fact that they are sharing the terrain with creatures that live there full time. Most of these animals prefer to do their hunting and foraging during the same time most of us humans like to do our sleeping. Being concerned about bears is a good idea, but it's also a good idea to go to bed at night and get some sleep. Living in a tent and starting at every sound in the night is going to make you a miserably tired outdoorsman in very few days.

It is wise to take some precautions to avoid inviting a large, furry camp visitor; be it black or brown, be it in Alaska, or down south in what some Alaskans call "America." The usual cause of most late-night visits are (1) people food in camp, (2) game meat in, or too close to camp, and (3) poor camp placement. These are numbered here in descending order of importance.

Culprit 1: People food in camp. Be careless about culprit number one and you stand the best chance of company if there are bears around, be it out in the wild or in a park campground. Cooking in tents and storing food inside, or nearby outside, increases your odds considerably for having bear trouble. Game meat may be more attractive to bears but game meat is not always around in camp. People provender, on the other hand, *is* nearly always around somewhere, making camp food the number one culprit.

Thinking of personal safety, as well as peace of mind while sleeping, you can improve the odds against a bear encounter by setting up a cook shack some distance from where you sleep. A poly-tarp cover or a rain-fly over a cook area is just as good as a tent for cooking and eating and considerably less risky. Have your food secured in some type of bearproof container or stored by elevating it, if you can, high enough in a tree with a rope over a branch. Plastic coolers are *not* bearproof—ask any experienced trained campground bear.

Culprit 2: Game meat in Camp. Few things are more attractive to a bear than fresh wild meat. Contrary to general thinking, bears do not live on meat. They love it, and eat it whenever they can, but they are primarily vegetarians, deriving 80 or more percent of what they eat from plant matter. But they know exactly what wild meat is and will take more risk to get to it than they would take for camp food. Because they place such high value on meat, they are inclined to be willing to fight for it. Especially once they have sampled and thereby claimed it. Hanging meat close to camp to protect it from bears is reverse logic and an invitation to trouble. Meat should be stored well away from camp and elevated in trees, or on meat poles, high enough to be above the tallest predator's ability to reach. Plans for a big-game hunt should always include provision for a means of easily lifting heavy pieces of game high enough to put them beyond a predator's reach. Novice hunters don't always consider this provision. If hunting in country where there are no trees large enough to accommodate this, at least make sure that meat is kept far enough from camp to provide a safety margin against a potentially testy claimant. When there is meat in or near camp, everyone should be constantly on guard against unplanned confrontations.

Culprit 3: Poor camp placement. Culprit 3, although considered least important of the three potential bear country problems, is the one that is probably the most easily overlooked. Camping along the edge of a stream or lake, though it may be attractive and handy, can inadvertently place you astride a bear highway. If there are visible trails in the area, and along lake or stream banks in bear country there usually are, camping in the middle of one, or even near it, is not the best choice of spots. If you can, pick a site some distance from a waterway, preferably one that it is relatively open and free of brush. Wild animals prefer good cover and, more often than not, will choose to walk around an opening rather than across it. Dense brush right up to your tent walls is an open invitation for close-up snooping.

Here are some real experiences where people I know, including myself, have failed to pay attention to one or more of these culprits:

I recall a friend telling me the story about sitting up all night in hunting camp, tending a fire under one end of a low meat pole, to keep brown bears off his cooling moose meat. He would periodically tap on the tree next to him with a stick; partly for noise to keep the bears away and partly as a means of keeping himself awake. Leaning against a tree, late in the night he dozed off and apparently slept for a considerable time. On awakening he found that a hind leg, which had been hanging quite close to him, was missing from the meat pole. Brown bears can get very testy and competitive about a moose kill, regardless of who killed it. Some hunters are very lucky and bears can be very quiet.

A few years ago I was sleeping in the cook tent (my idea—and a bad

Chapter 35—Three Culprits in Bear Country

one—to spare guided clients my snoring). This was in good brown bear country, not far off the edge of a premiere salmon stream. Added to the incident, I was guiding a hunter from New Zealand and he had killed a large bull moose. We had the meat hanging about 40 yards from camp, as high in a leaning spruce tree as we could raise the heavy pieces. In the middle of a pitch-black night I was awakened suddenly by what sounded like the clanking of a fry pan. Hearing nothing further after a few minutes, I chalked off what I thought I had heard to imagination and rolled over to go back to sleep. A few minutes later there was no doubt about it when I again heard clanking pans. There was a bear outside, blindly sliding his paws under the tent wall feeling for cooking pans we had in a box on the floor inside the cook shack. I immediately created a whole lot of hollering in the night.

A hunter friend of mine took turns with his hunting companion shouting and firing their rifles out the tent door all night—for a number of nights—to keep Kodiak bears out of camp. They had venison stored high in a cottonwood tree a short distance from their tent. Bears in many places on Kodiak Island are trained to come to the sound of shots fired. To many bears within the Kodiak National Wildlife Refuge, a shot is a dinner bell. It spells easy deer pickings, either in the form of a hide and viscera or the whole animal. My friend came home after a week of hunting—very tired and completely out of ammunition.

Early one morning while I was assistant-guiding for another brown-bear guide on the Alaska Peninsula, a whole bunkhouse full of us was awakened when the first man up at dawn announced that there was a bear molesting bear hides and skulls stored in waxed meat boxes outside in the backyard. These bear parts were awaiting shipment home with hunting clients. We watched out a window as the boss beaned that bear on the head with a large rock, running him out of camp and away from the salted trophy parts. A bear is not always particular about what attracts him into a camp. In this case, parts of other bears did the job.

When my partner caved in on a Dall sheep permit hunt with me at the last minute, years ago, I packed off by myself (another bad idea!) to hunt sheep in the Tok Management Area in the Alaska Range. That trip I had the pleasure of rattling rocks in a saucepan most of one night to keep a wheezing grizzly away from my tent. Two inches of new snow in the morning told the story. He had circled my camp, several feet beyond the perimeter of the tent, a number of times in the night.

Not smelling any food, which I had carefully stored high in a tree away from camp, he left before dawn. Where was I camped? In the funnel of a narrow valley bottom along the edge of a mountain stream—not the best choice of spots.

Visiting a local taxidermy shop several years ago I paused in front of a trophy-sized brown bear rug. There was a large, obvious patch on one side of the bear's face. Noticing me studying the oddity, the shop owner volunteered the story. The bear had been shot from a sleeping bag, and died half in, half outside, a tent door. Despite his best effort, and the fact that he is an excellent taxidermist, he could not disguise the fact that this animal had lost an argument with a shotgun. I never did learn what the culprit was in this case, but there probably was one.

Hopefully our great-grandchildren will still be able to enjoy having bears around, and be able to hunt them. In the meantime, if you spend a lot of time in wild country and you are not paying attention, there is a good chance of hearing something go bump outside in the night. Keeping the three culprits in mind before that happens could help swing the odds in your favor against having a furry late-night visitor outside in the dark, closer than you might like him to be.

Remember what Heston said. "There's *always* something out there."

Chapter 36
How Fairbanks Came to Be

IN 1901 TRADER E.T. BARNETTE, ABOARD THE HIRED stern-wheeler *Lavelle Young*, steamed up the Yukon River and into the Tanana River. The trip had the purpose of establishing a trading post to cater to miners and trappers in the vicinity. Barnette had planned to have himself and his goods set down along the Tanana a considerable distance above its confluence with the Yukon River. However, travel in that direction was hampered by a combination of rapids and low water. A decision was made to ascend the Chena River, a smaller tributary on the east side of the Tanana, in hopes of finding passage around the troublesome rapids; but the water level was also dropping in the Chena River, so this plan didn't work either. The captain of the *Lavelle Young*, fearing his loaded boat might ground going back down the shrinking Chena, insisted he had completed the task Barnette had hired him for and the trader and his 130 tons of supplies were unloaded on the first spot where the captain could nose his sternwheeler ashore.

Barnette wanted the site of his new trading post to be named Chenoa City. Apparently the Chena River was then known as the Chenoa River. Some locals in the early days apparently referred to the new trading post as Barnette's Cache. The accidental location on the Chena turned out to be most fortuitous, for in 1902 a major gold strike was made by one Felix Pedro in the hills about 10 miles to the north of the trading post. In that same year the new gold rush town was officially named Fairbanks, not by Barnette, but by a vote of a miners meeting. The name had nothing to do with the quality of the banks of the Chena

River. Apparently as a political favor, the naming was made in honor of Senator Charles Warren Fairbanks of Indiana, who was destined later to be vice president under Theodore Roosevelt.

And that is how Fairbanks came to be Fairbanks.

Chapter 37
A Hunting Partner

AFTER PONDERING THIS SUBJECT FOR A TIME, I FOUND that in the past I had never looked seriously at what goes into selecting a hunting partner, or tried to identify the factors I must have always inadvertently considered in the process. Pondering lead to the conclusion that the best way to identify the factors was to look at the best of my past hunting companions, partners slowly and meticulously accumulated over the last fifty years, at what had worked in these past relationships, and why.

Let me preface this little analysis with the comment that, to me, hunting time is quality personal time. Each year I head for the woods to recreate or, more precisely, to *re-create* myself. Hunting, why men hunt, and what draws us to the sport with such compulsion, is an elusive mystery. I have tried to put this mystery into words a number of times, only to fail miserably with each try. I only know that I selfishly treasure every moment spent when the cool fall days pull me away into the hills, and how generally intolerant I am of being distracted from its siren call by less than almost perfect company.

Few things can have a greater effect on the success or failure of a hunt than whom you choose to hunt with. A good, steady, dependable companion (or companions), is a key ingredient in the making of a memorable hunting experience. A good partner is like a favorite barber, one that cuts your hair just the way you like it—every time. Or a trusted auto mechanic, who fixes your car right the first time—every time, and always charges what you consider a fair price. These people, once you locate them, are valuable treasures to cultivate and keep. The loss of an ideal hunting partner, for whatever reason, creates a void that can take years to fill.

Alaska is my home. It's been almost twenty years since I received word that an old hunting partner of mine had died of cancer. In a business move, he had taken a job in Idaho and he and his family had left Alaska and moved on to another life. Neither of us were good letter writers. We were both busy earning a living and raising families and outside of the occasional note, usually regarding the latest hunt, we generally lost touch over the years. But still, from time to time, his line of work brought him back to Alaska. On several of these occasions he called ahead and we set up a hunt. I never hesitated to accommodate. We both loved to hunt, there was always the respect each of us had for the other's ability and dependability, and we worked together in the woods like a pair of wolves. I always pause for a moment, remembering this good campmate, especially when viewing treasured video copies of old 8 mm movies we took on past hunts and this old friend flashes across the screen.

Embarking on a new partner relationship requires a good bit of advance knowledge about the other person, and then at least a couple of short field trials. Before a serious hunt is planned, here are several things that might be considered about a potential candidate.

First is a question of compatibility. Is this the kind of guy you could stand to be cooped up with if the weather goes bad and you can't leave the tent for days? Do you hate his bad jokes? Does his smutty language bug you? My perception of how personalities will mesh is important. I always cringe when I recall a friend telling me about a (one-time) hunting companion who began every morning with a Tarzan call from his sleeping bag. Some things you just won't know about people until after you have been in camp with them for a time. But you had best have a good idea, in advance, about compatibility before you even consider a field trial.

Another stalwart companion, whom I usually introduce to strangers as "one of my deer hunting cronies," has been a fixture complementing my Sitka black tail camp in the Kodiak area for many of the years I have hunted there since I bought the place in 1982. A more levelheaded and dependable guy you will never meet. He is first in line for camp chores, always in the right spot on a deer drive, and selflessly tries to overload his own pack when there is venison to be carried back to camp. He loves the open Kodiak hills in November almost as much as I do, and he has the irritatingly friendly habit of sneaking along a cabin gift on every hunt. This man can hunt with me anytime.

Next—is the candidate dependable and does he appear to know what he's doing? If you get sick or hurt, will he do the right things and keep a cool head? If you're hunting within earshot of town this is not such a big deal, but when the bush plane drones off and leaves you in the middle of nowhere, and won't return for ten days, you had best be with someone you can depend on.

I have an old, trusted hunting companion I want with me any time I might get in a real pinch. I have never told him this, and I probably should, but if, for instance, I am ever in Africa, faced with a charging Cape buffalo, with potential death flashing before my eyes, he is the guy I want standing at my side backing me up.

Based on what you know about a prospective partner, does he come across as a guy who will pull his own weight? Hunting can be hard work at times. Do you think he will hang in there at the end of a long day when most of the party wants to make one more deer drive? If the weather is not quite what it should be, will he fold on you and head for camp? There are always things to be done on a hunt, as well as hunting. Will this guy pitch in and do his share or not? I'm not talking about the novice, who requires and deserves some slack along the learning curve. I'm talking about the guy who knows better and, out of laziness, will deliberately choose to let you do many things he *knows* he should pitch in and lend a hand with.

Years ago I had the distinct displeasure, while working as an assistant, guiding for another guide, of being stuck in a spike camp with another assistant guide who would never lift a finger to help anyone but himself and the client *he* was guiding. At the end of the day, if my client and I got back to camp first, dinner was ready for all of us when he and his client stumbled in. If he got back to camp first I always found that he had fed himself and his client and we were left to fend for ourselves. His stated reasoning was, "Hey, I was hired as a guide, not as a camp cook." I filed away this man's attitude should I ever be asked for an observation about his performance.

Keeping tabs of the cost of a trip, and who pays for what—equally, you hope—can easily get members of a party out of joint and be cause for hard feelings. Have you found that the candidate you're considering always out-fumbles you when it comes time to pay the lunch check? Did he have you pick up the tab for that last fishing trip, because he forgot his checkbook, and then later also forgot that you paid his share? Do you end up driving your rig every trip, and when hauling this guy along find that you always end up paying for all the gas? A candidate with these qualifications is waving a red flag and unless he is your boss, or your father-in-law, and it would be politically unwise to leave him behind, this guy has already flunked the hunting partner test.

There may be trips on which you find too late that you are saddled with a deadbeat. In a situation where you may be concerned about this happening I recommend that you announce, in advance, that you have estimated a trip cost and that you are collecting a kitty, an equal share from every member of the party, to cover all expenses. This is justified by pointing out that one person handles all the money, pays all expenses out of the kitty, keeps receipts and provides for a reckoning of the remaining money when the trip is over. If more money is needed in the course of the trip each member coughs up another equal amount—and everyone is advised in advance that this could happen. Even when there is no deadbeat involved, this is a good system for an accurate accounting of trip costs that guarantees that each member pays an equal share of expenses.

If someone you're considering for a partner performs well on these four tests he's probably worth taking a chance on. Even then, you really will not know for certain how a person will handle himself, or how really compatible the two of you will be, until the acid test of a hunt.

Good luck to you!

Chapter 38
West Kodiak Passage

Published in abbreviated form, and titled *Point-Blank Bear*, in *Outdoor Life*, December/January, 2002

"Above all, what I have tried to relate to you was the sense of fear in me as I kneeled in the grass waiting for the bear's next move. The hair still stands up on the back of my neck when I think of it."
Bowhunter Bob Ameen to the author, March 30, 1999.

I KNEELED THERE IN A HUGE, FLATTENED SPOT IN A SEA of waist-high, honey-colored grass. I knew this was an animal bed and from its size there was little doubt that a Kodiak bear had rested here, probably within the last day, if not the last few hours. The imprint in the grass was oval shaped, roughly the size of a king-sized bed with the corners cut off—testament to the size of the animal. The surrounding terrain was flat as a billiard table. All around the tall grass stretched out

Bow hunter Bob Ameen poses with his huge Kodiak brown bear.

of view toward the low hills on either side of the valley, the monotony of the scene broken only by the occasional willow bush. It was wet, my rain gear was cold and clammy, and I was getting stiff from the past three hours of silent inactivity.

Off in front of me was the object of my being here, and the reason

I knew I probably knelt in a bear bed. A huge Kodiak Island brown bear lay sleeping in another bed of grass, scarcely 20 yards away. I knew he was there and that he was asleep, I could hear him snoring. I also knew exactly where he was because at one point earlier—by this time I had lost track of exactly how long ago—he had rolled over in his bed. As he did so, a huge front paw, with a pad the size of a tennis racket, momentarily came up above the grass. I had no trouble seeing the long, curving white claws on the pad, a classic characteristic of a large, older bear. A bow hunter likes to get close for the sake of an easy, well-placed, shot but I had never planned on anything like this!

I had begun my stalk, closing the distance to the bear from 50 yards to the present 20, over three hours ago. Mercifully, the cold wind and driving rain that had plagued my partner and me all morning had backed off to a point where the temperature was almost tolerable—at least to a person swathed in polar fleece and pricey rain gear. Although three hours is a long time to be exposed to the kind of tension the current situation generated, I now realize there was a benefit to be gained from the waiting. Earlier, when we began the stalk, I had butterflies the size of bats in my stomach and my legs were weak and rubbery. All my natural defense mechanisms were advising me to get out of there! Even my hunting partner, Jim Hayes, who now stood, also dead still and freezing, 15 yards behind me with his .338 Winchester Magnum at the ready, had counseled earlier, "Bob, this is a really *big* bear! Maybe you should shoot him with the rifle." In addition to being a good friend and coworker Jim is a registered Alaska big-game guide with a number of successful guided bear hunts under his belt. That's why he was here as my backup and his advice was so important to me. I have never told him how perfectly logical his suggestion was that I shoot this bear with a rifle, and how tempting the idea was at the time. The long three-hour stalk had given me time to evaluate all the things the early afternoon had brought rushing at me so fast, time to calm down and think a little. My shaken resolve to face up to this bear with archery tackle was given the time it needed to become stronger than the fear—for the moment at least. Over the hours it had gradually become clear to me that there was no alternative to waiting out this bear's next move and doing this thing, as I had planned, with my compound bow.

These last hours also provided plenty of time to contemplate the events that brought us here.

The year was 1994. In July, after ten years of trying, I had finally

Chapter 38—West Kodiak Passage

drawn a Kodiak brown-bear permit in the Alaska Department of Fish and Game's annual permit lottery. After so long a wait I wasn't sure if it was good luck or that the Fish and Game drawing computer had just finally taken pity on me. At any rate, I quickly enlisted the help of my guide friend, Jim, and we laid on a hunt for early November.

We both live and work in the Wasilla, Alaska area, north of Anchorage. I had bow-hunted deer on Kodiak Island every season for years and during that time developed a considerable body of knowledge regarding the best deer holes on the south and west sides of Kodiak Island. In the course of my studies, one particular drainage stuck in my mind as having the best potential for bear. Jim's guiding experience was gained at locations in the state other than Kodiak and so the choice of a specific hunting spot, within the permit area I had drawn, was generally left to me. After talking with Jack Lechner, bush pilot and owner of Cub Air out of Kodiak, all the signs pointed to this small drainage and low range of hills on the west side of the island. For the sake of maintaining the anonymity of one of my favorite Sitka black-tailed deer spots, I will just say that this drainage empties into salt water on Shelikof Straits somewhere on the west side of Kodiak Island.

After drawing the permit, and prior to this bear hunt, I had also organized a deer hunt into this same spot with two other longtime hunting partners. This gave me the opportunity to scout the country for bear.

On Kodiak deer hunts we purposely avoid all thought of bears. They pose quite a hazard to a bow hunter who doesn't want the burden of packing a firearm large enough to be effective against one of these monsters. The bear problem is even more acute if there is an active salmon stream around and on west Kodiak, in the fall, every stream large enough to float a duck is usually choked with salmon. There is a large degree of comfort in never seeing a bear on a deer hunt here. You really don't want to. It is sort of like denial, a false sense of security that maybe there really aren't any bears around, when you damn well know there are! On Kodiak you are a wise hunter if you swivel-head as you dress a deer, or someone keeps watch, and then you get out of there and away from the kill site as quickly as possible. For safety's sake, meat is stored *more* than a respectable distance from camp. There is hardly a tree above head-high in many areas on west Kodiak, so there is nowhere to elevate game meat to keep it safe. You can shoot a brown bear in defense of life and property but you can't shoot a bear to protect game meat. If he can take it away from you it is his. Getting home with venison from some of my past deer hunts many times in the past was a matter of luck.

Our advance deer hunt to this spot had been a success. Between the three of us we had taken eight nice Sitka black tail bucks, all of which exceeded minimum scores for the Pope&Young bowhunting records book. We saw a few bear this season but not as many as I had expected. It was advice from our pilot, Jack Lechner, to concentrate on an area about 2 miles upstream from where we had chased deer. That clinched where Jim and I would hunt during the first week of November. Jack's comment that, "if I have seen one bear in that spot I have seen a hundred," was the clincher.

After spending several days weather-bound in the city of Kodiak, on October 25 Jack dropped us, our camp, and a motorized raft off on a sandbar along our stream, using his balloon-tired Super Cub aircraft. It was several miles upstream to the spot where we planned to camp and a bit farther yet to where we would hunt. Because of all the rain the water level was very high and we were able to motor our gear and ourselves upstream to the campsite with the raft by late afternoon of the first day.

Jim and I hunted this drainage for a very eventful seven days, mainly by sitting quietly and glassing the hills and the valley bottom from high spotting positions in the hills on the north side of the valley. During that week we located twenty-one bears, at different times and places, and we bagged three more Pope&Young qualifying black tails that ventured too close to our spotting positions to resist.

The bear had either been sows with cubs, too small, too far away, or were spotted too late in the day to take a run at. Several had been real bruisers, or "Bobos" as Jim calls a big bear. On two occasions we had spotted one exceptionally nice bear, probably the same one each time, along a brush-fringed creek coursing through the middle of the valley. We correctly assumed this little stream to be full of salmon. In all probability, we figured, this bear was feeding on fish somewhere near the same open spot where we were catching glimpses of him. Each time we caught him in the open he was in the vicinity of what appeared to be a beaver lodge. The willows along the creek were head-high and easily hid him from view nearly 100 percent of the time. The dead grass alone was high enough to hide most of any bear. All he needed to do to completely disappear was to lie down.

In camp the evening before we had discussed the chances of finding

Chapter 38—West Kodiak Passage

this bear in the dense cover at the beaver lodge. We carefully weighed the wisdom of venturing out into the valley the next morning to check out the spot. This was a coldly calculated move, since to date we had avoided smelling up the flats with human scent. These animals make a living with their noses. They know if a human has passed by within one hour, or several days, and react accordingly. If we missed him in the brush, Jim advised, and laid down our scent out there, there was a good probability this bear would be history.

We had started out from camp this morning through wind-driven rain. It was an uncomfortable, cold day. I was already half numb at that point, but as much from the thought of possibly facing a huge bear in the brush as from the effects of the weather.

We crossed the creek and slowly hunted our way along the valley floor, carefully glassing as we moved, until we located the beaver lodge. The lodge was occupied and the beaver had dammed the creek, creating a large pond upstream and backing up salmon below the dam. A small spillway over the beaver obstruction was a bottleneck that created a natural feeding site, as evidenced by the beds, scat, fresh salmon bones, skins, and heads we found littering the banks in the area. This spot was being fished regularly by a bear.

After scoping out the area, we decided to utilize the top of the beaver lodge, one of the highest points in the valley, as a spotting platform. After about two hours Jim caught a glimpse of a bear in the brush about 100 yards upstream. If it came past us going to the fishing hole, we hoped, I could ambush it from the top of the beaver lodge. We waited another two hours but the bear had vanished as quickly as it had appeared.

After another two hours of waiting, with no further activity, we began to get cold and impatient. I suggested that we move slowly upstream into the wind and see what we could find.

We had gone only a short distance when Jim arose to full height, gazing intently ahead of us. He lowered himself again and whispered to me, pointing. "Bob, is that a bear over there, lying in the grass?" I had a look and, sure enough, I could make out what appeared to be a rough, dark line of bear fur against the tops of the lighter-colored grass. "Yes," I whispered back. "I can see fur waving in the wind." We were looking at a sleeping bear, at a distance of about 30 yards. "Should I sneak in there and shoot?" I asked somewhat incredulously. "No" Jim replied. "We have been seeing that sow with cubs in this area. If it is *her*, and you sneak in there, you won't know it until the last second. We had best back out of here and look this thing over from the beaver lodge."

We had no more than completed backtracking to the beaver house when the bear stood up and began slowly ambling in our direction. I dropped out of sight behind the top of the lodge and rapidly began peeling off rain gear. I wanted to be ready to shoot in the event he kept coming and passed close by. However, he walked only a few yards toward us, then lay down out of sight again. He was well upwind from the spot we had been when we first saw him and still a considerable distance from where he might pick up our scent. In the rush, peeling off the raingear, I had still not had more than a glimpse of him. Jim had a good look. This was not the smaller sow we had seen on previous occasions, he advised me. It was a real monster bear and it was at this point that he suggested—more like recommended—that I shoot him with the rifle. This advice was not offered unwittingly. Out of respect for the size of the bear he meant it, and he had me questioning myself! By this time it was 3 p.m.

As we waited I mentally considered the possibilities. An alternative to a shot from the beaver lodge would be to ambush him in the creek. If he started fishing, I could stalk up and shoot from the stream bank. In mid-thought the bear rose from his bed one more time and began walking in our direction. I had an arrow nocked in my compound, ready to shoot, but just when an ambush began looking like a possibility he lay down in the grass again. This time I got a good look at him and I think my temperature must have dropped a good ten degrees.

We played the waiting game for a considerable amount of additional time before I finally made up my mind to make a move on the bear where he lay. I cannot describe the jumbled thoughts in my mind before I was able to muster the courage to take a step forward. In the end, inside myself, I guess, I was more concerned with copping out as a bow hunter than with facing up to this bear. It took forever for me to make my way through the tall grass to the point where I was close enough to hear him snoring.

I turned my head. Jim was there behind me, at port arms and off to one side, intently looking past me into the tall grass. I mustered a questioning shrug at him and he returned one likewise. By now it was 6 p.m. and the short Alaska November day was fading into evening. Shortly, shooting light would be gone and, along with it, this great opportunity. In anticipation of shooting I had shed my heavy rubber gloves a few yards behind me. I soundlessly stepped back to retrieve

Chapter 38—West Kodiak Passage

them and then moved forward again. I pitched them ahead into the grass, off to one side of the bedded bear, in an effort to mildly alarm him and make him rise. He never budged. Then I threw my Bic lighter. Same effect, nothing. I was out of things to throw, so next I elected to move forward, my progress perhaps a tad noisier than before. I took only two steps. He heard this, lifted his head and then sat up on his haunches like some sort of colossal dog. My entire body felt like it was tingling with electricity as I brought my bow to full draw. The way the bear sat, the front of his huge body quartered just slightly to my left. There was no opportunity for a clean arrow shot except head-on, through the armor of his rib cage. Even a compound bow, with its forgiving let-off at full draw, cannot be held back indefinitely. I soon had to let the bowstring ease forward. As the string and my arm relaxed, the bear and I made eye contact for a fraction of a second—which seemed like an eternity. I thought he had caught me but he had not. Something had to give here. My throat was dry as sandpaper but, in an effort to make him move, I attempted to clear it. What came out of my mouth was an ungodly sound, something halfway between a gurgle and a growl. Jim told me later he thought the bear had growled! At the sound, instead of turning tail to run, or standing up on his hind legs, perhaps offering some sort of better shot, he came slowly up on all fours and started walking toward me!

I didn't want a frontal shot but he was as close as I wanted him to get. It was either shoot him with the bow, now, or fall down and place my fate in Jim's hands. The chest which faced me was broad as a refrigerator. At less than 20 yards I knew I could easily place an arrow into his vitals—provided the hunting point could get through all the bone ringing that cavernous chest. I actually remember mentally coaching myself to place the arrow just under his chin and slightly to my right, to concentrate on that spot, release clean, and follow through.

The arrow went out of the bow like a BB, downrange, and completely disappeared into the bear's chest. Jim had a bird's-eye view of the shot through his rifle scope. At first the bear never even acknowledged he had been hit and continued a few more steps in my direction. When he suddenly realized something was wrong he calmly swapped ends and made a generally unhurried retreat. Here was an animal, so huge and well protected by virtue of his size and status in the world, that panic appeared to be scarcely a part of him!

After releasing the arrow I turned my back on the bear and began *my* retreat. At this distance there was no chance for a second shot anyway. "Should I shoot?" Jim urgently inquired. "No." I replied. "I think it was a good hit." As I reached my partner and the comparative safety of the rifle, the whole experience came crashing down on me. The adrenaline had been flowing too long and my legs just plain gave out and I half fell and half sat down in the grass. As I did so Jim yelled out "He went down!" I could sense the excitement in his voice. This got me back up on my shaky legs again for a look—but the bear was out of sight, down in the grass again. Jim added that he had seen the bear stumble several times before he fell. Miraculously, it was all over.

To allow a respectable amount of time to pass before approaching the bear, we walked back to the beaver dam to retrieve our packs. We found him before dark. I had made the shot at a measured 18 yards. He had traveled 26 yards before going down. Unbelievably, the arrow, tipped with a single-blade Phantom broadhead, had passed completely through the bear's chest and body cavity, piercing every major organ except the kidneys and one lung, and then lodged in a hind quarter. His chocolate-colored hide squared 9 feet 6 inches and was in perfect condition, except for the absence of most of his right ear. This was an old wound, probably gained in a fight as an adolescent, perhaps defending the same fishing hole where Jim and I found him. His skull measured 27 5/16 inches, putting him in fourth place in the Pope & Young records at the time he was scored in 1995. It is an extra special honor for me that this bear's score dwells in the Pope & Young records book between the larger and the smaller of two great brown bears taken by the incomparable Fred Bear!

I don't think I will live long enough not to be overwhelmed by the raw power and majesty which the life and death of this great bear represents. Whenever I look at him, or pause as I often do to think back on the experience, I am filled with a personal mix of awe, admiration, regret, and the ghost of my fear. A mix perhaps only I can understand—and one that I still cannot adequately put into words that do the feeling justice.

Since that hunt Jim and I have relived that rainy Kodiak afternoon many times. As he reads this, of all people I know he will understand my feelings. After all, he was right there with me and it was as much his experience and his trophy as mine.

Chapter 39
Lamentations of a Camp Cook

IT IS PROBABLY A SIGN OF CREEPING OLD AGE WHEN you notice that an increasing number of good things that used to be on the market are no longer available. I know that books go out of print and styles change, but that's not the kind of thing I'm talking about. What I'm referring to are familiar little things it seemed you could always buy, that you used regularly and really liked, that all of a sudden are no longer around. Good, functional, appreciated items that just disappeared and are no longer available—anywhere!

Never mind that lean pork doesn't taste like pork anymore, or that flabby chickens raised in shoeboxes don't taste like chicken used to. What I miss are some good, handy items that were once common but which you can no longer buy. A number of these items were as functional, in terms of transportation and storage, as they were easy and convenient to use or prepare, particularly out in a remote camp.

Whatever happened to canned corn on the cob? These came packed four cobs per container in an unusually sized can. Pulled from the can and warmed in their own vegetable broth, ears of corn were a welcome, unusual change, particularly in a remote diet. This food item was a great thing accompanying garlic bread and a feed of steamer clams, dug fresh from the beach in front of our deer cabin. No need to worry about bruising or babying fresh corn or wondering if the frozen stuff, coddled without refrigeration in camp, was thawing and growing soggy. You just opened the can and there it was!

Speaking of clams, why did they stop canning whole clams? It used to be you could buy the real article—large, whole clams packed in delightful clam nectar. I'm not talking about those wussy canned baby clams from Taiwan that you can still find in any canned seafood section. I'm talking the *real* thing! I believe this was a Pacific Coast, Canadian product. Even at the cabin, where we usually dig and eat our own clams, there are frequent paralytic shellfish poisoning scares that keep a prudent person away from a clam shovel. Good chowder is a tradition in our camp, even in the midst of a PSP scare, and canned clams, *real* canned clams, were the answer. These may be available in other parts of the country but I haven't seen them where I live for years. I would pay a completely unreasonable price per can if I could buy them in my local supermarket again!

Does anyone remember canned sweet-cream butter? In our neck of the woods the brand was Darigold. It came in a flat, yellow, 1-pound can with red lettering. It looked like a huge tuna can and at the market you found it in the freezer section. In camp it stayed fresh for weeks in its own container which could be conveniently resealed with its own plastic lid. Not only was it convenient, it was absolutely delicious. Eating is was as much like eating a fine mild cheese as eating butter. I haven't tasted what I think real butter should taste like since canned Darigold disappeared from the market *many* years ago.

Probably not a lot of Alaskans remember when canned whole milk was common. I'm not talking about canned evaporated milk, I'm talking canned, 100 percent whole milk. Neither am I describing the stuff that comes in a foil-lined cardboard box these days; boxes that crush, leak, are as tedious to transport as fresh eggs and squirt all over the place when you lift an opened container out of a cooler. This milk was sealed in steel cans and had an unopened shelf life of months, well beyond the time boxed milk containers these days deteriorate, spoil, turn mushy and leak all over the cook shack. The common brand names I remember were Avo and Real Fresh. I grew up with canned milk. At the time it worked well, much better than the pricey, and most often lumpy, "fresh" stuff that arrived off the boat once or twice a month in bulging frozen cardboard cartons. Served as cold as you could make it, canned whole milk was as good as you could get in the absence of the real thing; and the steel cans would still be as functional as they ever were.

Another item was packaged instant sour cream. All you had to do was add cold (canned!) milk to a package of this stuff, beat it well and

Chapter 39—Lamentations of a Camp Cook

you had a fine, thick topping for baked potatoes or a good sauce to use in casseroles, on pasta, or with meats. In its absence, it has been necessary to replace this convenient, light, foil-packaged product with heavy pints of the real article, which require refrigeration from the get-go.

How about topping for desserts? Another item gone from the grocer's shelves these days is packaged Dream Whip. Like the sour-cream mix, this came in light, convenient foil packages and all that was needed was to add cold milk and beat well. This produced a sweet, creamy topping for puddings, Jell-O, canned fruit, fresh berries, or pie. The Dream Whip we are used to now can only be bought in frozen tubs in the grocery freezer section. It is either kept frozen or thawed and then refrigerated. A nice deal if you have a freezer, or even a refrigerator, in camp!

I miss the small, c-ration-sized cans of beef or chicken tamales we used to buy. The inside bottom and sides of the can were thickly lined with cornmeal and the center was filled with sauce and meat. The socially acceptable method of preparing and serving them was to remove the paper label, open the top with a can opener and set it down in a hot water bath about halfway up the outside of the can. Lightly boil the water about ten minutes and, bingo, you had a delicious hot tamale, which you could dump in a bowl or eat right out of the can if you chose to. You can still buy long, skinny, canned tamales in taller cans these days. They are passable, if you don't mind lame cornmeal and watery sauce.

It is a well-known fact that in the bush the cook is generally the recognized camp doctor. It is also a fact that I have had to be content with keeping some other kind of medicinal spirits in the cookhouse since they took Vat 69 Black Label scotch off the store shelves years ago.

Civilization is highly overrated.

Chapter 40
"Oh My God, I'm Dead!"
Previously published in *Bear Hunting Magazine*,
November/December 2005, under the title *Oh no, I'm Dead*

THE GULF OF ALASKA COAST BETWEEN THE CITIES OF Cordova and Yakutat is a 200-mile expanse of wild, lonely, and generally uninhabited country. One would need to look hard to find a more remote area anywhere in Alaska these days. Ships pass by, miles offshore, and big jets fly overhead daily, most times so high it is impossible to locate them without a visible contrail, but most of the year this country is deserted. Fishermen come here in the early fall, either to net the huge silver salmon from its rivers commercially or to patronize the few sport fishing lodges that are found here. In Alaska, big numbers of fish typically mean big numbers of brown bears and the big bears abound along this remote stretch of coastline.

It was moose that attracted Vern Kuder, a Cordova, Alaska resident, and his hunting friend, Peter Bierle, of Escondido, California, to this area during September of 2002. Whereas the bears thrive along the salmon streams, moose do nearly as well on the lush vegetation in the surrounding swamps that feed these same streams. Peter and his wife had flown their Cessna 180 from California to Cordova that fall, as he had done so many times in the past. Peter is a bow hunter who has taken many species of American big game with archery tackle, but the chance for this hunt found him too near the end of his vacation. In the time he had left he agreed to fly Vern south down the coast from Cordova to hunt. This would be a meat hunt. Vern would do the hunting with his rifle and Peter would be his cameraman. Arrangements were made by Vern to use a friend's commercial fish camp cabin near

Chapter 40—"Oh My God, I'm Dead!"

the mouth of the Tsivat River (pronounced sigh-vat). The Tsivat is a premier silver salmon stream about 10 miles south and east of the foot of Bering Glacier. Along with the cabin they would have a skiff and outboard to use on the river.

The afternoon of September 16 the pair motored up the Tsivat to a temporary moose-hunting spike camp belonging to another friend. The camp was situated in a grove of spruce along the river. Passing through, they found that everything in camp a bear could reach had been trashed. A large tent, left erected and waiting for the hunters to return, had been torn to pieces. They left the boat there, angling north and east into moose country, off the river on foot. The afternoon was warm and both men left their jackets in the boat. Their goal was the open swamps off the river where they hoped to call a moose into the open.

Vern used a walking stick in the woods. He was nearly recovered from a year-old knee operation but still didn't trust himself to climb spruce trees to spot for moose—the proven method for locating animals in this brushy country. Peter did the climbing and spotting while Vern stayed on the ground and did the calling. They had no luck finding moose.

Early in the afternoon they heard a tremendous roaring off in the woods. Vern thought it sounded like a jet plane but Peter, with his better hearing, thought it must be a bear, or perhaps two bears fighting. The general direction of the commotion was behind and to the west of them, back toward the river. This roaring continued, off and on, all afternoon.

As the sun dipped in the west they started back to the boat. Peter had a GPS and walked ahead of Vern. Some distance before they reached the river Vern halted his partner. He knew of a small swamp slightly off their line of travel and wanted to check it out for moose sign. He handed Peter his rifle and told him to return to the boat. He would have a quick look into the swamp and then rejoin his partner at the river. Peter headed for the boat carrying both the GPS and their one rifle.

Peter arrived at camp about 5 p.m. He expected Vern to join him at any moment. The roaring of bears, now only a short distance off to the west across the river, sporadically continued. About an hour later Peter was suddenly faced off by a sow brown bear, accompanied by a cub, walking into camp. She was the apparent camp wrecker, immediately belligerent, and attempted to intimidate him with three bluffing charges. Protecting himself behind a huge spruce tree he was able to holler her away without having to shoot. In camp, with the rifle, he was reasonably safe. Vern, still a considerable distance to the north and east up the river, was not to be so fortunate.

After checking out the swamp Vern proceeded generally west toward the sunset. Without a GPS to guide him in that over-head jungle his idea was to find the river, then find camp. Reaching the Tsivat he first headed upstream, hoping shortly to locate the spruce grove. He soon realized this was a mistake and turned around and headed downstream again. It was getting dark. It would have been reassuring if he could have hollered at Peter, and received a reply from camp, but his reasoning was that they were still hunting and he didn't want to risk running off a moose. He was walking along, parallel to the river, when a huge brown head appeared, rising above the cut bank of the stream, scarcely 20 feet away.

Vern's first thought was "Oh my God, I'm dead!" This was undoubtedly the biggest brown bear he had ever seen in all his years in the Alaska wilds. He recalls the tiny ears extending from the sides of this gruesome head, a characteristic of old, large bears. (Younger bear's ears are carried more on the top of the head, and appear progressively lower toward the sides as the bear ages and its head grows.) Vern estimates it took only two to three seconds for the bear to reach him. "I would never have had time for a shot if I'd had my rifle," he asserts. "All I had time to do was spin around, throw my walking stick in the general direction of the bear and dive under some alders." He tried to jam himself under the angling trees for protection, clutching the trunks as hard as he could. The bear bite down on his right leg, above the knee. It picked him up, pulled his 200-pound frame from under the trees like a rag doll, then apparently dropped him.

From that point, details of exactly what the bear did next get understandably vague. Vern pulled his hands up around the back of his neck and head and played dead. The bear apparently stood over him, he has no idea how long, and he could both hear and feel the animal breathing on him. He knows the bear nudged him, apparently looking for signs of life, but he is not sure how many times.

After a while the bear appeared to leave. By now Vern's senses were coming back. He was cold, shaking, and hyperventilating—not good things for a person trying to play dead. He was afraid to look up for fear the bear would return and attack him again if he did. The bite on his leg didn't hurt that much; more accurately, he recalls, it was more

Chapter 40—"Oh My God, I'm Dead!"

of a sting than bad pain. After an estimated ten minutes he could no longer lie still and rose slowly for a look. His glasses had been brushed off in the mauling but he could still see that the bear was gone.

By this time it was getting dark. He knew he had to get out of there as fast as possible and get medical attention. He *had* to get downstream to Peter and the boat. The quickest way, he reasoned, was to wade right down the river. "I knew it was a risk," he says. "In my mind I gave myself about a fifty-fifty chance of being mauled again if I tried." To aggravate the situation, because he had lost his glasses he had some trouble seeing. He stepped out into the river and started downstream. "Sometimes the river was only knee-deep, and sometimes it was up to my armpits." The cold water aggravated his hypothermic condition but, he now recollects, probably served to ease most of the sting from his wounded leg. He had gone only about 100 feet when he reached a bend in the river. In the fading light, even without his glasses, he could see ahead around the bend and a distance downstream. There, standing in the river, was a huge bear; the same size and color as his antagonist—and likely the same bear.

The bear was facing downstream, away from him. It was apparently involved with fishing and had not heard him. As quietly as possible Vern climbed out of the river. He knew he would need to swing well out through the woods to get around this animal. "Earlier I had no time to be afraid. Too much happened, too fast, to allow it. Now I had to leave the river (with each hip boot full of 20 pounds of water) and didn't know if I could make it. It was *then* that I began to get concerned."

Vern detoured out into the woods around the bear. All the while he was getting colder, weaker and more disoriented. Shock was becoming an enemy. He wandered around in the alder swamp, trying to locate the big grove of spruce and camp. It was his experience in the area that helped him. Out in the woods, against the last rays of twilight, he recognized an old eagle's nest in a cottonwood tree. He had seen it many times and now knew where he was. Once more he headed west to the river and began wading again. It was then he heard Peter whistle from camp. Vern hollered and got a reply.

It was about 7 p.m. when Peter reached Vern with the boat. At first he didn't believe that Vern had been mauled. The only visible evidence was his torn right hip boot—that and his uncontrolled shaking. Peter got him into a warm jacket, set him in the boat and headed downstream.

The trip down the shallow river in the dark was quite remarkable. Fortunately Peter had been running the boat the whole trip due to Vern's problem knee and cranky back. With its deep holes, shallows, submerged logs, and overhanging trees, the narrow, braided Tsivat is difficult enough to navigate in broad daylight, let alone at night.

They arrived at the landing downriver in the dark. It was still a considerable distance from the river to the cabin. The borrowed four-wheeler they had parked at the landing had water in the gas and quit on them before they made it to the cabin. So, to add insult to injury, Vern had to walk on his own the last 300 to 400 yards to the shelter.

It was not until they removed his hip boot that they learned the extent of Vern's leg injury. Blood oozed from two huge puncture holes, each visibly at least an inch wide and deep. Both of either the upper or lower canine teeth of the old bear had apparently been broken off. Broken teeth are also typical of old bears. This left

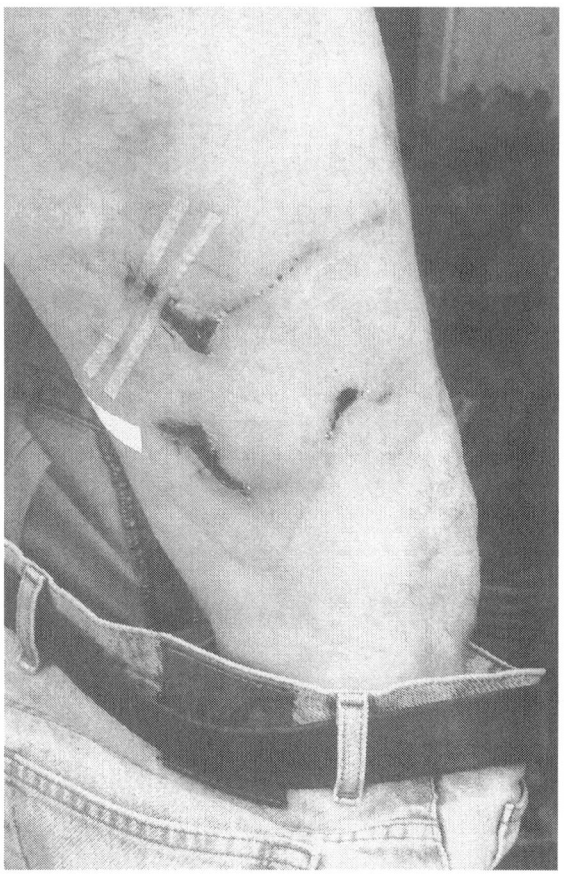

Cordova moose hunter Vern Kuder poses to show his bear bites. photo courtesy of the Cordova Times

Vern with only torn and bruised skin where the missing teeth should have punctured two more gaping holes in the other side of his leg. The fisherman's cabin had been cleaned out after last fishing season and there were no first-aid materials. They used folded paper towels pressed down firmly over the wounds to stop the bleeding and cause the blood

Chapter 40—"Oh My God, I'm Dead!"

to coagulate. That was after they had flushed each puncture wound with the only disinfectant available—half a bottle of vodka! Once the bleeding slowed they tightly wrapped the paper towel bandage with plastic packaging tape. Vern swears that getting that tape off his skin later was the most painful experience of the entire episode!

It was not until early in the morning that they were able to heat Vern up enough to stop his shaking. A warm cabin and hot tomato soup slowly brought him back from the edge of hypothermia. Carefully considering his condition, the two elected to wait until daylight the next morning to evacuate Vern to the hospital in Cordova. This, rather than risking a night takeoff from the sand flats along the river. As it turned out, bad weather, come morning, delayed flying to Cordova until early afternoon.

Vern is a tough guy, especially tough for a man of his sixty-six years. Upon arriving at the airport, he hopped into his own pickup truck and drove himself to the hospital!

Later, I asked him if he would be concerned about those big bears along the Tsivat in the future. Would he ever go back in there again moose hunting—or for any other reason? "Of course I will," he replied. "That bear knocked my glasses off. I got to go back in and get 'em."

Chapter 41
The Fly Fishing Malady
Previously published in *Fish Alaska* magazine, *Final Drift* section. August 2004

A FLY FISHERMAN I'M NOT. I AM, HOWEVER, CURIOUSLY curious about those afflicted with this illness and the strange behavior of people under the influence.

This fall I had cause to journey to a fishing lodge on the Tsiu (pronounced "sigh-you") River along the coast of the Gulf of Alaska. The Tsiu drains the low coastal plain to the east of the foot of Bering Glacier, approximately midway between Cordova and Yakutat, Alaska. Driftwood Lodge, where I stayed, is owned and operated by Charles and Jody Allen. This is one of three fishing lodges near the mouth of the Tsiu, all of which cater mainly to people addicted to the process of leading fish out by the lip, using flies.

Charles informs us that the Tsiu River has a consistently huge, and one of the most consistently dependable runs of silver salmon in Alaska. This means few slow spells and clients booking a one-week fishing expedition here can typically catch silver salmon anytime beginning the last week of August and extending through the first week of October, until their arms are sore. A "slow spell" appears to mean not catching fish quite so fast.

To me, a person standing waist-deep in cold water, catching and releasing 8- to 12-pound silvers, one after the other, for seven days, is certifiably insane. In a bold, intimidating mood I conveyed this opinion (in so many words!) to several of Charles' fishing clients at the lodge. I found myself invariably talking to a repeat customer, people who have fished the Tsiu from several to as many as eight straight years. I wasn't able to provoke anybody.

Chapter 41—The Fly Fishing Malady

During gourmet supper every evening at the lodge, the conversation is a continual roar of stories about the day on the river. Topics can run from fishing technique to the types of flies used, the variety of fish knots tied (including the holding strength of each knot—and I thought hand loaders were weird about their ballistics talk!) and even who fell in the river. Remember now, these stories are being told among the same guys that have fished together all day!

A frequent dinner topic is: Who caught and released the most fish for the day? Like the red badge of courage, it is a status thing to be the person who abused him or herself the most and has the sorest fishing shoulder (never mind that there are numerous fish guides standing by to unhook and release each fish for you).

Leaking waders are ignored. Cold, wind, and rain are irrelevant. Broken poles or messed-up reels are no deterrent. Like friendly winos sharing a bottle, a spare pole or part comes from out of nowhere and the relentless catch-and-release continues.

Democracy is the rule here. Every evening after supper a quick town meeting is held and fishing plans for the next day discussed. Usually, most want to be on their way at first light and on the river, fishing, as soon as humanly possible. That means breakfast at 6 or 7 a.m. for the hard chargers. The few souls that are more casual about this fish hunt are free to delay departure to the fishing hole until later in the morning—after a hot shower and a leisurely breakfast.

Despite the fine food available at the lodge for those who choose to avail themselves of it, many days I observed the entire complement of fishermen electing to eat a "shore lunch." During nice weather this often amounted to a cold sandwich, cookies, and a cup of thermos coffee delivered to the river. Shore lunch serves to spare fanatics the loss of precious hours of fishing time that coming, going, and eating a hot lunch in the lodge dining hall would have required—another testament to the self-inflicted sacrifice and zeal of these fly folks. I wonder what would happen if, God forbid, one of them expired on the river. I have this picture of the body being dragged by the chest wader suspenders from hot spot to hot spot, up and down the river, until the end of the fishing day when a break for a decent burial could be arranged.

Knowing nothing about fly-fishing, and fearing I might catch the bug if I even touched a fly pole, I elected to try my luck the first morning with a spinning rod. First, I moved downriver to some shallow water, below where the main group was beating the water to froth with fly lines. No one else fished in my spot. Surely this patch of faster water was less than optimum and would be more of a challenge than the "hot spot" above, where fish were being caught at a rate of one after the other. As I stood on the bank rigging my line I heard a rushing sound, mindful of floating up into Class II water on a canoe trip. I looked down the river to see a wall of fish ascending the shallows, heading toward me. We were fishing near the river mouth. The tide was coming in and so were the fish. It was unbelievable. One third the width of the river was being pitched and worried by salmon, frantic to get through the shallows and up into deeper holes. In that "bad spot" I caught and released three fish in five casts—and I'm not a good fisherman. After that I put the pole away for the day.

Many places in Alaska that are good for catching salmon are also good for seeing bears. This river is one of them. Fishermen coming to the Tsiu with a pricey pole for the fish should also bring a good camera for the bruins. The sight of a brown bear crossing the river toward them, bent on stealing a free salmon, is one of the few things I have seen that is capable of distracting a dedicated fly fisherman from the heat of pursuit.

For those who appreciate the challenge of combat fishing, this river would certainly be a disappointment. You can still snap a fly line here without the annoyance and downtime involved in hooking a neighbor. Although the word is out, and hoards of fly aficionados are planning their way to this river, bookings are usually available and there's plenty of room to accommodate your wildest salmon-fishing fantasy along the acres of open gravel bars on the Tsiu.

Chapter 42
Powerful Confused, but Never Lost
First published in *Bowhunting World EXTREME* magazine, 2003, under the title *A Long, Long Night in Kodiak Country*

THE BRIGHT BLUE SKY OF MORNING WAS FAST GIVING way to A graying afternoon. A weather front was moving in from the northeast—the typical scenario for a December storm rolling in off the Gulf of Alaska over the Kodiak Island area.

Long before, I had turned around and begun a gradual descent off the mountain, toward camp, through the giant spruce forest. Our tent home for this five-day deer hunt stood hundreds of feet below, at tidewater, behind a sheltering point of land along the east shoreline of Izhut Bay, a rugged indentation in the coast on the southeast end of Afognak Island.

This was the last month of 1981. Little did I realize that I would be a tad more humble, and a considerably wiser woodsman, at the end of this hunt.

That morning I had left my four rifle-hunting companions in camp and, against collective judgment, headed off on my own for a day of hunting. I am a bow hunter and saw the need to be far away from their choice of weapons and other hunting activity. We would all meet late in the afternoon and swap tales.

Sneaking my way through the mossy undergrowth, I jumped several Sitka black tail deer during the course of the day. All easily eluded me. These close encounters had piqued my instincts and I moved slowly and hunted hard on the return to camp, despite the distance and the lateness of the day. Not wanting to retrace my exact steps, I climbed 100 yards uphill before turning to angle downhill again in the direction of the beach. This would put my ascent over some undisturbed terrain. A light snow began to fall on top of the 4 or so inches already on the ground.

Soon after turning toward camp I cut a set of brown-bear tracks. They were fresh enough to warrant a nervous swivel-head. It could not have been more than minutes before this bear had laid down a path for me to cross. Concentrating more on the tracks and hunting than on where I was going could have caused me to miss the momentary, ever so slight leveling of the terrain before it slowly began dropping off again in front of me. Bearing slightly to the left, a natural navigation tendency of mine, I continued the gradual descent down the side of the valley.

I t was getting dark now and the snow began to swirl in a rising wind. I mused that I had timed my return exactly right. I would step out of the tree line onto the beach in the fading light, the last hunter in camp and just in time for the cocktail hour and fish fry planned for the evening. I like it this way. I have always taken a silent, private pride in being the last hunter in for the night. However, as I approached the beach fringe of trees I recall a feeling of misgiving. Something was not right. Pushing the last few yards through brush and a dense wall of young spruce, I stepped out onto the beach. I recalled a mental note of this iced-in lagoon, made as we flew past in the Grumman Goose yesterday during the flight in. I had angled off course and down into the wrong bay! Camp was in the next gouge in the coast to the north, now about a mile away, with a near-vertical 500-foot ridge between me and safety and comfort for the night. It was getting darker by the minute and the snowfall, furious by now, was quickly obliterating everything beyond a few yards.

Every time I recall this misadventure I think of the movie *Mountain Men*. In that movie, when asked if he had ever been lost in his wanderings in the Rocky Mountains, actor Brian Keith, playing the role of a grizzled old trapper, replied, "No, powerful confused for a month or two, but never lost."

So, here *I* was, not exactly lost but, for the moment, definitely in a state of powerful confusion. My immediate impulse was to make a run for it. I had 500 feet of altitude to negotiate and then something more than ½ mile of dense woods and shin tangle beyond that. Darkness by now was near complete so it wasn't a question of reaching anywhere *before* dark.

I unsnapped my army web belt and rummaged around in my butt pack for my flashlight. The batteries were in good shape but the light was a chronic quitter—bad connection or something—and I had to

Chapter 42—Powerful Confused, but Never Lost

beat on it periodically to keep it working. Not the most dependable tool. This would be all I would have between me and being effectively blind in the blackness of the woods. If I tried for camp, and the flashlight quit, the only options I would have would be to feel my way along, until I hurt myself, or sit out the night under a tree in the freezing temperature and falling snow. Either was a blueprint for disaster.

My impulse to run for it won the moment. I pushed through the beach fringe and back into the woods. In front of me was a blow-down. Four huge spruce trees had toppled upon each other in the wind and gone down in a broken tangle, probably last year, or earlier. I could see well enough to know the branches were brown and dead. Working my way around this mess I started up the steep hillside. I went only 30 yards or so when reason took hold again. Trying for camp, much as I wanted to, was not the thing to do. Staying where I was until morning was not going to be a fun thing, but I knew it was the right thing.

The Kodiak Island area, like Southeast Alaska, has a soggy maritime climate. What looks dry rarely is and starting a fire, especially in a snowstorm, is a survival test all on its own. On the coldest night a decent fire will keep a person alive, even one soaked with sweat, as I was. If I was to spend the night out here I *had* to have a fire. With the aid of my cranky flashlight, I gathered up and dragged in dead spruce limbs from the blow-down for firewood, piling up a heap the size of a Volkswagen. It took half my matches, my airline ticket jacket, a roll of nylon cord and my soggy underwear to get a fire started. I piled up green branches 16 inches deep, as insulation against the frozen ground, for a reasonably comfortable seat by the fire. An army poncho, carried in my butt pack for emergencies, spent the night wrapped around me, a much better arrangement, I soon found, than using it as the lean-to I first fashioned to "reflect" the rays of the fire upon me. It worked better, and produced more reflected heat, as I held it out around the fire, like batwings in the night, to warm me again each time my fitful dozing was interrupted by the uncontrolled shaking of early hypothermia.

Far-off booms, periodic shots fired by my companions, came to me through the snow and wind over much of the night. I was downwind of camp and my pistol shot replies to their signals went unheard, lost across the vastness of Izhut Bay.

Later accounts told me there was fear for me in camp that night. Most were unspoken thoughts involving the huge bears still roaming

175

these hills in December when the weather is warm. Several times during the night, awakening abruptly in a fitful state, I hallucinated. I saw an image of a person clad in white furs, standing, watching me through the snow from the woods at the far edge of the firelight. Several other times the dark form of a huge bear appeared to me, crouching on all fours, glaring at me with red coal eyes—only to disappear the instant my mind cleared. Imagination can be a cruel thing in the dark of night—especially when you are alone.

The Afognak beach was my classroom that night and I sat in the swirling snow being taught some humbling lessons.

Lesson one came to me as a statement of the obvious. Hunting alone in wild country is a fool's game. Because of the storm, nobody would know for sure where to look for me. I had covered miles, in all directions, since leaving camp that morning. Had I been badly hurt, or become hopelessly lost, where would anyone have searched for me, especially after the new snow had obliterated every track in the wood? In an emergency, hunting with a good partner doubles both your chances. The need for others to find you, or at least to know where to look for you, has to outweigh the macho of wandering the wood alone.

Lesson two was nearly as obvious. Had I not turned around in the growing dark at the head of the evening, and stayed where I was safe for the night, preparing early on to survive, things could have easily turned for the worse. I have always maintained that Alaska will kill you in a heartbeat, if you give her half a chance, and this experience just reinforced that conviction. But I could just as easily have been a hunter caught away from camp at night anywhere in the world where the temperature and weather have such potential for mischief.

Lesson three was to be thankful for the things that I had carried with me. What I had in my pack and my pockets was all there was—there was nothing else to work with. Any one thing less, the poncho, my flashlight, dry matches, or even the warm wool hat I had tucked in my butt pack, and that long night could easily have been a much larger slice of hell. In such a fix there is no substitute for being as well prepared as you can make yourself in advance.

Lesson four came out of the hours I had to sit and think about the things I *could* have had with me. It is clear that my life may have depended on a fire that night, which I had so much difficulty starting. A modest amount of some kind of flammable fuel in my little pack

Chapter 42—Powerful Confused, but Never Lost

would have spared a lot of grief. Then there was the cranky flashlight. Even in its testy state it did a yeoman's job of lighting the way to firewood and it was a comfort against the dark many times. Had there been a more dependable light in my kit, would I have gone for broke and struck out over the mountain for camp; and would I have made it? Up to that point I had never carried much more than a modest lunch while hunting. Now I will always remember how willingly, late in the night on that Afognak beach, I would have gladly paid a hundred dollars for a can of Spam!

In the early morning, rummy with fatigue after a night of feeding the fire, I was ready to move at first light. The last thing within easy reach to go on the fire was my bush bough seat. As the first glow of day began peeking through the timber, the storm had the last laugh. I no sooner took the first step away from the fire, heading for camp, and the snow abruptly quit. Climbing through 16 inches of new snow, I topped the ridge just as the full light of day brightened that end of the island. I popped a pistol round from there, announcing my ability to still do so, and the grim rescue force in camp, preparing for a search—with no idea of where to begin—immediately disbanded, heading off instead for deer hunting.

Later, one of the band, the one I would have expected, came around the beach to meet me to confirm that I was still in one piece. Then he too wandered off to hunt.

Inside the big tent, my undisturbed sleeping bag proved a stronger draw than a day of chasing deer in my exhausted state. I must have fallen asleep as I began lowering my head toward the pillow. I recall my last thought was that, as soon as possible, the gang off hunting must know that, while I may have been powerful confused for a while, I was never lost.

Chapter 43
Have We Been Here Before?

TWO MOOSE HUNTERS WATCHED INTENTLY AS THE De Havilland Beaver aircraft landed on their lake and taxied up to where they stood on shore. The hunters had been lucky. Each had shot a huge bull moose. The Beaver was here to pick them up and haul them home.

After the pilot came ashore he surveyed the pile of gear and moose meat on the bank and quickly announced that this was too much to haul out in one trip. A second flight would be required to get all their goods off this lake, and for this they would have to pay for the extra flight.

"Why is that?" inquired one of the hunters. "We took two moose off this lake last year and *that* pilot never said we needed two flights," he argued. A lengthy discussion ensued with the result that the pilot finally gave in and consented to try hauling everything in one trip.

The overloaded Beaver used up most of the short lake surface in take-off and, barely airborne by the time it reached the end of the lake, crashed into the timber along the shore.

All three people in the plane were knocked cold but, luckily, were otherwise uninjured. Both hunters came to at about the same time and one, a bit dazed, asked the other, "Where are we?" The second hunter replied, "Oh, just about in the same place we were at this time last year."

Chapter 44
Bear-Baiting Myths

Author's note: This article editorializes my position in support of the free choice Alaskan hunters currently have under the law to harvest, or refuse to harvest, black bears using bait materials. This is written from the viewpoint of a bow hunter, although all *hunters are currently free to use this method of hunting if that is their choice—which is as it should be.*

HUNTING BLACK BEARS OVER BAIT IS CURRENTLY, CIRCA 2005, legal in Alaska, although a voter initiative was attempted in 2004 calling for a ballot-box ban on this method of hunting. A flurry of anti-baiting letters appeared in the press prior to the 2004 election. This was countered by an equal flurry of letters from writers who had no ethical problem with hunting black bears over bait. As the debate escalated, the previously innocuous little black bear suddenly found itself elevated to poster-baby status.

Nearly every year, protesters come out of the woodwork and appear in Alaska newspapers, or at State Game Board hearings, in opposition to the hunting of black bear using bait.

It is rare that opposition to the use of bait for attracting and hunting black bears is attacked on biological grounds. Objection typically comes from the heart, not from the head, and the status, management, or the well-being of the bear population are rarely issues. A majority of opponents testifying in opposition to bear baiting typically represent one of several animal-rights groups. Most often the spokesman lodging a protest are quick to note the organization which sent him or her. A display of power and membership numbers is an important part of the game.

My issue with their issues is that the act of baiting bears is neither unfair, lazy, unsporting, or unethical, as is maintained. I will attempt to defend this proposition using my head, not my heart.

My bowhunting career in Alaska seriously began the moment I returned after mustering out of the army in the fall of 1969. I did most of my bear hunting during those early years, soon after returning from the service. Heading into the field in the spring was a highly relished tonic after a long, inactive winter. Fall hunting rarely involved black bear, except by accidental encounter. There are just too many other more prized animals in Alaska to hunt during the autumn. Spring was always my black bear season and tree stands over bait my method of choice.

Over time I built a string of tree stands at various locations. I recently paused to count how many during those early years. I counted only the stands I had built just for the purpose of hunting bear—both black and brown. I don't doubt that I have missed a few but I'm reasonably sure I haven't counted the same stand more than once. The number I can recollect building came to forty-eight.

My bowhunting career extends back into the "good old days." We hardly knew what camo was then and the newfangled portable tree stands never won favor with me. Although I *did* buy a portable rig once, I found it generally so bothersome I used it only a few times and eventually ended up giving it away. Instead, I opted to construct my platforms from scrap lumber and natural material out of the woods. I don't recall anyone ever objecting to any of my hunting stands. Other people rarely found them. I kept them simple, hard to see, and placed them far out in the woods off the beaten path.

This array of tree stands varied from a 2-by-6 board nailed between a tree fork, to covered platforms on which I could camp, day and night, sometimes for longer than a week at a time without coming down from the tree.

For black bear I came and went daily from planted baits. For brown bear I was always stationary for days on end, either along a salmon stream, a well-used bear trail, or over an old kill of some kind. Brown bear cannot be purposely baited; however, the head, hide, and viscera of legally killed game animals, as well as natural kills, are legal bait materials. One of the best natural baits for brown bears, provided you can stand the incredibly horrible smell, is a beached dead whale.

I will leave the brown bear behind and only discuss the bear that can legally be baited, Ursus Americanus, the black bear. Of the forty-eight tree stands I have constructed, an estimated forty-two were built to hunt black bear.

People opposed to baiting typically maintain that this method of hunting is too easy. *Easy* seems to be the key word here. Because bear baiting easily works so well, they maintain, it follows that it is patently unfair, a lazy method of hunting, and, therefore, unethical. If it were *that* easy to harvest a bear over bait I might agree. However, unless I did something drastically wrong during my earlier hunting days it was my experience that exactly the opposite is true.

Chapter 44—Bear-Baiting Myths

I have successfully taken four black bear over baits and a fifth on an open hillside feeding on blueberries. The hillside black, a fall bear engrossed with the berries, was considerably easier to stalk and harvest than any of the other bears which were taken over bait. This was not a fluke. I have had a number of opportunities to harvest other bears since, while afoot on the ground, at just as close a range or closer. Those opportunities were offered by bears in berries, along salmon streams, on beaches, animals caught feeding on winter kills, or just by inadvertent contact out in the woods. For various reasons I have chosen to leave a substantial number of such bears alone. Had I elected to harvest any of these other animals I would never have had to pass a bow hunter education course or attend a bear-baiting clinic. There would have been no need to obtain a baiting permit. I wouldn't have had to travel to and select a site at a remote spot, beyond roads, trails and habitation, post warning signs around that location, pack in materials, and build a stand. Neither would I have had to locate a bait supply, transport the food materials to the site once or twice a week and then spend weeks of evenings and early mornings, cold and bug-bitten, waiting for a legal bear to appear. I do not concur that hunting over a bait is either easy or lazy!

Legal bait materials are limited to biodegradable items which quickly disappear into the remote environment when hunting is completed. What doesn't disappear must legally be cleaned up and hauled away. Opponents of baiting are partial to using horror stories of doughnuts and bacon grease smeared across the countryside to paint as distasteful a picture as possible to suit their emotional argument. The fact is that hunting bears over bait, including the food materials used at a bait site, is one of the most closely regulated hunting practices in Alaska.

As I have noted, the four blacks I have taken over bait required building forty-odd tree stands over the years. That equates to ten-plus stands per bear. To me, at least, this attests to the efficiency of the hunting method and the "ease" with which a black bear can be harvested using this means of hunting.

Many stands produce nothing—a bear never comes. Some sites bears will hit but never show themselves when you are there—regardless of what time of day you choose to try to sneak in and catch them. Other sites produce sows with cubs. If that happens, you might as well pull up stakes and go home. You cannot legally hunt sows with cubs and once a family has found a bait it will not leave, even for a considerable time after you cease placing out food.

Occasionally, while bait hunting in Alaska, a brown bear is attracted. Again, you might as well pack up and leave. This has happened to me several times and in such cases weeks of preparation and work flew out the window.

Another argument used by people opposing bear baiting is to assert that a person hunting over bait has an unethical advantage in being able to pick and choose a larger animal from the multitude of animals which, supposedly, flock to bait sites. I would like to know where these people hunt and how they obtained this knowledge. There are many more small bears than there are large ones. An average black bear will tend to measure 5 feet, usually a bit less, from nose to tail. Small, inexperienced bears will come to bait more readily than bigger, smarter ones. Bigger black bears did not get big by being stupid. I have sat on stands on numerous occasions and caught glimpses of truly big bears off through the woods checking out the situation—only to have them back away and leave. After studying these bears I knew they were coming in to the bait only after dark, after I had left. The idea that hunters over bait have the easy choosing of big animals is part of the myth that bear baiting is so easy and effective that it simply must be unfair.

Another argument people opposed to baiting like to use is that bruins eating food off a bait station become habituated to handouts and eventually evolve into trouble bears. There is no evidence to support this claim; especially if a hunter is following the law and operating as far from human habitation as the law requires. Black bear are opportunists. They will eat whatever is available, wherever it is, and they will feed on a bait as long as food continues to be provided. Once the food supply ceases they will eventually move on to whatever else is available. The likelihood of bears having the mentality to equate food placed out in the woods, as bait, to humans at other locations is a convenient stretch. Common sense dictates that if a rural dweller leaves chicken feed, dog food or garbage about on his property he will have trouble with black bears. *Every* black bear is a potential trouble bear! This is a fact of life to people who live on the fringes of wild country, regardless if a hunter is baiting bears miles away or not.

Proposition Number 3, a ban-bear-baiting initiative appearing on the November, 2004 statewide Alaska election ballot, was soundly defeated by a three to one voter margin.

Chapter 45
Sourdough Don't Fly

First printed in *Fish Alaska* magazine, *Final Drift* section, May 2006

A BUNCH OF YEARS AGO FIVE OF US PILED ONTO A WEIN Airlines jet at Anchorage, Alaska bound for a fishing experience in the Kodiak area. The names of most of the members of the party are irrelevant and, to protect the innocent, will not be mentioned here. The tale I am about to relate significantly involved only myself and one other member of the group. To protect that one person I will refer to him only as "Big Bill."

On most shared adventures I am the self-appointed camp cook, partly because no one else usually wants the job but mostly because I like to cook. To get a leg up on my responsibility as provender provider in this case, I had carried aboard the Wien jet that morning a quart mayonnaise jar containing an active sourdough starter. One should bear in mind that this event occurred long ago, during those carefree days when travel was void of strip searches and other personal violations in the name of modern airport security. The starter sponge was to be used over the next few days in camp to prepare sourdough hotcake and fried fish breakfasts.

Just before takeoff I had some sort of premonition, an instant attack of worry about the jar. If I had the same shudder run down my back today as happened to me then, I would swear it was nothing less than the ghost of Julia Child whispering a warning to me.

The ominous batter was tucked away in my hand carry. What if the gases from the dough built up and burst the jug? Who knew what would happen, especially once the plane reached cruising altitude and the cabin pressurized? I loosened, then quickly retightened the jar lid.

This produced an immediate hissing, gurgling sound. Quick action was obviously needed or, I feared, the interior of my carry-on was going to be the site of a culinary disaster! Big Bill was in the aisle seat next to me. I handed over the jar and told him to slip back to the toilet, loosen the top in the sink and let off some pressure. This he did, returning to his seat just in time for takeoff.

Now, Big Bill is prone to a ruddy kind of red face anyway, but when he plunked down in his chair he was giggling so hard his cheeks were crimson and his eyes wet with tears. He advised me that the jar had all but exploded, blowing pancake starter over much of the bathroom when he let loose the top. He had tried to clean up the mess but it was far too extensive, plus he had been pressed for time by the impending takeoff. He handed me the sticky, but now less deadly, jar. We were already off the end of the runway and well into one of the steepest power climbs I have ever experienced in a jet plane. The craft seem to be going straight up. I made sure the lid remained loose and reaching down, set the jar on the floor between my shoes, clamping onto it as best I could with both feet. It seemed like forever before we leveled off and the pilot reduced power. At that point I looked down between my legs to my feet. Never think that things are so bad they couldn't possibly get worse. The jar was gone!

I turned my head and found the seat directly behind me occupied by a young gentleman in a coal black suit with starched white collar—obviously a priest. Big Bill, by this time, was near hysterical. I was having trouble controlling myself but I was concerned that he might bust a gasket. Two others of our party, across the aisle from us, had picked up on the story and by this time were both also in a helpless giggle. The other passengers aboard the plane were craning their necks trying to figure out what all the ruckus was about. This hysteria was to continue, nonstop, all the way to Kodiak.

Bending my head down as low as possible I could see down the deck under my seat. Spilling an 8-inch line of sourdough all the way, the jar had slipped from between my feet during the dizzy power climb and rolled back, coming to rest against a large paper shopping bag the young priest had stowed under my seat in front of him. Despite his state of mind, Big Bill managed to deftly reach down and retrieved the now mostly empty jar, slipped it cleverly into an airsick bag, and sealed the twist ties. If worse came to worst and we got caught and had to account for this mess, I quickly reasoned, we could maybe get away with claiming that one of us had been airsick.

Next, to my credit I guess, I turned and informed the priest that we were sorry but we had spilled something on the floor. I told him there was a chance that some of the liquid might have wet his carry-on and that he should handle his paper bag carefully. Not the whole story, but at least an effort. By that time we were descending into Kodiak airport and the young Father was more interested in landing than he was in the detail of what I was saying or the misfortune that had fallen on his hand-carry. I did note that, contrary to airline policy, he had retrieved his paper bag from under the seat and now had it resting on his lap.

Like thieves in the night we vacated the aircraft, walking behind the padre, who now clutched the large paper bag to his breast. I noted that he was met inside the terminal by two ladies in gray and white habit. As we passed them I saw the paper bag as he lowered it to his side, in the process of shaking hands with the ladies. I also saw the streaks of white pancake batter rubbed up and down the front of his handsome black suit.

We claimed our luggage and quietly slipped out of the airport.

In revealing this unintended wrongdoing I now assume full responsibility for the whole affair. The idea of carrying the starter along to camp that day was entirely my own. I imagine the mess created by the mayonnaise jar is now long forgotten by the people who cleaned aircraft cabins for Wien Airlines during that year. Legally, I am quite sure that any applicable statute of limitations has long since expired. I hope that by now the messy affair has slipped the mind of the priest—along with any thought of theological reprisal. Wherever he is, if he reads this, may the good Father find enough space in his heart to forgive the old sourdough—no pun intended.

Chapter 46
Remembering Fred Bear

IN 1985 THE ALASKAN BOWHUNTERS ASSOCIATION extended an invitation to Fred Bear to be guest speaker at our annual awards banquet. Although we were blessed with having some weighty, nationally known guest speakers, both before and after Mr. Bear—Doug Kitteridge, Jim Dougherty, Tom Jennings, and Glenn St. Charles, to name a few—we were stunned when Mr. Bear gladly accepted the invitation. "It will give me a chance to touch base with a few of my old bowhunting buddies in your area," he said.

Fred Bear addresses a packed house as guest speaker at the 1985 annual Alaskan Bowhunters Banquet.

Typically, the ABA banquet day begins each year with vendor displays, seminars, and an annual membership meeting. Hundreds of

Chapter 46—Remembering Fred Bear

people mill through the banquet hall checking out the latest archery doodads, the hunting videos and a world-class trophy display which is always mounted behind the stage as the centerpiece for the evening banquet. Fred was there, moving about through the crowd, shaking hands and meeting people. He was as comfortable as a pair of favorite old shoes. In bowhunting circles here was a walking legend, but you never would have known it by watching him. A crowd of admirers surrounded him wherever he went. He chatted casually with whoever was in earshot and graciously consented to pose for pictures with anyone who asked. You knew in an instant that here was a special person.

That evening Fred took the podium for his mid-dinner talk in front of a packed hall. He had no prepared speech. He just got up and started talking. He reminisced about friends mostly, and the old days when he was in our end of the country bowhunting. He poked fun at many people and told a few good stories. Some of his tales made you laugh, others made you to wince at their boldness and honesty. Here was a man who had spent his life hunting things with a bow and arrow and offered no apology to anyone for doing so, although in this group he didn't have to. After twenty minutes he paused and looked down at the master of ceremonies, asking, "I see I have talked for over twenty minutes. Is that enough or should I continue?" Our MC, God bless him, stood up and replied, "Mr. Bear, you have all our ears, you talk as long as you want to." And he carried on some more.

The evening banquet is a long affair and usually runs quite late, typically until about midnight. After such a long day the hall usually empties out fast, everyone heading quickly for their cars and homes. We had put Fred up in the hotel at the banquet site so *he* was already home. He wandered up to me through the rapidly thinning crowd and asked, "Where's the party?" "That's it," I replied. "I guess the party's over."

It was not until I was outside, nearly to my car, that I realized what a cosmic blunder I had made. I had unwittingly passed up an opportunity to spend some time with God! I should have checked into a room on the spot and invited him and some friends up for a drink and a visit. I will regret that lapse in social skill for as long as I live.

Two years later I was president of the Alaskan Bowhunters Association and called Fred to invite him to be with us again as guest speaker. But his health was failing fast at that point and he delayed committing for weeks, waiting for permission from his doctor to fly to us from his

Florida home one more time—permission that would never be given. He finally called me and, with regret, declined the invitation. He died not many months later.

I have an autographed photo of Fred posing with me at that 1985 banquet. The sentiment, like the man himself, is simple but far more than adequate. It reads, "Happy Hunting Dennis Lattery, Fred Bear."

Chapter 47
A Memorial for the Futz

THE SPRING OF 2001 HAS BEEN A DRY ONE. SNOWFALL during the winter was well below average for southcentral Alaska and we had no rain to speak of during April and May. We live in Chugiak, a bedroom community about 20 miles north of Anchorage. Our home comes close to backing up against the Chugach Mountains and we usually get more rain here, because of the mountains, than they do in the Anchorage bowl—but not this year. It is getting dry, and several years of leaf buildup from our birch trees has me worried about fire danger. I find myself lying awake at night thinking about a Marlboro Man tossing a careless cigarette butt out a pickup truck window, leaving me to contend with a brush fire—or perhaps the burning of my home. This chilling thought spurs me to rake and clear a fire line around the house—not the most welcome plan for spending a precious Memorial Day weekend.

My daughter Denise and her dog, The Futz, near Talkeetna, years ago.

Cutting trees and brush, and raking out around the back shed, I crossed the burial plot of my old basset hound. The registered name on his papers was "The Acorn Saynard," the exact name offered up by my four-year-old daughter years ago when asked what she wanted to name her new puppy. From the start most folks called him Saynard, even me, when I got mad at him. But after a while I took to calling him The Futz and, finally, just Futz, and the name stuck—mostly a private thing between him and me.

A more disgusting dog you never did see! He was flatulent, his eyes ran, he drooled constantly, his long ears smelled—no matter how many times you cleaned them—and he shed his short, tricolor hair everywhere. But a better, more gentle, pet for your child you could never find. The first twelve years of my daughter's life can hardly be discussed without the mention of his name.

I probably would have raked right past the grave, but years ago I placed a set of moose antlers on the spot to mark the spot where The Futz was buried. At that time the antlers were pretty respectable. They were among the top three Alaska/Yukon moose taken with a bow and arrow during the early 1980s, placing thirty-seventh overall in the 1981 Pope&Young records book. I was asked to send the antlers down to the Pope&Young banquet that year for display, and I would have, had the rack not been frozen in a snow bank at the time the request was made. Admittedly, I could have made more of an effort. Later, I intended to nail the antlers up on the peak of our horse barn but over the winter the neighbor's dogs chewed off several of the handsome points and the antler was left in unimportance where it lay beside the barn.

The old Futz went blind the next winter and slowly started going deaf. Each time we let him out of the house we had to put a bell on him so we could find him by sound if he wandered too far. Every outing we had to shout him back to the door, or go outside and direct him home by touch. We kept him as long as love allowed but, finally, in the spring, it was that same love that dictated we have him put to sleep. I felt his last quiver of life as he died in my arms at the veterinarian's office.

Once on his grave, I never moved the antlers again. Since 1982 the fall leaves and high-bush cranberry brush had combined to hide the spot and green algae slowly began to coat the palms and what was left of the long handsome points. Even when rescued and mostly uncovered again by the raking project, the rack still looked as if it was growing up out of the ground.

Like the priceless marks on the wall in our kitchen, pokes in the sheetrock with a paring knife marking our daughter's height increase as she grew into a young woman, those antlers will remain as they are where they are. It is far more appropriate that the headgear of that great moose mark the spot where our old pet rests than if they hung over a fireplace or the peak of a barn, one set of memories complementing the other, a fitting memorial to both.

Chapter 48
A Good Mulligan
First printed in *Bowhunting World – EXTREME* magazine,
Volume 55, No. 6, 2006

FOR MANY YEARS I HAVE CONTRIBUTED TO THE COOKING for our family. During that time I have somewhat proudly developed a personal philosophy about preparing food and my role in a kitchen

All the essential elements for Deer Neck Stew.

as a male. My wife finds my view on the subject amusing and often brings it up in front of company when talk about food takes the floor.

Chapter 48—A Good Mulligan

It has become quite a joke for her to ask, "Tell them how you feel about cooking, Dennis." My reply is that "no man should ever find himself completely dependent on a woman for his food."

As a big-game guide, it has been my responsibility to feed clients. I run a small operation and I can't afford, nor do I want, a camp cook. Accordingly, my time in the kitchen at home has served me well. It doesn't take long in the guide business to learn that a well fed camper is a (more) happy camper. Canned Dinty Moore beef stew or Chung King chop suey, or other complete meal-in-a-can items off the grocery store shelf just don't cut it. One of the quickest ways to blow off the chance for a repeat customer is to produce lousy provender. My brag for years has been that my camp will always provide the best food that field conditions will allow.

Pointing out the necessity for all guys to possess *some* amount of cooking skill leads to the subject at hand—a good stew. This is a camp basic. Any male who might ever stand a chance of getting stuck with the job of camp cook should at least, in my estimation, be capable of preparing a passable mulligan.

This meal has always been a regular at deer camp. It serves two purposes. Number one, it is good, hot, filling food and, number two, it answers the question: What can we serve for dinner two nights in a row and spare the cook some work? On the first night the menu item calls for stew with steaming garlic bread. The second night it is stew with that great meal stretcher—dumplings. The recipe I provide here will feed three big eaters for two nights or five to six big eaters for one meal.

This dish is referred to in our camp as deer neck stew because I usually use most of the neck meat off one of our little Sitka black tail deer to make one. As a side note, people who have tried all the various species of deer, and talk like they really know, maintain that our Alaska island deer are by far the best eating. Neck meat makes either good hamburger or very good stew meat, and that's about all. Rolled neck roast has never caught my fancy. Approximately 4 pounds of well-trimmed, 1-inch-cubed meat are required for this big, meaty stew. Other game meat or beef can be substituted but, to me, nothing else has the flavor of our island black tail for making a good mulligan.

A word of caution here: This recipe requires a *very* large pot! Anyone who has made a number of stews will remember the times the ingredients outgrew the pot, necessitating a switch to a bigger one, sometimes a couple bigger ones! Spare yourself, and the camp dishwasher, such poor management.

Yet another common camp name for this meal, in our camp, is milk bucket stew. This is because I have a special stainless steel milk bucket at my Raspberry Island (Kodiak area) camp just for this purpose. I have never measured this bucket's capacity but it must be at least ten to twelve quarts. This recipe fills the bucket to near the top. People new to camp always balk at the size of my stew as it grows. As I build on it, and the bigger it gets, the louder the outcry expressed by cook watchers that we will never eat it all—but there is usually very little left after the meal on the second night.

A few comments about ingredients: Much of what goes into preparing this meal comes out of a can. While that makes "cooking" easier it also adds big weight, which will need to be hauled to camp—an important consideration if your goods will travel by bush aircraft. I find a two-night meal for camp well worth the extra weight. A number of ingredients are fresh and will perish if held too long. If the weather is warm, this may cause some refrigeration problems. A solution is to plan on this big stew early on in the menu, while the veggies are fresh, a day or so after the first deer is brought into camp (hopefully) by one of your hunters. In Alaska on some hunts it can be as much a problem keeping things from freezing as it can be to keep them from spoiling. There are a number of ingredients, such as salt, pepper, granulated garlic, soy sauce, and so forth, I assume any cook would normally have along in a well organized cook box. If they are not, and you plan to use this recipe, make sure you have what is needed on your camp grocery list. If you're making this stew at home in Ma's kitchen for Super Bowl Sunday, and a market is only minutes away, then such careful attention to ingredients is not so important.

This recipe will produce a decent mulligan:
Ingredients:
4 lbs. trimmed, roughly 1-inch-cubed venison (neck meat or otherwise) or other red meat
3 tbsp. flour
3 tbsp. cooking oil
10 cups water
1½ tsp granulated garlic (or more, usually, to taste)
3 tbsp. soy sauce
2 packages au jus mix, any brand

2 large onions, quartered and thickly sliced
4 large russet potatoes, peeled, cut in 1-inch cubes
5 large carrots, washed and sliced (¼ inch)
2 large turnips, peeled and cut (1-inch cubes)
1 medium green cabbage, cored, cut in sixths lengthwise, then coarsely cross-sliced
4 ribs of celery, cut in ½-inch pieces
2 16 oz. cans of diced tomatoes
1 6 oz. can of green peas
1 6 oz. can of corn
1 6 oz can of cut green beans
1 6 oz can of sliced mushrooms (optional)
salt

pepper

2 16 oz cans of beef broth (Hold in reserve for added moisture the second night.)

2 cups Bisquick baking mix (Hold in reserve for dumplings the second night. If you don't bring along the whole box, make sure you write down instructions off the box for preparing dumpling dough.)

Garlic bread sufficient for your party.

Red wine?

<u>To prepare:</u>

Add ten cups of water to a large pot and place over high heat.

Season the cubed meat well with salt, pepper, and granulated garlic. Dust and lightly coat the meat with flour.

Lightly brown all the meat in small batches in a frying pan with some of the cooking oil. Dump each batch into the stew pot after browning.

Add the remaining granulated garlic, soy sauce, and one package of the au jus mix to the stew pot.

Add onion, potatoes, carrots, turnips, and celery. Bring the pot to a boil, then reduce heat to maintain a good simmer. Allow to simmer, as is, about thirty minutes.

Then add canned tomatoes, peas, corn, and green beans, including the juices. Add the optional can of sliced mushrooms, with its juice, at this point if you don't object to mushrooms in the stew. (I kind of like them.)

Simmer at a low boil for another hour, stirring frequently

to assure the bottom does not stick and burn, then taste. If the flavor is a bit bland, add either part or all of the second package of au jus mix and stir well. If the flavor is still a bit lame, slowly add more soy sauce, a bit at a time, carefully stirring and tasting, until the flavor suits you.

After adjusting the flavor, add and thoroughly stir in the sliced cabbage.

Allow the stew to simmer for at least another half hour to fully cook the cabbage—a whole hour would not hurt as this dish improves with a long, slow cooking time, allowing it to "stew" and meld the various flavors of the ingredients. It is then ready to eat.

<u>First night:</u>
Serve with steaming garlic bread. If your camp is not averse to pulling a cork, a little red wine makes this meal even more robust. Store the remaining stew in a cool place.

<u>Second night:</u>
Add the reserved cans of beef broth to the remaining stew; heat to a moderate boil while stirring well. The broth should assure that adequate moisture is present to steam-cook dumplings and prevent burning on the inside bottom of the pot—add a little water if necessary. Prepare the Bisquick mix according to instructions on the box for making dumplings. Using a large spoon, measure and drop golf-ball-sized dollops of dumpling mix on top of the boiling stew, taking care to spread them evenly over the surface. A good-sized pot will accommodate about ten to twelve dumplings. When cooked, dumplings will swell to about three times the raw dough size. Without disturbing, allow them to cook on top of the boiling stew, uncovered, for ten minutes. After ten minutes (still without disturbing the dumplings!), place a lid on the pot (or cover with aluminum foil) and continue cooking, covered, for another ten minutes; then reduce the heat and this meal is ready to eat.

With dumplings, no bread is necessary. A little red wine is just as nice the second night.

Enjoy.

Chapter 49
The Rock and the Hard Place

ONE WINTER WEEK NIGHT IN A KODIAK WATERFRONT bar, business was slow. It was bitterly cold and most of the regulars were absent. Only two or three customers were present, catered to by a bartender named Bill. Bill had served drinks at this waterhole for many years.

One of the customers present was an older lady named Nelly. Nelly was *really* one of the regulars. Tonight, for reasons known only to her, besides being "in the cups," she was in a bad mood—more like depressed. After consuming several more than her usual number of Oly (Olympia) beers, Nelly stood up and made an announcement. "I've had it!" she said. "I'm going to commit suicide! I'm going to go down on the beach, put a big rock on my chest and let the tide come in and drown me." Saying this, she headed for the door.

Business was slow and Bill wanted to see this for himself, so he shooed the remaining barflies out of the place, locked the door, and he and the group followed Nelly down to the beach amid the pilings underneath the bar. Sure enough, she was lying on the gravel near the edge of the water with a large rock balanced on her chest and hands just as she had proposed.

Bill and company watched the intense event for quite a while but nobody was really dressed for the raw evening and soon they all got chilled. Finally the Bill had had enough and headed back up the bank to the bar, followed by his now very thirsty patrons. A number of new people were waiting at the door, bewildered about the unusual establishment closure, and soon loud music was playing and the place hopping. In the revelry Nelly and her determination to end it all was forgotten.

About an hour later, Bill was pouring drinks for a party of fishermen fresh off the boat when suddenly the front door opened with a crash. In staggered Nelly, almost purple with cold and mad as a hatter. "Damn you, Bill," she hollered. "Why didn't you tell me the tide was going out? I lay there on that beach for over an hour and almost froze to death!"

(This story is a paraphrase of one that came to me courtesy of now deceased Smoky Stover, City of Kodiak comedian, ex-unofficial mayor of Onion Bay, and, once upon a time, cabin neighbor. Any resemblance to anyone in the story, living or dead, is probably an accident. Any and all blame or offense should be placed on Smoky.)

Chapter 50
Picking the Ideal Client
First Published in *Outdoor Life*, November, 2002, under the title *Be My Guest*

TYPICALLY, SOON AFTER THE CHRISTMAS HOLIDAYS ARE over, a majority of the hunters who are planning a guided hunt for this year start shopping. Beginning about mid-January, and extending about through the end of March, hunting consultants, guides and outfitters experience a flurry of mail and Internet activity from potential clients seeking hunt information.

About this same time we start to see "how to" articles appear in most hunting magazines. A favorite subject is usually the offering of advice on choosing a guide, lots of good stuff about success ratios, client references, guiding history, hunting areas, facilities, and cost comparisons. According to the articles, these are things the sportsman needs to know who is looking for a dream hunt for the least amount of money possible.

As a result, the average guide or outfitter is questioned, examined, investigated—about everything but x-rayed—and held up against every other guide the potential client may contact. If he's worth his salt and survives this process of elimination, the guide hopefully ends up with the clients he needs to fill his season. But once the deposit is paid, and the hunter booked, it is an indisputable fact that a first-time client knows much more about the guide than the guide knows about him. When a new guy climbs off the plane, what the guide sees is usually what the guide gets, having had little opportunity himself to kick any tires.

This little bit of how-to info is a slightly different twist on hunt shopping—a hypothetical from the guide's point of view. For what it's worth, here are a few things a guide might look for in a client, if the tables were turned and the guide got to ask all the questions and had a crack at choosing who his client would be—or not be. Not a dream hunt, but a dream hunter! No disrespect intended, but it doesn't hurt for any of us to take a hard look at ourselves once in a while.

What might be some criteria for assessing this dream hunter and, from a guide's point of view, what might be expected of that hunter?

First consideration, in my book, would be attitude. Above all, I'm hoping for a guy arriving with a total adventure in mind. True, the client has usually had to pay a lot of money for what he is doing. He's footing the bill and that fact alone entitles him to have about whatever attitude he wants about what he's paying for. But in my view, my perfect client isn't just buying a kill—he is hiring me to take him on a hunt, a total experience, not just for one rifle shot and then a fast trip back to Chicago!

I like the guy who is really aware of what's going on around him, a guy who asks a lot of questions, one who brings his camera and uses it a lot, a man who admires sunsets, the geology, the fall colors, and the occasional bald eagle.

I serve the best food in camp that hunt conditions will allow. Despite my asking each client beforehand if there are food preferences, or dislikes, after arriving at camp some like the food, some never do. My perfect guy remembers he had the chance for a say about the food, so as long as it's hot, tastes good and there is lots of it, he digs in and enjoys it. Hell, he might even offer to cook a time or two!

He doesn't grouse about bad weather (contrary to popular opinion, guides have no control over what God does with his weather!); he takes it in stride as part of the hunt. If spruce trees and cow moose are blowing past outside the tent he takes my advice and we stay in camp that day. Take a bath, clean your rifle, or read some of that book I told you to bring. And if my man rolls up his shirtsleeves and takes out his skinning knife when his animal is down—now this is a guy who came for the entire experience! Everyone isn't Mr. Attitude, but that's what I hope for.

Item two would be physical condition. There is too strong a tendency for many hunters to book hunts which are beyond either their medical or physical ability. Too many others *could* have been physically prepared but failed to follow through. In either case, this is not necessarily the fault of the guide. Admittedly, responsibility for the proper level of physical condition is a two-sided deal, and either the guide or the client can drop the ball. A conscientious guide carefully and thoroughly advises his client of the rigors involved in a hunt, and based on that, expects him to arrive in good enough shape to participate in what is planned. A few steps up a steep hillside, on the first day out of camp, is not the place or time to learn a client is not up to it. If this guy's not physically ready he won't enjoy his hunt, and I know he won't be back to hunt with me again. My ideal guy works on his conditioning and arrives in good shape. Either that or he is the type that will accurately and honestly advise me of his limitations and, armed with that knowledge, there are no surprises and I will have a chance to adjust things to accommodate with a hunt my client can handle.

Item three would be weapon proficiency. First, I will never turn around and find myself looking down the bore of this guy's rifle. He knows his firearm is always loaded, whether it is or not. Whatever weapon my perfect client chooses to hunt with, he arrives with all the ammunition he will need and everything in working order. One of his first concerns is for a careful check that everything survived the cross-country flight in a cargo hold and arrived at camp functioning. He can shoot his weapon with dependable accuracy. The caliber of his rifle is matched to the game he is hunting—as we discussed in advance. Talk is cheap, but my guy has obviously done a lot of shooting before the hunt. His weapon is test-fired, either at a range in town before coming to camp, or at camp, and it is either right on or it's the fault of the air cargo handler. On that same steep hillside, hunting that first morning out of camp is not the time to learn that the client has only fired a few rounds through his new rifle, or that his scope is rattling around inside its mounts!

Item four would be equipment. The ideal client I choose is very attentive to the gear list I send him. If I tell him to bring a good sleeping bag, one rated to minus five degrees, or colder, that's what he brings. I'm not the one who will have to lie all night shivering in cold bedding, with every donated coat in camp piled on top of me. He will bring good rain gear (not a plastic poncho!), the footwear I advise, well broken in, and a range of good-quality clothing that will keep him comfortable through the gamut of weather we are likely to encounter, from hot, to wet, to freezing.

Many Alaska guides operate on the water. We do a lot of hunts with rafts. When the sun is shining, rafters are throwing water on each other. But when the clouds roll in, and there's a fall wind driving some rain, the two available options can quickly become either we are properly dressed, and we keep on hunting, or we stop, make camp, and put a hypothermic member of the party in a sleeping bag.

Item five is a catchall that would best be described under the heading of "horse sense." These are a multitude of small things the guide knows about a client *after* a hunt is over that would have been useful to know before the hunt began. Of all the criteria for selecting a perfect client, horse sense, in total, is perhaps the most important and yet the most difficult of all to assess without spending days in the field with a hunter. This is not something that is learned. Either a person has it or he doesn't, and there is never a list of guides a potential client has provided that can be used to check for this kind of information. On the one hand, it is neither practical nor necessary that every client be the consummate woodsman. That is why guides are required to have an above-average level of experience and skill in the woods. But on the other hand, people not paying attention, every minute, can get lost, hurt, or in serious trouble in a heartbeat. If you have an extra sweater or a raincoat in your daypack, later on in the day you can put it on, or if you don't, you can't. Bullets are mindless, they go wherever they are pointed when the trigger is pulled. Knives are designed to cut many things. An ax can split open a knee quicker than a chunk of wood, and stove fuel has no regard for the surface on which it burns. Knowing in advance, somehow, that my ideal client has a tendency to be calculating and cautious, good attributes in the wilderness, hours, or perhaps even days, from help, would be a great comfort.

From my point of view at least, these five factors are the big ticket items that play heaviest in a guide/client relationship. Realistically, if most of these click along fairly well a hunt will usually work out fine.

It may be with my tongue in my cheek that I offer this pipe dream idea of a pre-hunt interview and background check before accepting a booking, but I am dead serious about what I would consider if I ever, just once, got the opportunity to shop for an ideal client!

Chapter 51
South Fork Reflections

WE DRIVE UP THE GLENN HIGHWAY HEADING NORTH from Anchorage. All around the country is ablaze with fall color. Contrasting the drab gray-black ribbon of the road, the birch, poplar, and wild rose make their brilliant statements. On the upper slopes, bearberry and low-bush blueberry command the view, bright and shocking up close, in patches, but a soft, blended red from a distance.

Another Alaska summer has slipped swiftly past us, despite our frenzy to keep pace with its endless daylight. Each day the sun drops a bit lower toward the horizon. It is two or three minutes lower than yesterday and two to three minutes later in rising. It's getting colder at night now, especially at this altitude. There is a sense of urgency in the morning air.

Somewhere just a few miles past Sheep Mountain Lodge I look to the right, across my passenger's nose, and my breath catches in my throat. Off to the south the Chugach Mountains lay, in differing hues of blue, arching across the landscape like a fortress, an ominous great wall protecting far-off Prince William Sound from an intruding world. At this point the Matanuska River makes a colossal sweep from the east-to-west course we have followed on the highway since passing Palmer, to cut a deep wound through the wall of the fortress toward the south. This is the South Fork of the Matanuska River. Eons must have been required for a grinding glacier to cut this gaping hole in the scenery.

I swear, every time I pass within view of this valley I can hear a choir of angels softly harmonizing. In one low, continuous, beautiful note they call to me, like some siren song, to come to them. But I have never gone. Every time I pass I'm already on my way to some other adventure. But still, when my gaze strikes those dark wooded valley sides, and I see that deep, white river bottom, curving off out of sight into those mountains, the same soft choral note comes to me. Each time this happens I wonder—if I heeded their call, what would I find?

On this occasion my split-second look is rewarded with a sheet of precipitation rolling in over the top from the west, far up inside the wound. A wall of blue-white haze is streaming in great fingers down over the upper slopes. This is something born back in the upper reaches of world-class glaciers, its birthing witnessed by surrounding peaks with Nordic names like Thor, Valhalla, and Norway, all near to or higher than 10,000 feet above the level of the sea. It's too high, too cold, and too late in the season for this to be rain. The wild sheep that live there know what it is and what it means.

I turn my head away, back to the road, and the chorus is gone. The passenger catches my brief departure from safe driving and his head swivels toward the south for a look where he saw my eyes wander. With an oblivious insult to my awe he silently turns forward again, his eyes fixed sleepily on the road passing rapidly under us.

After a brief time I ask, "Did you hear that?"

"What?" he replies, his eyes still ahead on the road. This is an astute woodsman, with an above-average eye for nature's details.

"Uh… it's nothing," I return after a brief pause.

The truck heater hums out warm comfortable air and I have aroused only a small amount of curiosity with my question. I guess either you can hear the music or not, and too much of that precious moment would have been lost had I made an effort to explain. I let it go…

Chapter 52
When Optics Are Your Best Friend

AT AGE FORTY-EIGHT, MY EYESIGHT TOOK A SUDDEN, drastic turn for the worse. I thought I had contracted some horrible eye disease. Following a hastily arranged eye exam my optometrist was heartlessly frank. "Hey," he said, "You're forty-eight. It's all downhill from here." From birth I'd had the eyes of a hawk. I couldn't stand to wear sunglasses, even for a short time. How the devil was I going to wear glasses now if they were needed? I have been an avid hunter all my life. I know some good hunters who are near-deaf but I don't know any good ones that are near-blind. Was this the beginning of the end?

The initial crash of my sight was followed several years later by cataracts in both eyes. So there really *was* a horrible disease. It is scary to witness your vision deteriorate from fairly decent to blurry shadows, especially as fast as this occurred in my case. First the left lens fogged up, then the right. Following operations to replace both bad lenses my sight was returned almost to the point where it had been at age forty-eight. My vision was now something less than 20/20, but that was most welcome when I looked back on the terror of foggy cataracts! Beggars can't be choosers. I would have to adapt to my changed eyesight if I was going to continue hunting—which I was determined to do. Good-quality field glasses would have to replace the hawk-eye vision of my youth.

It took some time to fully realize how good optics can compensate for fading, or faded, vision. Of course I had always had binoculars hanging around my neck while hunting, most hunters usually do, but they are mostly used for distance spotting. I rarely put them to my face for close-range stuff. I always depended on hawk eyes for that—the hawk eyes that were no longer there. Now I had to train myself to use the glasses for close-in work. I needed them to detect that flick of an ear, a blending face in the brush or to discern a leg in the alders from the alders themselves. This meant having the glasses in my face most of the time, not just when scanning a mountainside. It is surprising what your poor old eyes will see when you work on your close-range spotting skills.

A friend and I were deer hunting in the Kodiak Island area a few years back. Hunting was slow, as the herd had suffered a bad winter kill two seasons before. The population was on the increase but on this trip sightings were spotty. It was tough to find a deer, any deer. The bag limit was still three animals, bucks *or* does after November 1, but this was considerably tougher hunting than was normal for Kodiak. We were used to seeing fifteen to twenty-five deer a day during good times, and to a bag limit from five to seven deer—either sex.

We paused at a spot on our favorite mountainside, overlooking a patch of alders. The upper tip of the patch was only about 20 yards below us. We had not seen a deer all morning. Putting the binoculars to my face, I first glassed down into the upper tip of the alder patch and found myself looking into the face of a huge buck lying just inside the brush, staring directly up at me. When I put the glasses down I couldn't even see the animal. He was perfectly camouflaged to my bare eyesight.

It took a lot of talking and pointing to show my partner where that deer was, even with his scoped rifle. Had I not had the binoculars in my face we would never have harvested that nice buck.

This last fall the same partner and I were raft-hunting moose on my favorite "secret" river in southcentral Alaska. Early one morning we were silently sneaking our way along an old dead river oxbow looking for a bull. I was not paying attention to my own close-range spotting rules. My partner was. I heard him whistle softly behind me and whisper that there was a bull lying in the open on the bank of the oxbow 50 yards ahead of us. To my unaided eyes he blended perfectly into the surroundings where he lay.

I was leading, and about to move off the river toward an open moose meadow I knew about. Had my partner not been carefully glassing the nearby area, like I should have been, I would have walked us right away from a winter's supply of moose meat.

When I say "good" binoculars I mean exactly that. If you are going to spend days on end looking through those things there is no substitute for the best. A pair of low to mid-priced glasses just doesn't have what it takes when it comes to industrial-strength use. You will find it startling how crisp you can adjust a good pair of binoculars to your eyesight, with no distortion or color haze. If you're like me, and the old eyes are already shaky, there is nothing to be gained by putting them through the strain of poor-quality optics.

I have found that binoculars with large objective lens, 40 millimeters or better, work best. This gives the user a wide field of vision and much better light-gathering ability when you need it most, later into the evenings and earlier in the mornings. A bigger objective lens means a heavier binocular; but to me the advantage gained is more than worth the tradeoff for the extra bit of weight. I am also a believer in higher power. For me, gone are the days of the old 7x35s. A minimum should be 8-power, and 10-power is better—although 10-power takes some getting used to. My old eyes now enjoy a pair of new-generation Leica 10x42s. I feel sorry for the guy who shows up in camp carrying a little pair of so-so quality, low-power, broomhandle binoculars.

If your eyes are like mine, or even if they are not, train yourself to use this tool more often. When you're in hunting country, even when sitting around, you should have them in your face. Make it a fast rule that, if your pants are on, your glasses are hanging around your neck and you're using them.

An old Indian once told me that when hunting I should move little and look a lot. Follow this advice with a good pair of binoculars. You will soon be glad you did.

Chapter 53
On Following Your Nose

WE WERE ON THE SIXTH DAY OF A TEN-DAY SITKA BLACK-tailed deer hunt at my Onion Bay camp on Raspberry Island. Raspberry is a long, skinny island sandwiched between Afognak Island on the north, and Kodiak Island on the south.

Since arriving, the three of us had hunted for five days and covered five of our six most dependable deer hot spots. It is standard practice to hunt one hot spot per day, either camped on well-worn deer trails or using short deer drives. Black tails are creatures of habit, so at the end of six days, we start all over again, by hunting the spot where we began the first day. After six days, just as many deer as we ran off or harvested on day one have typically moved back into the country. This six-day rotation system works well where we hunt and provides a dependable, endless supply of venison.

On day six we used the skiff and motored up Onion Bay about a mile from camp to a place we call The Point. We beached the boat and began climbing the steep, open, grassy slope extending upward from the beach. The terrain rises from the beach to an elevation of about 2,000 feet. This open hillside is cut with a number of gullies which are choked with alders. Alder patches, especially in steep gully chutes, are favored hiding spots for Kodiak area deer.

Standard procedure is to send two hunters around to the top of one of these alder chutes. With one hunter in place on each side at the top of the patch, situated so they can see each other well, a third hunter functions as a bird dog. He drives uphill slowly from the bottom, making a lot of

Chapter 53—On Following Your Nose

noise—a thoroughly miserable job. The deer move up through the finger of alders, ahead of the noisy driver, and are pushed to the waiting hunters at the top of the patch.

On this drive it was my turn to climb up around one side of the patch and position myself as a shooter. But on the way up the hill a Kodiak bear spooked out of another patch of brush several hundred yards below me. We frequently see brown bear on our deer hunts. Distracted from the drive, I watched him until he moved away, out of sight around the hillside. About the time the bear disappeared, I was then distracted by the appearance of a nice buck on the open hillside several hundred yards above me. He ran around the hill, away from the top of the alder chute where I was supposed to position myself. The temptation was too great. I deserted the drive plan, and my partners, and worked my way up and around the hill after the buck.

I never saw that deer again. I had blown the drive for my companions by not sticking to the plan. To compound my lack of consideration, I elected to continue up and around the hill in the general direction the big buck had gone, hoping to get to a position where I could glass the area into which he had headed. I climbed for about thirty minutes, until I reached open hillside where I could see fairly well. I had hardly arrived and settled down to glass when a large doe jumped into view about 30 yards away. I aimed and shot quickly and she disappeared, running away from me and down into a gully. As I took a few steps in her direction she suddenly reappeared, a bit farther away and angling downhill. I shot one more time and she disappeared again into another draw. In a flash she appeared on an open flat below me. I shot again and she fell over dead.

Unable to descend directly to where the deer lay, I angled along the hillside to find the best route down. Reaching the spot where I had shot at her the first time, I found a dead deer lying on the hillside. There had been two deer! Dragging this doe downhill toward the deer I knew for sure I had killed, I found another expired doe, just a few feet out of sight of the spot where I had shot at the second deer. Now I had three deer on my hands! All three were legal. At the time there was a five-deer, either-sex limit, and these three tagged me out. We would all have a freezer full of top-rate game meat this year!

With three deer in tow, each of them trying to slide downhill between my legs, I worked my way down the steep mountainside toward the beach. Half way down I found my two near hysterical hunting companions, sitting by the edge of the alders. After we were reunited, it was quickly obvious that they were as mad as they were relieved to see me. They had figured I was dead for sure; that I had been mauled by a bear in the alders. Losing track of me before I went off alone around the mountain, they had regrouped and become quickly concerned when they couldn't find me. They then found the remains of a bright-colored hat along the edge of the alders. It was torn to pieces. They had figured it had to be mine and feared the worst. I had been too far up and around the mountain for them to hear my shooting, and by the time I reappeared dragging the deer, a gloomy plan was being discussed about the safest way to search the alders for my remains.

My efforts to joke and make light of the episode met with miserable failure. The fear they had for my welfare had been too real and come too close to home. Considering my sudden, unexplained disappearance, as well as the destroyed hat, their displeasure was certainly understandable. Every bit of the cool treatment I got that morning I had coming. Both these gentlemen were older than I am, experienced hunters who knew better than to pull such a stunt on a companion. Each of them was more than kind and diplomatic in conveying their thoughts about my inconsiderate behavior.

I had let them down by ignoring the game plan and striking off on my own, a mistake I have avoided ever making again on subsequent hunts. This has been a difficult thing for a hunter who, by nature, likes to trust his instincts and follow his nose wherever it leads him.

Chapter 54
In the Midst of Bears
First published in *Traditional Bowhunter* magazine, February-March 2000

ON THIS TRIP I WAS ABOUT HALF-WAY UP THE MOUNTAIN, near timberline, at a place called Fog Lakes. I was in the Talkeetna Mountains about 60 miles northeast of Talkeetna, Alaska, on the second night of a bow hunt for brown bear. I sat in my tree stand, in the dead of night, and a rotten fall storm was blowing in on me. I was alone.

My Fog Lakes brown bear.

Scoping out my predicament in the gathering darkness that night I had a flashback of a similar experience in a tree stand in weather like this the previous fall. I recalled from that experience that, even though the decking of my tree stand sat astride heavy planks that had been carefully spiked to big spruce trees, the spikes I thought would hold fast had pulled free. I snuggled down into my sleeping bag in the storm on that trip after buttoning down a poly-tarp shelter over the tree camp. There had been little sleep due to the violence of the storm and the rocking and rolling of the trees. The next morning I found that all the spikes had pulled out during the night. They were bent like pretzels and the entire tree stand and I were hanging by rope, swinging in the wind.

Whatever possessed me on that Kodiak trip to tie off the deck supports with safety line is a mystery. I had never taken the precaution before. Maybe it was the ready supply of Japanese fishing rope that littered the beach in front of my stand, and most of the beaches in the Kodiak area these days. I can't explain why, but the action prevented a 20-foot fall in the night and saved my bacon for sure.

Now, this year, here I was in a similar situation on another hunt. I huddled in the middle of the night, in another tree stand, in another storm. But here in the Talkeetna Mountains there was no handy supply of Japanese rope and I had never expected the heavy weather that was now bearing down on me.

This was mid-September in the fall of 1985. I was heavy into bowhunting and determined to take a brown bear with archery tackle. This Fog Lakes trip was the fourth in a series of hunts I had been on in my determination to harvest a brown bear the hard way.

I had lived in Alaska at that point for all but a few of my forty-four years. Since I began hunting as a teenager I had walked around a good number of brown bear while hunting with a rifle. I never wanted to take a bear until after I began hunting with archery tackle. My priorities had changed and I had developed a plan to harvest a bear—but I was determined to do it *my* way.

There were four standing rules I had adopted for brown bear:

> First and foremost, everything had to be legal. If I couldn't look someone in the face who wanted to hear the story, with a clear conscience, I didn't want a bear. No jack lights, or illegal baits and no electronic devices or lighted sight pins on any hunt!
>
> Second, I chose to hunt alone. Two people make as much noise as three people and ultimately tend to distract each

Chapter 54—In the Midst of Bears

other, especially when the hours get long and the waiting gets boring. Being alone in the Alaska wilderness never bothered me. For the sake of my game plan I was prepared to accept the danger of hunting alone and the possible consequences, if any.

Third, if I hunted alone, for the sake of my safety, I would set up to hunt from a tree stand.

Fourth, I would try to utilize some natural advantage to improve my chances, like a salmon stream I knew attracted brown bears, or a frequently used bear trail I could count on. For example, a narrow spit connecting two islands—a natural crossing pointed out to me by a logger friend—was what drew me to the Kodiak area to hunt. An ancient bear trail crossing that spit was exactly the kind of situation I was looking for. If a bear crossed the spit while I was there, in the stand, the advantage was mine.

I had a number of bush pilots in the Kodiak area watching the beaches for dead beached whale or sea lion carcasses, in either case a good natural and legal means of attracting bears to a specific location—and keeping them there with some degree of predictability. Another possibility I concentrated on was big-game kills. The head, hide, and viscera of big game animals, leftovers from the legal harvesting of an animal, are legal bait materials. Many hunters keeping a watchful eye on a moose or caribou kill site have been rewarded with a bear for the trouble. In good country a bear will quickly claim a kill, sometimes before all the meat is removed, and they are sometimes prepared to fight to the death to keep it! Our Alaska game laws contain a provision providing for the desperate killing of big game animals in defense of life and property. However, under this law killing a bear in a dispute over game meat is not considered defending property. If he claims it, the game meat belongs to the bear, and you cannot legally shoot him—unless bear season is open and you have a bear tag in your pocket. The law also provides that the deliberate placing of *any* bait to attract a brown bear is illegal.

Some bush pilot friends at Talkeetna Air Service had been on the lookout for a moose kill setup. This one was perfect, as they had advised. They could show me the kill site from the air, there was timber surrounding it, and the location was within reasonable packing distance of a lake (Fog Lakes) I could be set off on with a floatplane. I was ready to get on their plane the morning after they called. Don Lee, my pilot, had dropped me off and I had humped my camp and tree stand materials up the mountainside and built the stand yesterday. I climbed up into the tree prepared to stay there for seven days without coming down. The objective was to become a fixture over the kill site, an accepted part of the landscape—no noise and as little motion as possible. This is a quiet, lonely way to hunt, but if I kept to established hunt discipline, I knew that sooner or later the bears would come.

Back to my predicament at Fog Lakes: When the storm hit I was in my stand in my sleeping bag and nearly asleep. A northwest wind came first, just after dark, followed by a driving rain. I stretched a parachute cord low over my deck and draped a heavy plastic sheet over that to cover myself. After tying down the corners as best I could, all I could do was hunker down and try to enjoy the ride—and hope this time the nails holding my decking to the trees held!

After a long and generally sleepless night, morning found the tail end of the storm passed through and the sky clearing. Glad to be in one piece, and still in the tree, I uncovered the stand at first light and slipped out of my sleeping bag. There was fresh show halfway down the mountainside behind me. Across Fog Lakes and the alpine landscape to the north I could see the escarpment of Devil's Canyon on the Susitna River and beyond that the Alaska (mountain) Range. The willows were decked out yellow and the bearberry, low-bush blueberries and dwarf birch were brilliant scarlet reds and warm purples. In the growing dawn I was slowly becoming the landscape fixture I wanted to be. I had a grandstand view from my tree perch and it was a sight to see!

It was quite cool until the sun came up; then the temperature turned pleasantly warm. During the course of the day several caribou passed by but there was no sign of bear. All the while a continuous flock of magpies and Canada jays came and went from the kill site. Scavengers by nature, and near the bottom of the food chain, they were busy packing off all they could before being displaced by a larger scavenger.

By 8 p.m. the light was fading fast, so I gave up for the day. I quietly made a cup of tea on my soundless Sterno stove and slipped down into my sleeping bag. About the third sip, all hell broke loose.

Chapter 54—In the Midst of Bears

From a short distance away in the brush, up the mountain behind me, came the most ungodly blowing and snorting I had ever heard. I still feel the hair prickle on the back of my neck when I think of it! In the waning light a huge sow brown bear slowly appeared out of the spruce, followed by three silver-colored cubs about half her size. She rocked from side to side, with her head held low, all the while expelling violent bursts of air through her nose and mouth. I don't know who was more terrified at the moment, I, because of the suddenness of the encounter in the eerie twilight, or she, of the intruder she knew was there but could not locate. The small spruce trees my stand hung from were situated on the steep side of a small, round hill. The remains of the moose were on the top of the hill in a little clearing just slightly below the level of my stand and about 10 yards distant. It was obvious that at the moment the sow was more interested in my tree stand than she was in the moose remains. The brush, off toward all the huffing and puffing, was alive with silver forms, shining and almost luminescent in the fading light; and they were all converging along the hillside toward the base of my tree stand!

I had never measured the height of my platform from the base of the tree. I would guess the height to be about 15 feet. I also guess that when the sow reached the tree, and stretched up her nose for a smell, it was only about 6 feet away from my face peering down into hers over the edge of the deck. It is generally held that brown bears cannot climb trees. Don't you believe it! Over the eons they may have lost the inclination to climb—but not the ability. I have seen them do it. In the gathering gloom I eased a handy sidearm out of its holster, preparing to make a whole lot of defensive noise if she started up the tree, but with a sharp huff she dropped down to the ground and the whole herd of them thundered off in the direction from which they had come. I was left alone, admittedly shaken, but, after a few minutes to ponder the personal value of the experience, a much richer person.

About an hour later the sow and cubs cautiously returned, this time coming in from the woods on the other side of the kill. On entering the clearing they immediately fell on the remains and horrible sounds of wild animals feeding came to me through the darkness. I soon realized that if I let them continue at this rate between the four of them they would probably clean out, or drag off, most of the kill that first night. This would leave nothing to attract the boar I wanted. I elected to run them off.

First I tried a flashlight. It allowed a good look at the bears in the darkness but the bright beam had no visible effect on them; they just kept on eating. Realizing that my chances were dwindling with every sickening crunch in the night, I took a deep breath and let out the loudest bellow I could muster. The effect was instantaneous and terrifying. The sow charged at the flashlight across the darkness. In the light, due to the lay of the land, it looked as if she would jump right off the top of the hill and onto my tree stand. Startled, I came close to falling off the deck backwards. Actually, the closer she got to me the more rapidly the hill dropped off. A few seconds later and she was thrashing around in the brush below my tree. Both she and the cubs promptly left and never came back that night.

The first encounter that evening was just a start. Over the course of the next three days and nights I had a parade of bears passing through the kill site, fifteen animals in all. There were two more sows, each with triplet cubs in tow, and four boars. One boar was a decent bear, a blocky, dark guy I judged would square between 7 1/2 and 8 1/2 feet, Another was medium sized, between 6 and 7 feet, and two were smaller, both probably two-year-olds that had either been orphaned or run off that summer by a sow preparing to breed again.

The boars were smart. During the morning and evening twilight they would show only at a distance, and then disappear. They would expose themselves only under cover of darkness. It was as if they knew I couldn't and wouldn't shoot then. The big guy never showed himself at all during the daylight, only after dark. Obviously he had not grown that large by being stupid.

Between 8 p.m. and 8 a.m. my time was occupied with running off sows and cubs. I hollered them off, threw branches at them, and shot so many in the rump with rubber tipped arrows that my arrow supply began to run alarmingly low. All this activity was strangely accepted by the bears as a part of the present situation. They were all aware that I was there but now it was like that fact really didn't matter. As soon as I ran one family off, another came in from another direction. Every once in a while, in the mayhem, a boar showed between the sows, but none of them would come any closer if there was enough light to shoot.

Despite my efforts at keeping the sows and cubs run off I still had to find some time to sleep. They were sneaking in while I was catnapping and were methodically cleaning up the kill a bit more every night. By the evening of the fifth day I knew I needed to review my strategy or the kill site would be cleaned out and this hunt would be over.

Chapter 54—In the Midst of Bears

Pondering the problem, I reasoned that maybe running the sows off created too much disturbance, causing the more cautious boars to keep their distance. Maybe if I let the sows feed, at the risk of being cleaned out completely, one of the boars might do something different.

The morning of the sixth day, at about 7 a.m., my original sow, with her triplet cubs in tow, poked out of the alders. Expecting the usual hazing, she was clearly nervous as they approached the kill and began eating. Unhindered, the whole family soon fell into a feeding frenzy. I stood motionless on the stand with my bow in hand and watched. In mid-bite the sow suddenly raised her head, peering into the alders behind her. With a warning snort from her the whole bunch cleared out in the opposite direction. Out of the brush, exactly where the sow had pointed, poked the head of a bear. It was the midsized boar. He appeared as much aware of the sow and cubs as she had been of him. He knew he had run them off and, apparently reasoning that the coast must be clear, came straight up the hill for his turn to feed.

There are tribes of American Indians that harbor a belief that a hunter takes only an animal that offers itself to be taken, and that taking the offered life incurs an obligation of respect and reverence which must be politely observed. To do otherwise would be an affront to the animal's spirit and bring bad luck down on the hunter. I submit that this belief is worthy of considering. All living things have a time to die. This is infinitely more certain than any prediction of the measure of time any one thing has to live. Few wild creatures have the luxury of meeting their end in peace, or dying of old age in their sleep. This only happens behind the walls of a pen, protected by humans, in a zoo or some other such facility where wild creatures have had their wildness removed from them. To think otherwise is an unrealistic view of wild animals and of things as they really are—an affliction of many people in this day and age.

Except to say that this animal's life ended quickly, and that he died as nobly as any of us could hope to, I prefer to keep that part of my little story a private thing—between the bear and me. In celebration of his life I will always hold this hunt up as the finest outdoor experience of my life. I will never forget my six days and nights on the edge of the northern forest in the midst of those beautiful bears.

Chapter 55
Calling All Moose
First published in *Traditional Bowhunter* magazine, August/September, 2006

THIS IS THE PRODUCT OF YEARS OF INTERACTION WITH and observation of *Alces alces gigas*, the Alaska/Yukon species of moose. I have no credentials as a scientist. Take what is written here for what it is worth.

Many wild animals and game birds are susceptible to having their means of communication and mating activities studied and then used to hunt them. All species of deer, moose, elk, ducks, geese, and wild turkey, just to name a few, are particularly suited to having their natural mating urges and instincts turned to a hunter's advantage. Moose are a fine example. Hunters have been calling birds and deer to them for generations but it has not been until relatively recently that the ease with which moose can be coaxed close to a hunter has become general knowledge. (Alaska Natives have known this for centuries.) On a historic note, you can see Art Young, in his 1923 movie about bowhunting in Alaska (2005 Pope & Young Club release *Art Young's Alaska Adventures*), using a birch-bark megaphone to call moose to him. For people who choose to hunt with a bow and arrow, having some knowledge of the mechanics of game calling could be especially useful.

For starters, it's important to understand that knowing the specifics of *exactly* how to call moose is less important than knowing that even bad calling can often produce good results. Sometimes even accidental calling can be turned to advantage.

Once, on a solo hunt in the Chugach Mountains, I called up a bull moose, unwittingly, by pounding on plastic tent pegs with an ax. The ax was an Estwing, which has a one-piece head and handle that I prefer. Beating the pegs into hard ground caused the ax head to set up a resonating ring like a tuning fork. This brought an inquiring grunt from a bull off in the woods. I immediately stopped camp work and went hunting. I didn't get the bull that windy morning but I did arrow a nice, fat cow he had with him, filling my either-sex archery permit on the first day of the hunt.

Like all large North American ungulates, moose breed in the fall. Mating is timed to provide for birth of the offspring early in the spring. Mother Nature's plan, obviously, is to offer the newborn calf the advantage of a jump start on life during her fat time—the warm, lush spring, summer, and early fall months. The role of a bull moose in this grand plan is that he is the one who pays the heaviest price for the timing of the fall breeding season. When the rut is over, the large herd bulls, like other species of deer, are generally spent, undernourished and quite often pathetically beat up and in poor shape for facing an approaching winter. In Alaska at present, the hunting of moose is typically restricted to small-spike/fork bulls, any bull having an antler spread of over 50 inches, or any bull with at least three brow tines (points) on at least one antler. (A moose with less than a 50-inch antler spread is a harvestable animal, provided he has three brow tines on at least one side of his antlers.) There is a reason for this. Studies apparently have shown that young bulls and larger old bulls are usually the first to perish during a severe winter. The thinking being that we should cull animals least likely to survive a hard winter.

Beginning as early as the last week of August, bulls begin to experience the first stirrings of the mating season. This period is generally referred to as the pre-rut. The onset is marked by an increase in bull movement. Generally solitary during other times of the year, bulls are now instinctively driven to be on the move in a search for cows.

As the fall progresses, cows take part by becoming increasingly vocal. With the onset of fall colors and cold nights they begin calling, particularly between the hours of beginning darkness and morning daylight. Cows remain vocal throughout most of the rut, a continuous proclamation of their intention to mate. They will even continue calling, if somewhat subdued, after they have been yarded up by a herd bull. It is the cow which determines when she is ready to mate. She will resist doing so until she is biologically ready, despite the amorous and dogged attempts by excited bulls trying to speed things along. To some extent, the cow may have some latitude even in selecting the bull she mates with. Calling cows are often observed being accompanied by bulls which they apparently find unacceptable. Continued calling could be her message that she is in the market for a better deal. It is likely that this mate shopping may be the cause of many a violent battle between rival bulls.

Other factors enter into the mating ritual. An excellent sense of smell is certainly important, but restless bulls and vocal cows are the two ingredients that figure most heavily in moose calling.

During the first half of the September season in Alaska, a cow call is best used to attract a bull. During this period an amorous male will usually approach the imitated call location of a potential mate quietly, with only very low grunting to announce his presence. A cow moose, with her great hearing, can hear these grunts while most of us humans cannot—at least until the bull works his way in quite close. Bulls tend to be very cautious during this phase of the rut, and in their caution, if the smallest thing is perceived as being the slightest bit wrong, they will back off and leave. It is interesting to watch the body language of a bull that has come in close to a caller and then senses trouble. Rather than turn and flee, which will happen if the wind carries a bad scent to him, there is a tendency to first freeze in place, dead still. Then, after a considerably longer time than I would consider prudent, he will begin backing up very slowly, turning his body around squarely without either bending his neck and without turning his head. All the while his eyes appear distended, peering straight forward, as if trying to catch movement in the direction from which he is turning, using his peripheral vision, but I am positive his great ears are really what is in play during this fine bit of silent choreography, rather than his notoriously poor eyesight. Once he has completely turned, the tendency then is to tiptoe cautiously and silently away. It is truly amazing how an animal this large can ghost away through the woods so silently, especially an animal with huge antlers! Special attention must be paid to wind direction, limiting movement and avoiding noise which will give away the caller's exact location. Hunters calling during the pre-rut should always be prepared for the appearance of a bull they have no idea was nearby. That bulls, or their low grunts, are not heard does not necessarily mean they are not around.

Chapter 55—Calling All Moose

Later in September mating gets into full swing and bulls begin aggressive rutting. They generally slow down on feeding, or quit eating nearly altogether for several weeks. Lower food intake and increased physical activity in defending their cows against challengers, real and imagined, causes their temperaments to go from bad to worse. Hormones cause their necks to swell. A large bull is generally prepared to fight almost any other bull over cows he has gathered around him during the pre-rut. This is the time for the hunter to concentrate on using bull-related calling techniques—perhaps mixed with an occasional cow call. A rutting bull, standing guard over his cows, will tend to react to almost any sound he interprets as a threat from a rival, and there appear to be many such sounds. Brush thrashing, breaking branches, and aggressive grunting work best. Some callers claim that the sound of water pouring into a lake or stream is an effective calling technique. This supposedly imitates the sound of a urinating cow standing in water. I have never had any noticeable luck using this technique!

It is my determination that an enraged bull responding to a hunter's taunting calls is often best handled by mimicking, that is by making the same sounds he makes as he approaches and challenges, right back at him. This seems to be particularly infuriating to a bull. Simple things like driving a tent peg or chopping wood in camp, even running a chainsaw, can attract them while in the heat of the rut.

A particularly offensive sound to a rutting bull is the sound of another bull's horns rattling in the brush. Brush and branches passing through a moose's antlers, even some distance off in the woods, makes a distinctive, hollow clatter. Once you have heard that sound you will never forget it. Although one may be hard to find, a dried shoulder blade from a moose makes one of the best brush-thrashing tools available. Scraped against trees and rubbed vigorously through heavy brush, a brittle shoulder blade sounds more like a bull thrashing with his antlers than any other tool you can use. An old plastic bleach bottle, with part of the bottom cut out, will serve as a calling tool in a pinch. I have seen Alaska Natives scrape 3-pound coffee cans on trees to call moose. Rub the tool you use against trees (the rough bark of spruce trees seem to produce the loudest racket) and thrash it in the brush. This reasonably imitates bull thrashing, an unmistakable challenge. In the right time and place this will work for you.

Don't call too often. Either cow-call (early season) or brush-thrash and bull-grunt (late season) for about a minute or so, then keep absolutely silent for about fifteen to twenty minutes and listen carefully. Repeat calling for another minute or so, and listen again. Repeat this sequence for about an hour. Give a bull a chance. He may be working his way to your call from a mile or more away. I have called for as long as two hours before having a bull present himself. Being patient while doing this is a good thing.

When you are convinced there is nothing around to come to the call, move a good distance away—at least a quarter to a half mile is a good rule of thumb—and begin calling again. When I set up to call, I like to get myself into a position where I can see some distance in at least one direction, where I am downwind and preferably on a high riverbank or hillside. Where the cover is thick all around, but there is obviously lots of fresh moose sign in the area, I will call from there, wherever it is. I also like to camp near where I have been doing extensive calling. My policy then is to maintain a relatively quiet camp and continue calling from there during the evening hours until well after dark. On several occasions, doing this has led to having a bull grunting at me just outside camp in the morning. Chances are he moved into the area during the night and was there at dawn listening and waiting.

Once you know you have a bull coming to a call, the rest is played by ear. Enticing it out of the brush is one thing, calling it into range for a good bow shot is quite another! I have never had a moose, bull or cow, do the same thing when coming to a call. Unpredictability of the outcome is the thing which makes calling and hunting moose with a bow such an exciting thing. Here are a few ideas:

A bull coming to a cow call during early season (pre-rut) will be more skittish than a late-season bull coming to challenge a rival. You have the advantage in both instances. He may be a little or a lot crazy and you are in control, provided you keep your wits about you. I have found that the best policy, once you know for sure a bull is coming to your calling, is to keep low and as well concealed as possible, allowing the bull to approach to a point where you can see him. Once you can see him, my advice is to stop calling. The bull already has the call direction accurately pegged in his personal computer. He knows where the calls are coming from but may not know exactly how far away the sounds are being made. Hopefully he will tend to keep going on the course that his senses direct. This could work to a clever hunter's advantage,

Chapter 55—Calling All Moose

especially a bowhunter's, offering the chance for a shot, sometimes an alarmingly close shot, as the inquisitive or intimidated bull passes his position. This could also work well for two hunters calling together. At the first sound of an approaching bull, one hunter remains stationary and concealed while the other moves off in the woods, in the opposite direction from where the bull is coming, and continues calling. Hopefully this setup will cause the distracted bull to pass close by the hidden shooter, offering a good bow shot.

I have proven to myself several times that aggressive bull grunting and brush thrashing at close range can run a bull off, especially if the approaching animal is not a large, really aggressive male. Stop thrashing and let the approaching bull worry about it. If you are working the moose alone, the last sound you should make, as the bull comes into view, is a low cow grunt or a very short moaning cow call.

An aggressive bull coming to challenging calls can arrive thrashing the trees with fire in his eyes accompanied by violent snorting and saliva drooling from his mouth! Upon learning that the caller is human, most bulls will quickly vacate the area. But remember, it is his time of year to be a bit crazy, and if surprised at close quarters, he could easily be dangerous!

The message here is that moose calling really works and if you understand a few moose basics, it is relatively easy. Don't be bashful; even bad calling, particularly during the late rut, is better than no calling at all. Most folks do not live in moose country, and as a result, a hunt could require considerable travel and expense. In Alaska the services of a guide are not required to hunt moose. Most guides worth their salt already know this moose-calling stuff, so if you go hunting unguided, don't go off on your own without first arming yourself with some calling knowledge!

Some good videos are on the market these days, and although I've never used them, there are also a number of audiotapes, electronic calls and some tube calls you blow on. The time you spend doing some research and studying these videos or tapes, could well be the key to success on your next moose hunt.

Chapter 56
"Packing" in Alaska
First published in *Traditional Bowhunter* magazine, August-September 2007

OUTSIDE OF A FEW SPECIAL HUNT AREAS, PLACES WHERE public safety issues limit use of the weapon one might choose to use for hunting, in Alaska we are generally free to hunt with whatever legal weapon we choose. Although bows are legal, firearms cannot be used to hunt inside the trans-Alaska pipeline corridor, for instance. This corridor is 10 miles wide, parallels much of Alaska's highway system run-

Looking over 20 Dall sheep on a mineral lick in the Alaska Range. I am bow hunting but the pistol is always with me.

ning north and south, and passes through a mix of some good hunting country. The 48-inch pipeline is exposed above ground for miles in many locations and does not react well to having holes shot in it!

Federal parks are off limits for most hunting, and much of our state park system, with a few exceptions, is generally restricted regarding the discharge of firearms, though, again, archery tackle may be used on those state parklands for hunting. Still, the great expanse of other open space in this state, and comparatively lower hunting pressure allows for a decent level of hunter dispersion, low user conflict and, thankfully, few weapons accidents. We can only hope that either/or seasons (restricting hunters to a choice of hunting with either a bow *or* a firearm during a season) are far off in the future—if there will ever be a need to have them at all. It is not unusual to see hunters coming to Alaska with both archery tackle *and* a firearm in their gear.

There is a standing joke in the Alaska outdoor community related to carrying "bear bells" and pepper spray on your person as protection against bears. These supposed deterrents were created for use by non-consumptive outdoor people. They are currently the politically correct alternative to self-defense with a weapon. According to the joke, it is not difficult to determine when bear bells and pepper spray have failed to work. One need only examine bear scat in the area to know for sure. If the scat is full of spandex, little silver bells, and smells of pepper, then keeping bears away using those defensive tools probably doesn't work well.

Most bow hunters in the contiguous United States would never think to carry along a sidearm while hunting; and probably, in many cases, packing a pistol would accomplish little more than burning calories by carrying around dead weight all day. In some jurisdictions it is probably even illegal to carry a sidearm while bowhunting. Not so in Alaska. Though many purist, dyed-in-the-wool, resident Alaskan bowhunters would be quick to disagree, I have always advocated that every person hunting with a bow in Alaska should carry a sidearm. For the sake of loud, defensive noise, if nothing else. And the larger and louder the caliber a person is capable of discharging the better. The bow is not known for being a good defensive weapon.

A bowhunter's disdain for the practice of carrying along a pistol is most often a philosophical issue. An issue, in my opinion, that has more minuses than pluses. I have had some very accomplished bowhunters describe their resistance to carrying a sidearm as a macho thing. I have never failed to be unimpressed by that reason. Living a hunting lifestyle, coupled with spending a lifetime in Alaska, has allowed me to take a number of big game animals with archery tackle; but my Ruger .44 Magnum has always been hanging at my side when I hunted with a bow. To date I have never had to put the bow down and use that pistol against any animal, yet it has always been there if an emergency had arisen.

The more a person hunts in Alaska, the greater the odds are of some form of contact with animals where having a handgun along would certainly be a comfort as well as a good idea. It has always amazed me how some people who bow hunt every year in this state, and never carry a sidearm, have so successfully avoided scrapes where a pistol might need to be drawn. Such people, in my estimation have been very lucky—so far at least.

In my case, the number of near emergencies where I felt it was necessary to at least lift the pistol out of the holster have mostly involved bears, black and brown, although I have had a couple of colorful experiences with rut-crazy bull moose. Three personal examples, and a fourth involving other hunters, come to mind.

In the '70s, while bowhunting black bear over bait, I walked in to my tree stand late one evening hoping to catch a very large boar which I knew was coming to the stand late every afternoon just about dark. I also knew this same bait had attracted a medium-sized sow towing a single cub. I was not interested in a bear of her size, nor was she legal owing to the presence of the cub. On the evening in question, 50 feet from the spruce tree supporting my stand, I was accosted by the sow, which suddenly broke from the brush and backed me up against a birch tree, popping her teeth all the while and blowing violently through her nose at me from a distance of about 30 feet. Picture being cornered by a very large dog, and then double that threat, and you almost have a fair idea of this predicament. I suspected she was conducting a rear guard action allowing her cub time to get away. Pistol in hand by my side, I leaned against the birch tree and kept dead still. She gradually calmed down and, after about fifteen minutes of standoff, backed off slowly and disappeared into the alders after her cub. No harm done to either side.

In another case, in the '80s, I was on a fly-in solo brown bear hunt in the Talkeetna Mountains north of Anchorage. I was camped in a tree stand over a fresh moose kill (I lived in the stand for seven days and nights that trip without coming down). It is illegal to deliberately place bait to attract brown bears. It *is* legal, however, to harvest brown bear off the head, hide, and viscera of harvested big game animals. On the second day of the hunt, in the middle of the night, I had a huge sow brown bear decide to try to climb up into the tree stand with me. She nearly succeeded. I had my pistol out, ready to make a lot of noise if she came up the tree one inch farther. I was in my sleeping bag peering down over the edge of my tree stand platform into the ghostly shape of her face in the near darkness. She was only about 6 feet below me when, suddenly, she abandoned the climb and backed off down the tree. I don't ever recall feeling as alone as I did at that particular moment. The pistol, although never discharged, was my only comfort.

In another instance in the 1980s, two of us were five days into a Dall sheep bow hunt in the Alaska Range. We were returning to our camp along the ridge tops after a frustrating day of trying to belly up on a couple of rams. We were camped in a huge protected bowl between two mountaintops. We reached the upper rim of the bowl just in time to look down and see a mountain grizzly less than 100 yards from our tent. It was obvious where the bear was headed and more than probable what he intended to do when he got there! A violent report from my .44 magnum echoing across the bowl put him to flight. We watched him run, without stopping or even slowing down, for more than a mile down the mountain before he dropped from sight.

An incident a number of years ago involved two bow hunters in the Fairbanks, Alaska area. The hunters, apparently working together, arrowed a big bull moose. As best as I can now recall the story, the bull either lay down, or collapsed, and was approached by the hunters. One of the two attempted to cut the animal's throat but was surprised when the bull suddenly came to life, arose, and picked the man off his feet between its antlers. Apparently his best defense was to hang on for dear life while the bull tried to shake him off. To make a very exciting story short, the moose was finally killed by the riding hunter's partner using the only weapon available other than a bow and arrow—a machete! This story is useful to make my point. I recall reading about this incident in the newspapers some years ago, although I cannot now vouch for details.

Hunting Alaska is a lifetime dream of many bow hunters. Come do it. But my advice, take it for what it is worth, is to leave the bear bells and pepper spray at home and bring along a good pistol!

Chapter 57
Mystery of the Kenai

IN SEPTEMBER 1996, RICK CLARK, THEN A RESIDENT OF Cooper Landing, Alaska, was moose hunting in the remote highlands east of Tustamena Lake on Alaska's Kenai Peninsula. Joining him was hunting partner Fran White of Seward, Alaska. This portion of the Kenai Peninsula is designated as a special trophy management area. Hunting moose there is dependent on first drawing a statewide lottery permit. Both hunters had the necessary permits for a late-September to mid-October hunt. Due to aircraft access restrictions applying to this management area, these hunters had arranged to have themselves and their outfit packed in by horses. Rick had gone ahead into the trophy area and already had camp established. Fran arrived on horseback a few days later, riding uphill to camp from Tustamena Lake through an early fall snow squall. The horse packer dropped Fran off about 5 p.m. Rick was off scouting for moose and joined up with Fran about 6 p.m.

Soon after his arrival, Fran was in the process of feverishly unpacking his gear, wanting to get on with hunting as soon as possible. Rick had completed all the work establishing camp, nestling their big tent in the protection of a spruce grove in the mostly open alpine moose country. In the rush to be off hunting, one daily chore remained unaccomplished—a short trip to a nearby spring stream for fresh drinking water.

Rick knew this area of the Kenai had a notorious history of obnoxious brown bears and that an encounter at any time was a possibility. As a result, his personal standard operating procedure, when moving about alone, was to do so with a loaded rifle, with a round at the ready in the

Chapter 57—Mystery of the Kenai

chamber. His concern over testy bears was so intense that his precaution included never carrying his rifle slung over his shoulder. It was always in his hands and, on occasions when hunting alone, with the safety off.

Water canteens in tow, and carrying his rifle, Rick headed down a game trail to the spring. He had gone only a few yards from the tent when, about 30 feet ahead of him, a brown bear sprang out from behind a spruce tree alongside the trail and charged at him. The animal rapidly closed the distance between them to a matter of feet. According to Rick, he only had time enough to let go of the canteens, raise the rifle, and fire. There was no time for analyzing the situation, to consider options, or second-guess the charge as a bluff. In the close quarters of the moment it was instantly his sense that the bear intended to attack him. Fortunately for Rick, the incident was over as quickly as it began. The bear was spun off the trail by the impact of the .375 H&H Magnum bullet hitting him in the shoulder. It fell and immediately died, just a scant number of feet to the right of the shaken hunter's boots.

Rick yelled for Fran to come, that he had just been charged by a brown bear. The shooting had occurred moments after Rick's departure. It happened so soon that it was Fran's first thought that he must have accidentally discharged his rifle!

Following the shooting, and a period of time to calm down and take stock of the incident, the hunters discovered from tracks in the new snow that the bear had circled and inspected the camp several times, at close range and in broad daylight. Unlike bears living in the vicinity of popular Alaska bear-viewing streams these days, where the animals are habituated to the sights and sounds of people, this behavior was uncharacteristic of a normally elusive, truly wild bear, as one would expect to find in these remote hills on the Kenai Peninsula.

The first thought of the pair, after considering how fortunate Rick had been to survive his brush with a potential mauling, or worse, was that this boar was just one of those occasional bears that does the unexpected—for lack of a better description, a rogue bear. It was not obvious until the next day when they rolled the 8-foot animal over and began skinning him that there was probably a better explanation for his generally bizarre behavior.

Bear season was not open at the time and, by Alaska law, the head and hide of a brown bear killed out of season in defense of life or property must be recovered and turned over to the Game Department within fifteen days of the incident. It is also necessary to complete a questionnaire concerning the circumstances of the shooting. Camp was within operating range of his cell phone and Rick called local game officials, reported the incident and the two dutifully set about recovering the head and hide to comply with the law.

Typically the first cut made when skinning a bear is a long incision in the hide extending from a point under the chin down the centerline of the chest and belly to, or to a point near, the rectum. Skinning back the hide along this first cut the hunters were confronted with what appeared to be a scar running parallel to the cut in the hide they had made down the center of the bear. This scar was approximately 3 feet long, involving a portion of the chest and part of the abdomen, several inches to the bear's right side of centerline. Further investigation revealed what appeared to be stitch marks along the entire length of the wound and there was a considerable amount of bruising and old blood under the hide and in the fat in the vicinity of the scar. Curiosity prompted Rick to photograph the wound.

Who did this to the bear, and for what reason? In view of the nature and size of the scar, Rick was certain that upon return from the hunt he would find an answer to the mystery from either state or federal game officials.

As a practical matter it appeared unlikely that such a surgery could have been accomplished in the woods under a spruce tree! Neither did it appear reasonable that a wild animal turned loose with an unhealed wound such as this could survive. If indeed surgery had been performed on the bear, how had the animal been cared for until it had healed sufficiently to be released again?

Rick knew that the location where the bear was shot was well within the Kenai National Wildlife Refuge, which is federally managed. After the hunt he reported to Refuge officials to hand over the hide and skull and to fill out the required incident questionnaire. There were no answers to his questions and, he felt, an obvious disinterest in his story. He was greeted with the same response from biologists from every agency that might possibly have been involved and advised that there was no type of research with brown bears, especially anything involving surgery, in progress. Officials could offer nothing to explain what might have caused the mysterious scar.

Rick had considerable time to dwell on this incident. He could not shake the thought that the scar under the hide of this bear was too obvious to be imagined and too incredibly unusual not to cause him to seek a reasonable explanation.

A recollection made later, after returning from the hunt, sticks in Rick's mind. "A day or two" into the hunt, after they had finished skinning the bear, a distant passing aircraft made an abrupt turn and flew directly over them. Their camp was literally miles from nowhere, on the remote bench-land above and to the east of Tustamena Lake, and their tent well hidden in the trees. The plane then continued on its way. Rick cannot help but wonder if that aircraft may have been on a radio-tracking run. Later, biologists would tell him that there *was* tracking activity being conducted in that area, but not on this bear.

It has since been learned that studies relative to the physiology of bear hibernation are being conducted at several locations in the American west. Biologists appear to be concentrating on the hibernation of black bears, because of the ease of working with them, but brown bears apparently have the same physiology. The purpose of this work is to learn more about the mechanics of hibernation. Mainly, how do bears use fat reserves, why bear's muscles don't atrophy during months of inactivity while hibernating, and how they cope with a toxic buildup of urine in their systems.

In recent years, these studies have been funded by the Colorado Division of Wildlife, the National Science Foundation, and NASA. NASA's interest is apparently due to the medical implications such research may have for future prolonged space travel.

There is no indication in the literature that hibernation studies are being conducted in Alaska. However, an interesting observation may be made of information obtained from Colorado and Wyoming studies and of the scar on Rick's bear. The study found that bears might survive starvation during hibernation by actually digesting part of their own gastrointestinal tracts. The digested portion of the tract apparently grows back quickly once the bear comes out of hibernation. One example offered by a party to the study noted that a bear's intestine could measure 20 feet at the onset of hibernation and end up only 7 feet long at the end. It is not clear how the study's measurements were obtained but the scar on Rick's bear would be explained if surgery had been performed on it for this purpose. Bears can apparently be easily manipulated and worked on during their long months of hibernation. Being left to sleep it off in a den could solve the problem of an adequate healing time after surgery. Could it be that hibernation data are quietly being obtained from bears in Alaska?

Looking back on the incident, Rick regrets that he did not open up the bear's chest and investigate the cavity beneath the scar. Later, he considered the idea of returning to the site in hopes of locating some remains and a possible answer, but this was never done. Remembering the overflight by the mysterious aircraft several days after the death of the bear, in the back of his mind he still suspects the possibility of a tracking device. Possibly inside the animal?

In addition to being disappointed at drawing a blank on obtaining any official information about the scar, Rick remains a trifle miffed at a remark made by one of the biologists. The poking comment was that perhaps a UFO might have been responsible for the mysterious operation.

The cause of the incision and apparent stitches in Rick Clark's bear remain a mystery.

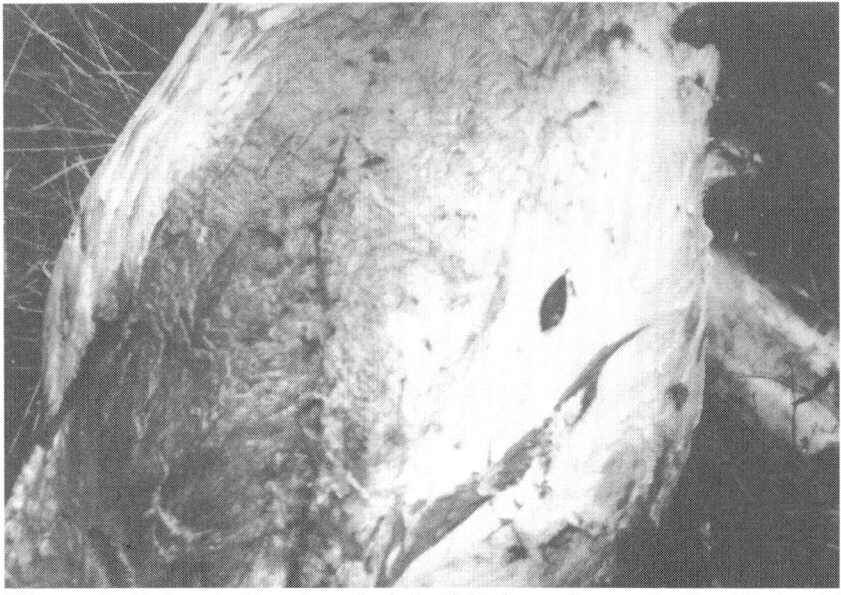

What made this huge incision down the belly of this brown bear on the Kenai Peninsula?

Chapter 58
Living in Earthquake Country

IF YOU HAVE GROWN UP IN ALASKA, FROM THE TIME you were old enough to remember things, to the present, there are probably several earthquake events that are stuck in your memory.

For those living in an active earthquake belt, as the majority of Alaskans do, life is punctuated by a series of periodic short shakers. When these occur, the thought in most of our minds as we are jolted awake in bed in the night, or as we cling to the sides of a door frame during the day awaiting the outcome, is "Oh my God, is this the Big One?" Small quakes are usually very impressive to people directly over the center (epicenter) of a seismic event, while people not paying close attention, just a few miles away, may not even feel the ground move. Despite the size of Alaska, *everyone* across the entire state knows by feel when a Big One occurs!

We all live with the knowledge, although it is largely unmentioned, that if a 10.0 quake occurs, a lot of bad things are going to happen and a horrible number of people are going to perish. This threat, to wise people, also means always being as prepared as you can make yourself for such an emergency.

Prevailing thinking is that occasional small quakes are a good thing, sort of like letting off steam in small batches instead of by an all-in-one explosion. Still, you never remember the small ones, just those big enough at the first jolt to give you the idea that things might really be about to go to hell.

In my experience the memory of three particular earthquakes dwarfs all others.

First was the July 10, 1958 quake centered somewhere in the Mount Fairweather vicinity along the southern Alaska Pacific coastline. This is a rather remote part of Alaska in terms of population, which was a good thing. Because of this, there was only limited property destruction or injury. This event measured something near 8.0 on the Richter scale of earthquake magnitude, depending upon which authority you rely on! Anything near 8.0 is about as bad as an earthquake should be. Severe damage to almost any structure within one hundred kilometers of the center of an 8.0 quake is likely. Anything much above 8.0 is a certain catastrophe.

The Fairweather quake manifested itself most at Lituya Bay. Lituya is a glacier-formed indentation in the Alaska coastline approximately 120 miles due west of Juneau. A huge chunk of mountain and glacier shook loose and fell into the bay, causing an enormous wave that scoured off all vegetation, huge trees included, at the bay's eastern end, up to the 1,700-foot level. Three small fishing boats were anchored in the bay at the time. One boat, along with two people, perished in the wave surge. The two other boats, with all passengers, somehow managed to survive the mountainous churning inside the bay.

I was in Skagway, 80 miles northeast of Lituya Bay, when this earthquake hit. I was at my girlfriend's house at the time, sitting, of all places, on the toilet!

After a hasty retreat outside from the creaking old two-story Keller House, the Gold Rush-vintage mansion owned by my girlfriends parents, we encountered violently swaying cottonwood trees and water sloshing from a large decorative fishpond in the yard. The ground was making a sort of squeaking sound and we could see shock waves, not unlike ocean swells, rippling across the large lawn from south to north.

The event lasted no more than two or three minutes, leaving us a bit giddy from the ground motion.

There was no significant damage in Skagway from this shaker, outside of a few cracked chimneys, books dumped from bookcases, and canned goods spilled in store aisles. Still, the violence and a feeling of helplessness and terror this quake brought with it made it one to remember—not to mention my sitting on the toilet at the time!

Skagway is situated only a few feet above sea level and for a time there was concern about the possibility of a tsunami. It would not take an

Chapter 59—Living in Earthquake Country

enormous wave coming up Lynn Canal from the south to flood the entire town. There was no tsunami.

The next most remembered quake was the Big One that shook all of Alaska on Good Friday, March 27, 1964. This was the *Big One*. It measured 9.2 on the Richter scale, the highest score ever recorded for an earthquake in North America. The epicenter was somewhere in Prince William Sound about 80 miles due east of Anchorage.

My wife and I were attending the University of Alaska at the time. We were in downtown Fairbanks in a building near the Chena River when the quake hit. When it started, we rushed outside into a large parking lot. The ground rolled and shook, accompanied by the same strange squeaking sound I remembered from the Lituya quake. The rolling continued for several minutes and left us, again as during the Lituya quake, with a queasy, almost mild seasick feeling. Bear in mind that where we were was almost 300 miles north of the epicenter of the quake.

Reports were immediately announced over radio where the worst damage had occurred. Anchorage, Seward, Valdez, and the village of Chenega in Prince William Sound got the worst of it. One hundred twenty-five people died as a result, fifteen killed directly by the quake itself and 110 perished from the accompanying tsunami. Property damage was later estimated to be over three hundred million dollars.

I recall there was some erroneous damage reported at the time. We were concerned about home and family and heard, on the radio, that Skagway had suffered major damage and flooding and that, apparently, fuel tanks in the waterfront area were on fire. None of this, thankfully, was true. Fate had placed us, and all our people, safely far away from the Big One. But living anywhere in earthquake country, at any time—you never know.

The third most memorable earthquake event in my life was a small one, caused no damage, and, as it affected us at least, was even a bit humorous.

My wife, Sharon, and I were at our remote cabin in the Kodiak area. This was late in the evening of July 27, 2001. Sharon was asleep in her bunk. I was up late sitting in the dining room trying to beat a game of single-pass solitaire. This is a 12-by-18-foot cabin, circa 1950s. The "dining room" is the plywood table we eat on, like the "parlor" is the edge of a bunk where visiting company sits. Definitely not the type of arrangement you would find in *Cabin Living Magazine*!

The event started like any other typical small one that occurs somewhere near directly underneath a person. First came a deep booming sound from underground, followed by a sudden shudder and then shaking. I sat at the kitchen table awaiting the outcome. The cabin wall behind me, over our little propane cook range, was covered with hanging kitchen pots and fry pans. At first shudder, the collection set up a clatter like a peddler's wagon going down a rough road, binga bong bung, banga bang bing. Every pot and pan made a different-pitched sound and the roar continued, nonstop. As the ruckus kept up, I turned to watch my wife, asleep in the bunk. All of a sudden, in the clatter, she awakened abruptly. Realizing what was going on, she sat up and hollered "Earthquake!" loud enough to broadcast a warning to the entire bay. Luckily she didn't bang her head on the bunk above her as both of us have done so many times.

Sharon, and our cabin, in earthquake country.

I tried to calm her, told her that for the moment we were okay, and to sit tight and ride it out. Bong bonga bing, binga bong bang. In less than a minute the pan clatter eased off, and then stopped. Once more we had ridden over a wave from the great unknown.

Our next concern, being a bit knowledgeable about such things, was the possibility of a tsunami. The cabin sits on the edge of a saltwater lagoon just a few feet above sea level. Even a minor wave generated by an earthquake could easily reach our front door. Our five acres, flat along the lagoon, backs up a steep wooded hill so, if necessary, we could instantly flee to higher ground. We tuned our AM/FM radio to KAKM, the Kodiak radio station, and listened for news. There was none, not a word about an earthquake. Apparently this was one of those shakers that only a few locals feel; it must have been right under us. The event was not even reported the following morning on the local news.

Where we live, we are faced with this threat every day, but like everybody else, we have learned to quietly ignore the possibilities. Like our heartbeats, or breathing in and breathing out, the movement of the earth beneath us is just the way of things. We take each shaker as it comes and, hopefully, the next will be a small one.

Chapter 59
Fire on the Tsiu

We assume so much these days, living the fat life, that we lose track and take too many things for granted. Things like a well-stocked supermarket close at hand, or an education for our children, or that the police will surely be here in minutes if we call. But fly out of the big city, any big city in Alaska these days, and most of the things we take for granted not only fall farther behind with every passing mile, but most of these city things we have come to depend on, daily, completely drop off the face of the earth. Imagine the terror of a raging fire in your home or business in the dark of night and no fire department, anyone, to turn to for help!

TODAY I ARRIVED AT THE LODGE FROM ANCHORAGE. I do some big-game guiding. Charles Allen, the owner and my partner in developing a small, quality guide service out of his Driftwood Lodge, located on the banks of the Tsiu (pronounced "sigh you") River, picked me up at the Cordova Airport. The 90 miles or so from the airport, east to the landing strip along the Tsiu, took a bit less than an hour in Charles' Cessna 206.

Today is April 18, 2001. My client, Joe Schmidt, a restaurant owner from Prescott, Arizona, will arrive May 1 for a spring brown-bear hunt. Two more hunters are waiting is Dallas, Texas, literally with the plane engine running, for word that the bears are moving. They are prepared to come when we call. Over the course of the next ten days we plan to do a lot of flying and scouting before Mr. Schmidt arrives.

The guys appeared to enjoy their steak and baked potato this evening. Without benefit of an election I have been elected cook and, out of my element in the lodge's stainless-steel kitchen, I served dinner late. After supper both Charles and his old friend, Dr. Bob Hansen, a retired mining engineering professor from Colorado, drifted off to their bunks. During silver-salmon season the lodge is generally crowded with fishermen, but now it is empty and we each have the luxury of our own private cabin with bath. Along with the cooking I have apparently also won dishwashing honors. About ten thirty I was scalding my hands with rinse water in the kitchen when suddenly the lights went out.

At first I thought the blackout must be a mistake, that one of the

Chapter 59—Fire on the Tsiu

guys had assumed everyone had tucked in for the night and shut off the power plant. I waited a few minutes in the pitch dark of the kitchen before feeling my way out to the front door, intending to give someone hell for the error. Stepping out the entry I saw a pall of black smoke rising from the vicinity of the shop/powerhouse building against the fading western twilight. I hollered out loud, to anyone who would listen, "Hey! Is that thing on fire?"

Running toward the power shed, I found myself falling in a few steps behind Charles, who had just bolted down the stairs from his second-floor apartment over the first floor crew's shower and bathroom, the only two-story structure of the thirteen buildings in the lodge complex. Charles opened the shop door to the red glow of a seething inferno at the far end of the building. The ominous light came from a back room housing the main and auxiliary power plants. He no more opened the door than a 12-inch sheet of flame came boiling across the ceiling toward us at the front door. In the search for quick answers, by opening the door we had unwittingly provided ventilation the pent-up blaze needed to *really* get going.

"Dennis," Charles hollered, "Get a fire extinguisher!" "From where?" I countered. "The lodge," he replied. There would be no reaching a fire extinguisher inside *this* building. Before he ended the instruction he was running past me after the extinguisher himself, realizing that nobody knew better than he did its exact location inside the dark lodge building. In moments he returned and turned the chemical spray loose into the shop. For a brief moment the flames retreated from the dousing, only to return with even greater fury once the extinguisher had vented itself. The upper interior of the building was soon completely involved in flame, the fire roaring. We had only seconds to drag a Honda ATC out of the building and push over a full drum of diesel fuel and roll it out the door, with fire at our backs as we did so.

At that point the hard truth came crashing down on us. This was a *real* fire. It was painfully clear that the shop building was lost, and who knew what else. We were never to know exactly where, or why, the fire started.

It is amazing how, when tested by panic, we do strange things. I will always remember looking at a small portable welder sitting just inside the door of the shop. It was painted bright red and it was brand-new. Bob Hansen had been welding on the frame of one of the Honda four-wheelers when I arrived that afternoon. It wasn't heavy. I could have easily pulled it out the door to safety, but in an instant my rescue plan was overpowered by some other more important things and the welder, only an arm's length away, was left to the fiery inferno.

The loss of the power plant left us helpless. What water we had came from a well, and without electricity there was no pump to draw the water. A hastily rigged garden hose soon slowed to a trickle as the last water pressure drained from the holding tank in the well house.

In minutes the shop was completely involved in flames. It was a close call where the fire would spread next. The situation was aggravated by a northeast wind, blowing several miles per hour around the flaming shop and directly toward the next building in line to the southwest, the lodge laundry. Beyond the laundry, and in a direct line of the wind and the fire, were four guest cabins.

On the other side of the shop, separated by only a few feet, was an old 12-by-12-foot storage shed. Proximity to the shop dictated this was going to burn for sure and, feeling around in the dark, we quickly removed three drums of aviation gas which were stored there. The shed lay about 25-feet from the southwest corner of the main lodge building. Had the fifty-five gallon drums of aviation gas been lit off, the lodge would have soon followed. If the shed burned, even without the aviation gas, the lodge was still in deadly peril. All the big building had going for it was the northeast wind, which carried the flames, heat, and flying debris in the opposite direction.

After removing everything we could get our hands on from the old shed, denying the fire more fuel if nothing else, we watched helplessly as the smoking corner nearest the shop burst into flames. Already, on the *other* side of the shop building, the roof of the laundry was ablaze.

During the course of the early hours of the fire there was one over-riding consideration—we must do whatever possible to save the main lodge. The wood-frame outbuildings and cabins could be replaced with comparative ease, but the lodge, laboriously built of beach logs in the early 1990s, would be a nightmare to replace. Charles voiced a woeful thought out loud into the wind. "If the lodge goes, it's all over."

In minutes, the shed was fully ablaze, aiming its wrath at the next downwind target, a two-story wood-frame structure housing the crew showers and washroom downstairs and Charles' apartment upstairs. In the golden glow of the fire it was easy to see the building's white-painted siding beginning to scorch and bubble. Its bursting into flames was only a matter of time.

Chapter 59—Fire on the Tsiu

Keeping a nervous eye on the main lodge, we shifted to a rescue mode. Near helpless to combat the fire itself, it came to us to concentrate on saving what we could from the next doomed building before it burst into flame. Only minutes ahead of the flames, Charles climbed the stairs to his apartment and began throwing down whatever he could feel in the smoke-filled dark. Shotguns, rifles, hip waders, and bundles of clothes came showering down on me on the ground from the upper doorway. Before being driven out by hot smoke, he rescued a very pricey satellite telephone off his office desk, but the equally pricey antenna was firmly attached to a post supporting the stairs. A short time later, accompanied by the discharge chorus of the hundreds of pistol, rifle, and shotgun rounds stored in the apartment, the antenna perished in the holocaust.

The battle to save the main lodge raged on for hours. We shoveled sand up onto the wood shake roof until we had the area nearest the fire buried to a depth of 3 inches. This insulated the flammable shake roof from the scorching heat of the flaming bath house/apartment building burning down only 25 feet away. The log walls of the lodge smoked in the heat. We bailed a meager amount of dish rinse water from a sink in the kitchen and resorted to splashing eight-dollar-per-gallon RV antifreeze on the logs in an effort to cool them down. A big thermopane window in the front of the building cracked from the heat in a spider web pattern. The deck in front of the lodge charred to within 8 feet of the log front of the building. More shoveled sand prevented the deck from burning through to the lodge like a fuse. Later, we would find the closest burn hole in that deck only 24 inches from the lodge wall.

In the front entry, a good 50 feet from the washroom/apartment fire, the yellow plastic backing on an outdoor thermometer, hanging on a wall, slowly began melting in the heat, oozing sideways. Later, as the fire gradually cooled, the thermometer frame solidified again in the shape of a grotesque banana.

Charles and I shoved the back wall of the burning two-story building, the wall closest to the lodge, over into its own fire, pushing it over using a long plank. Better to have if fall in that direction and burn than to fall outward onto the front deck of the lodge.

Gradually, over the next few hours, the intensity of the washroom/apartment fire, and the danger to the lodge, began to lessen. We were now able to direct our attention to the line of burning guest cabins. By this time two cabins west of the laundry had already gone up in flames and the third in line was blistering in the heat from its burning neighbor. A quick decision was made to haul some water from the river with a Honda four-wheeler and trailer. A plastic garbage can of water proved adequate to douse the superheated wall of the next endangered cabin, preventing it from burning.

And that is how and where we stopped that cursed fire. It was four in the morning. We had been fighting this thing, nonstop, since ten thirty the evening before.

The morning after the fire. Somehow, the log lodge building in the background was spared.

Of the thirteen buildings in the complex six were lost—but we had somehow managed to save the old log lodge. What kept another line of cabins from burning, the row lying immediately west of the washroom/apartment building, we will never understand. The wall of the first cabin in that line, downwind of the burning washroom/apartment building, and facing the blaze, was scorched from heat so intense that it broke the window on the exposed side and melted the vinyl window casing out of shape. The only explanation that can be offered is that God did not intend for any more buildings to burn, even though all the elements for complete disaster were present at the time.

As this is being written, building materials, equipment and a crew are en route to the Tsiu to rebuild. Charles expects to have his lodge fully operational to accommodate arrival of his first silver-salmon clients in

Chapter 59—Fire on the Tsiu

August. Joe Schmidt, my Prescott, Arizona bear hunter, is a very understanding man. He has consented to come and hunt with us next spring—under much better conditions.

Something must be said here about good neighbors. Selfless offers of assistance, loans of equipment, days of donated cleanup work and hours of free flying time are testimony to the fact that a frontier spirit is alive and well in remote Alaska. The people who helped know who they are and to whom a debt is owed.

We are all a lot wiser now about fire, and of being left to your own devices in a remote location. When considering the *down* side of this misadventure we need to remember that there was an *up* side. Not counting scratches, bruised shins and dinged heads in dark buildings, none of us was seriously injured. It is unlikely the near catastrophe and terror of that dark night will ever be repeated on the Tsiu. A number of things have been incorporated into a rebuilding plan which will considerably lessen the chances of such a thing happening again. But still, out there beyond the fat life, nothing should ever be taken for granted.

Chapter 60
Octopus—Care and Cleaning

Octopus—The new seafood?

In Alaska, octopus is still a much maligned and, with the possible exception of sushi lovers, generally avoided seafood. It is rare that an octopus is caught on saltwater sport gear. But occasionally, an eight-legger is hauled up from the depths while bottom fishing. Such catches are most often released, with the typical degree of repulsion, or, occasionally, may be saved for use as either crab or halibut bait. Used as bait, octopus flesh is renowned among commercial fishermen for its tough ability to stay on a hook, long after herring or other bait fish has been pulled off the lower end of a fish line by scavengers.

Being a bit selfish, I hesitate to make the case that octopus, when properly prepared and cooked, is as delightful a seafood as any I can name. Few people seek them out to eat as my wife and I do and I really don't mind the lack of competition. The idea of combat octopus fishing, or a much higher local demand for this sea creature for eating purposes than already exists in this state, is to me unthinkable! Be advised, that if you happen to hook one accidentally during a fishing adventure, don't you dare throw it back until you have tried it at least once for eating. If you do not, I assure you, the loss will be yours.

Octopus — Getting Past the Name Is the Hardest Part:

Obviously, the hardest thing about using octopus for food is getting past the idea that it is… octopus! It is a fact that this sinister-looking critter, that crawls across the ocean's floor making its living, eating whatever it can find, is little different from the comparable scavenging life of prawns, lobster, or king crab. The uninitiated may find little comfort in the fact that millions of people across the world probably consume thousands of tons of octopus every year in their diets. Those people have no qualms about eating them, nor do they suffer any ill effects. It is used just like any other delicious seafood. Recognizing that people will be people, and that American diets definitely differ from that of much of the rest of the world, and some people are more squeamish than others, I am going to demonstrate here, as inoffensively as possible, how I prepare the octopus we catch for eating. We can usually find one during a good minus tide under the huge beach rocks near our cabin at Onion Bay.

Octopus live on the ocean floor in water-filled cavities they excavate under huge rocks. Typically, there are two entrances to an octopus' home. These creatures extract oxygen from sea water and an entry and exit hole assures circulation of fresh water for breathing. The presence of one of these creatures under a rock at low tide is confirmed by small sand deltas which appear, usually on opposite sides of a boulder. This sand is part of housekeeping, during which the resident maintains its chamber under the rock by blowing sand, small pebbles and shells out through each of the two openings. It is near impossible to dig an octopus out from under its rock. However, they can be forced into the open by squirting a mix of bleach and water into one of the two entrances. If an octopus is present, it will exit on the side opposite the opening where the bleach was administered. Allow ample time for the creature to fully exit the opening. If it becomes alarmed it will withdraw back under the rock from where it will not be forced, by any means, to show itself again.

There is no catch limit on octopus. They are not even mentioned in the sport fishing regulations.

When we capture an octopus at the cabin, my first consideration, especially for uninitiated friends or guests, is to assure that no one is offended by watching me prepare it for eating. I try, unless they insist on taking part, to clean the subject away from everyone, especially someone who has never tried this seafood before. Why provide for a potential turn-off if unnecessary? Once a person has tried octopus the way my wife cooks it, and likes it, and still remains curious about preparation before it goes into the frying pan, then I will accommodate with a demonstration the next time we harvest one. Although someone could easily be fooled by the taste and quality of this seafood the way we eat it, easily thinking it was something else, we would never serve it to people without telling them in advance we were going to do so.

The end product of cleaning and preparation is a bowl of white meat very much resembling strips of halibut. This is hardly intimidating to anyone, especially to the cook. These pieces my wife seasons, coats with Panco Japanese-style breading, and then fries in deep vegetable oil. The eating is delicious. To me, it very much resembles the deep-sea scallop in flavor and lobster tail in texture.

Care and Cleaning:

The tools necessary for cleaning an octopus are a very sharp knife (razor-sharp is best); a good sharpening tool to assure your knife stays razor sharp; a cleaning table with plenty of room to maneuver; a meat mallet for tenderizing (I have a special wood mallet, made of a spruce 2-by-4, at our Raspberry Island cabin just for this purpose.); half a bucket of fresh seawater (or cold fresh water if you are away from the salt chuck); and a bowl to hold the finished product.

Keep the octopus alive in a bucket of sea water until butchering. Change the water periodically as needed to maintain freshness until cleaning. A live octopus will climb out of a bucket with no water in it. He will usually not climb if he is kept in water.

Begin the process by first removing the cap (head), along with the black beak, which is located under the cap in the center of the legs. The black beak resembles the beak of a parrot and functions as the octopus' mouth and teeth. Discard the cap and beak.

A bundle of eight connected legs remains. Separate each leg from the bundle with the knife, lengthways, and drop all of them into the bucket of sea water and allow to stand for about fifteen minutes. Octopus bodies are literally a bundle of muscle. The legs will continue involuntary motion for some time after the cap head has been removed. Not a convenient thing to work with. In a short period of time—ten to fifteen minutes—most of these muscle contractions will cease.

Next, move the legs from the water onto the cleaning table and allow them to air-dry; this will facilitate skinning.

Continue by skinning each leg. This is a bit tricky, so be patient. Doing this will really make you appreciate the value of a very sharp knife! Once it is skinned, hold each leg with the suckers sideways and trim the suckers off. You will end up with eight tubes of very tough white muscle.

Chapter 60—Octopus—Care and Cleaning

There is nothing wrong with using the suckers or the skin for food. Most of the rest of the world eats the entire octopus, including the skin and suckers. Boiled octopus, or *taco* in Japanese, is one of a variety of different seafood which is used for making sushi. The leg meat is sliced diagonally, including the skin and suckers, and served on small rolls of specially prepared rice. The meat prepared this way is quite chewy but is delicious. All types of sushi are typically eaten using soy sauce as a dipping sauce. I prefer my soy sauce laced with a bit of Japanese Wasabi; a hot, green, horseradish paste. Be very careful with Wasabi, it is very hot and a little goes a long way! Hawaiian *taco poki* is another delightful seafood dish prepared with boiled, unskinned, roughly chopped octopus leg meat.

Next, cut each leg into 2- or 3-inch pieces. Pound each cut piece with the meat mallet until tenderized. Don't be bashful, if you don't tenderize the pieces enough they will be tough. Pound each piece until it is almost mush!

Here is the makings for three excellent meals.

Last, put the meat in the bowl and hand it over to the cook!

Give It a Try—You'll Like It!:

Next to fresh deer liver, my favorite cabin fare is my wife Sharon's breaded octopus. It is a special treat I look forward to every year during our August sojourn to the cabin. And, by the way, finding an octopus is much easier on my old bones than chasing down a deer liver during the bucks-only restriction in effect at that time of year!

Chapter 61
Test Your Dead Reckoning

ON A RECENT MOOSE HUNT, ON A SOUTHCENTRAL Alaska river, I was once again reminded of the need to exercise caution about getting far enough away from a point where I know where I am, to another point where I do not. The name of that game is called getting lost!

In my defense, the situation I describe here was not actually a case of getting lost. It was more of a test, a test of my natural dead-reckoning ability, or lack of ability, to arrive back where I wanted to be without the aid of a compass or a Global Processing System (GPS). I had both a compass and a programmed GPS with me. I was in woods where the trees were far overhead. Low overcast and fog obscured everything except gray daylight, allowing no opportunity to see the sun, a skyline, or any landmark that would help me establish direction. These are textbook conditions for getting lost.

That morning my hunting partner and I had traveled northeast off the river we were float-hunting by raft. We will call this river the Nunyabiz, short for *none of your business*, to afford whatever level of protection I can for my favorite, not-so-secret-anymore, late-season moose-hunting stream. This river, by the way, is beyond range for calling home on a cell phone.

It was late morning and we had tried moose calling without success for about an hour from the brush on the edge of a large, open muskeg. At this point we were through hunting for the morning and now planned on a beeline return to camp over on the river. For grins and giggles I

Chapter 61—Test Your Dead Reckoning

checked the return route with my GPS. The instrument pointed directly behind us into the thick black spruce and informed me that we were .35 miles from the front door of our tent over on the river bar. From where we stood on the muskeg I would return to camp, I thought, using dead reckoning. Dead reckoning, in this case, included my natural instincts regarding direction, what I already knew about the lay of the land, and a GPS compass heading to start with. Boy! Was I in for a surprise!

I was in the lead as we traveled the first several hundred yards. I expected any minute to pop out into a long narrow meadow, which I knew for a fact lay across our return route. There was no meadow and suddenly the slope of the terrain seemed wrong. It now sloped off to our left when, my memory told me, it should be dropping off gradually downhill in front of us toward the river. The sameness of black spruce and thick brush surrounded us in all directions. Everywhere I looked were dense woods that looked exactly the same. In that short space of time my sense of direction and dead reckoning had failed me. But what was really surprising was the short travel distance required for the failure! Time to check the instruments.

My GPS showed how much I had strayed. I was now heading in the wrong direction on a bearing almost directly southeast. I should have been heading southwest. The Garmin told me the correct direction to camp was near behind me now, still .23 miles distant. In the brush, my internal compass had pulled me off course by nearly forty-five degrees! During this short dead-reckoning experiment I had failed to consider a built-in tendency of mine, to naturally stray off course to the left. This was a wakeup call. I already knew about this internal compass problem. Here is how.

Years ago, while walking back across a large lake from ice fishing, I happened on this simple dead-reckoning test. Far out on the lake, with about 6 inches of snow, and nothing in any direction to trip me up, I made careful note of a distant landmark, closed my eyes, and imagined myself walking directly toward that landmark. I continued, all the while visualizing the chosen spot in my mind's eye and trying to the best of my blind ability to walk directly toward it. After a considerable distance, several hundred yards, I opened my eyes and found that my tracks in the snow described a perfect circle, to the left, that would have had a diameter of about 300 yards had I kept on moving ahead with my eyes closed. I tried this a second time, with exactly the same result, confirming that my internal dead reckoning tends to draw me off beam rather dramatically to the left. This natural, and apparently predictable, tendency to stray from an imagined straight course could explain why lost people are prone to wander in circles.

This simple test requires a large, flat, unobstructed area, such as a frozen lake or a sand or salt flat—any sizeable, level, area where you can walk a considerable distance with complete confidence that you will not be tripped up by obstacles. The area should also be quiet. There should be no sound you can home in on to help direct you during what should be a completely deaf and blind test. If there are sounds which will give you direction, plug your ears. The object is to learn what you will do naturally if you find yourself traveling under conditions where there is nothing more to guide you than an internal sense of direction, or dead reckoning.

This test demonstrated to me that under certain conditions, which can arise in the woods in a heartbeat, I had best never find myself in the position of relying completely on my sense of direction. The dead reckoning test tells me that relying on my sense of direction would probably put me on a course unwittingly turning in a wide circle to my left. At the first sign of things getting tight, like an aircraft pilot I now *know* I will need to rely on my instruments; and better sooner than later! This offers an immediate, knowledgeable alternative to wandering in circles in dense cover, a heavy fog, or a swirling snowstorm.

I once heard of a foolproof way to stay on course in thick country. I was told (probably not by a Norwegian!) about the Norwegian compass. This instrument is a 30-foot-long pole. The user starts by carrying the pole which is first lined up in the direction he intends to travel, and then proceeds walking. In thick cover the long pole prevents the traveler from turning from his starting direction, keeping him on course. As a practical matter, a good GPS, backed up by a reliable compass, is probably a better deal for most of us than a 30-foot pole, especially for those of us who have tested themselves and know for sure what their tendency is to wander off a dead reckoning course.

Chapter 62
Dipping Copper River Salmon

NO DISCUSSION OF THE MARVELOUS THINGS I HAVE been able to do, spending a lifetime in Alaska, would be complete without mention of dip-netting for king and sockeye salmon in the Copper River.

For years the Copper River dip net fishery was the only one of its kind in the state. I drove to Chitna, Alaska for the first time in 1976 and harvested a twenty-five-fish limit, a mix of mostly reds (sockeye) and a few king salmon. With the exception of two years since that first 1976 adventure, I

Dipping salmon in the muddy Copper River: you can't see the fish and they can't see you.

have journeyed to the muddy Copper every June or July and dipped my year's supply of fish. Every one of those years—with the exception of a few bad seasons when the river was so high it was up in the trees, ruining any chance for decent dipping—this fishing privilege has allowed me to fill my family's diet with top-quality canned, smoked, and fresh-frozen salmon.

Since the time I began dipping fish from the Copper River, the opportunities for catching fish with a dip net have been expanded by allowing the practice in the Kasilof River (1981) and the Kenai River (1982), both on the Kenai Peninsula. These two relatively new fisheries are much closer to where I live in southcentral Alaska, but the old habit of fishing the Copper has kept me taking the long drive to Chitna every year to net my fish. So far, I have never dipped in the Kasilof or the Kenai River, which are much closer to the population center of the state, and because of that, more subject to crowds and "combat" fishing, which I do not appreciate. So far at least, I have always been able to find my own private rock or stretch of beach along the Copper River, below the village of Chitna, where I can still enjoy the experience and catch a year's supply of fish in the process.

The salmon-dipping fishery in these three rivers is limited to Alaska residents. A resident fishing license must be obtained and a dip net permit, available at almost any Alaska Department of Fish and Game office, is required. At this writing there is no charge for the permit, although thousands of Alaska residents are now taking part in the program and, since the fountain of money from Alaska's oil wealth will inevitably dwindle in the future, the revenue potential from permit fees will probably, one day, prove to be too hard to resist!

The three rivers where dipping is allowed have one thing in common. They all have muddy, or at least very murky, water. The dipper cannot see the fish, and the fish, feeling their way upstream in these sediment-laden rivers, cannot see a net. All that is necessary is to sit on the bank in a backwater, or eddy, and hold a long handled net down in the water. The fish, swimming upstream in the backwater of an eddy, simply swims into the net. His presence is advertised by the bump, or thump, when he hits the end of the net. A *big* bump denotes that the dipper has probably netted a king salmon. A smaller bump, sometimes almost imperceptible in the swirling current, usually means a red.

More ambitious fishermen can fish by sweeping. Sweeping is fishing directly in the passing river current, typically on a rock jutting out into the river, or at the end of a point. The process involves placing the net in the river, upstream, and having the current push the net outward and downstream. Along the arc of this "sweep" the dip netter hopes to net fish struggling to swim upstream against the current. At the end of a sweep the net handle is pointing downriver. It is then pulled in, hand over hand, lifted up and out of the water, turned, and placed back in the river again, upstream, for another sweep. This type of fishing is hard and strenuous. Many who prefer sweeping choose to fish off gravel bars, wading out into the river with chest waders to reach water deep enough to effectively fish. Sweeping off a gravel bar, with the river washing around the dipnetter, can be an especially dangerous practice. Some fishermen secure themselves to shore by rope, but many do not bother.

A large king can jerk a dip netter who is not paying attention off his rock, or off his gravel bar, and into the river if that person is foolishly fishing in a precarious position. Every year, it seems, the Copper River claims the lives of several people who play Russian roulette with its muddy water and fail to safely rope themselves to shore. Once you are adrift in the icy river, the odds of survival are slim. It is a lucky person indeed who is able to keep afloat long enough to be pulled from the water by one of the boats which pass by only occasionally. Many is the time I have stopped fishing and turned my head away from the scene of a careless person taking his chances—preferring not to witness the death of a fool.

Sockeye salmon are schooling fish which enter the mouth of the river from the Gulf of Alaska in bunches and proceed upstream together. If a big run is coming through, everyone with a net in the water catches fish. At times, between schools, dipping can be agonizingly slow. If a person is unfortunately on the river at the wrong time he might not catch a fish for hours. At other times the reds may come through in small spurts. The trick is to not succumb to boredom and quit fishing. If a dipper is not straining water when the fish pass he or she will not catch any! Sooner or later they will come and a good rule to follow is to keep fishing!

Unlike red salmon, the king salmon typically do not run in tight schools. They seem more inclined to move upriver as singles or pairs and may pass by a dip netter at any time, even when sockeye fishing is slow. You never know when a king will pass by. A constant trickle of these bigger fish coming up-river is another good reason to keep that net in the water.

In past years there was no limit on the number of Copper River king salmon that could be included in a limit of fish. If a dip netter caught twenty-five kings he could keep them all—an absurd amount of fish even if a family lived on a steady diet of salmon! At this writing only one king may be retained in a catch limit.

Every year since I began dipping in the Copper, charter boat services have been available at O'Brien Creek. O'Brien Creek may be reached by driving about 2 miles south of the community of Chitna on a maintained, single-lane gravel road. This road follows the old historic Copper River & Northwest Railroad right-of-way to the river, and O'Brien Creek. For a fee, these charter operators will haul dip netters downriver and place them at better-producing fishing sites in Woods Canyon, sites which usually can be reached only by water. These charter river craft can haul up to six people and getting on one when the fish are running steady is on a first-come, first-served, basis.

A favorite means of preserving our family's catch of sockeye salmon is canning. We put the fish up in glass pint Mason jars, following canning instructions which come with the jars. To each jar of fish we add ¼ teaspoon of salt, two teaspoons of vegetable oil (one teaspoon on the bottom and one on the top), and two teaspoons of bottled Catalina salad dressing (one on bottom and one on the top). The Catalina dressing, straight from the bottle, is dark red. This assures a lovely pink color to the processed fish and a delicately delicious flavor. We use such canned fish for salmon patties, in casseroles, eat it creamed over new potatoes or toast, or, my favorite, right out of the jar with crackers! Preserve salmon in this manner and you will never buy canned tuna for sandwiches again!

See you on the Copper!

Bibliography

Russell Annabel. *Adventure Is in My Blood*. Safari Press. 1997.

Mary J. Barry. *A History of Mining on the Kenai Peninsula*. Alaska Northwest Publishing, 1973.

Mary Giraudo Beck. *Shamans and Kushtakas – North Coast Tales of the Supernatural*. Alaska Northwest Books. 1992.

Stan Cohen. *The White Pass and Yukon Route: A Pictorial History.* Pictorial Histories Publishing. 1980.

Terrence Cole. *E.T. Barnette: The Strange Story of the Man Who Founded Fairbanks*. Alaska Northwest Publishing. 1984.

Ed Ferrell. *Strange Stories of Alaska and the Yukon*. Epicenter Press. 1996.

Bob Forker. *Ammo and Ballistics*. Safari Press. 2000.

Basil Hedrick & Susan Savage. *Steamboats on the Chena: The Founding and Development of Fairbanks, Alaska*. Epicenter Press. 1988.

James W. Phillips. *Alaska-Yukon Place Names*. University of Washington Press. 1973.

O.M. Salisbury. *The Customs and Legends of the Thlinget Indians Of Alaska*. Bonanza Books. 1962.

Roberta Sheldon. *The Mystery of the Cache Creek Murders* (Sic). Talkeetna Editions/Publications Consultants. 2004.

Arthur R. Thompson. *Gold-Seeking on the Dalton Trail*. Wolf Creek Books, Inc. 1900.

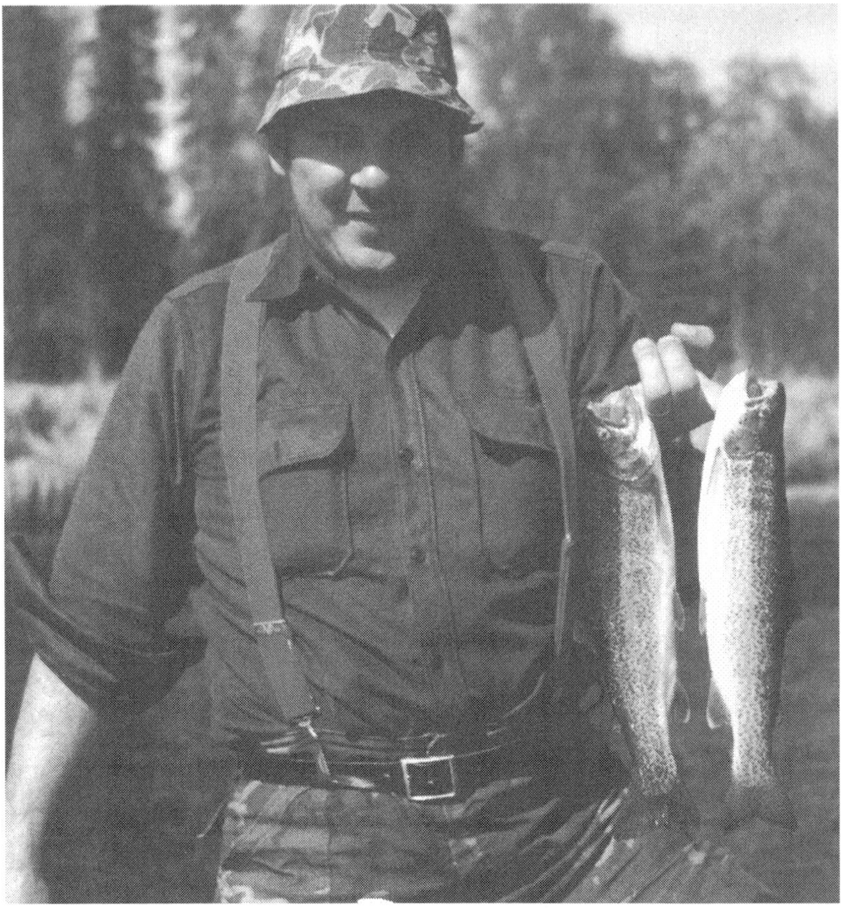